THE CORPSE IN CUYLER'S ALLEY

Castle Clinton
or
Garden

U. S. Revenue Office

Whitehall St.

BATTERY

State Street

Whitehall St.

South

Front

Broad

Bridge St.

Cornelius Slip

Moore St.

Pearl St.

Stone Street

Stone Street

Mill St.

Beaver Street

Marketfield St.

Bowling
Green

Battery Pl.

Washington

Greenwich St.

Morris St.

Rector Str.

Cedar Str.

BRO

New St.

Broad

Street

Broad Street

New

Street

Hanover
Sq.

Wall Street

Pine Street

Water
Street

Old
Slip

Coffee H. Slip

Front Street

Water
Street

Street

Exchange
Place

Beaver Street

William Street

Lane

William
Street

Maiden

Street

Burling

2

3

4

1

5

6

7

8

800 x 2000

Albany Basin

Albany St.

E   A   S   T

THE CORPSE IN CUYLER'S ALLEY

A Mystery of Old New York

Paul Amber

Gratacap Press
New York

Published by the Gratacap Press, New York

Design by Blair Cummock
Cover design by Peter Gammie & Roz Akin
Cover photography by Graham Haber
Text set in 11pt Sabon
Printed in the United States of America by CreateSpace, an Amazon.com company

Library of Congress Control Number: 2014919118
ISBN: 978-0-692-31902-4

For Betty

CHAPTER 1

Miller walked south on Front Street. At every corner he stopped and peered—first west toward Pearl then east to the waterfront where, a block away, beyond the glare of the gas-lamps, loomed a dense thicket of masts and spars jostling in the biting November wind.

Past warehouses, sail-lofts and ship-chandleries shuttered fast, decaying clapboard houses and wooden shanties, Eli Miller patrolled the same stretch every night like an old horse that plods back and forth across a field. There was a certain irony, he sometimes reflected, on being put out to pasture on the very streets which once were the theater of his youthful heroics. In those days, a volunteer fireman, he lived for alarm bells, never considering their implication for death and destruction, just glad for the chance to run with the boys. The Phenix Fire Insurance Company had tossed him this fire watchman's job as a kind of bone. At least he was getting paid. All he ever got from fighting fires was a wheezy lung.

In the partial shelter of a corner storefront Miller pulled a flask from an inner pocket and fortified himself against the chill. The nights so far had been mild for the time of year, but winter was starting to flex its muscles. The plaintive creak of an overhead signboard attested to that, and the sharp snap-snap of a billowing canvas banner. The sort of wind that could knock over a lamp and bellows a fire out of control in min-utes. Whole city blocks, in his day, he'd seen engulfed. Nothing you could do save look and hope. Miller's eyes blurred and shapes became softer as he submerged into a warm, infantile stupor.

Jerking his head up, Miller cursed himself. One of these days, if he wasn't careful, he'd be a goner. The only things moving hereabouts at this time of night were footpads, garrotters and river pirates. It was another hour before the first market men would trudge towards the workday.

A few blocks further on Miller turned into the pitch blackness of Cuyler's Alley. Fetid smells, undispersed here by the wind, rose familiarly from musty cellars as he relieved himself in his usual spot. As he backed off, his gaze fell on something several yards further into the alley and he wondered if his old eyes weren't playing tricks on him. Gingerly, grasping the knife that he always carried on his rounds, Miller advanced on the mysterious shape. A human body, no two ways about it; some sailor, he decided, soused out of his mind, from one of the nearby boarding houses, so-called. Stashing his knife, Miller probed the prostrate figure with his foot. Nothing doing. He bent his head for a closer look.

Eli Miller had seen a thing or two in the course of his sixty-one years in the City of New York, but this close encounter with a fresh corpse in that dark waterfront alley was almost more than he could stomach. Fumbling for his flask, he had the presence of mind to drain it at a gulp. Only then did he feel ready for another look.

A short while later two workers from a nearby slaughterhouse were startled to see an old man stumble headfirst out of an alley, pull something from his pocket, and start twirling it violently. They were quick to recognize the tinny, grinding drone of a watchman's rattle.

CHAPTER 2

Oliver W. Matson sat behind his desk in the basement of City Hall. A shaft of pale morning light from an overhead window threw a diagonal sash across his massive torso. In its beam it caught the edge of an eight-point copper star pinned to his brown velvet jacket. The star bore the seal of the City of New York and the legend, "Chief of Police." A yellow silk vest struggled to confine the vast expanse of the chief's stomach; huge hands gripped the armrests of his chair. His gaze—through square-framed spectacles rendered tiny by the craggy nose upon which they perched—spoke of the stolid inquisition of a stern headmaster. The thrust of his rock-like jaw spelled trouble.

Or so it seemed to the man sitting on the opposite side of the slab of gleaming mahogany. Frank Harrington, Inspector of Hacks and Cabs and the chief's de facto deputy, knew well that "stare of cold command" which made malefactors tremble and throw themselves on its wearer's mercy. The look had served Matson well back when he was an examining magistrate. The ease with which he'd extracted confessions had caused admiring colleagues to dub him "The Father."

"Well, Harrington?"

Harrington laid the newspaper he'd been reading on the desk and weighed his words carefully. The front page editorial in that morning's *Daily Argus*, thrust at him by his boss the moment he entered the office, had struck him as not entirely disastrous. To be sure it attacked the new police as being "no more effective than the old watch system," but its real focus seemed to be an assault on the person of the chief himself. And Harrington—though he hadn't breathed a word of this, not even to Mrs. Harrington—was not averse to the idea of the chief subsiding into a premature but doubtless comfortable retirement. What the new department needed was a fresh, vigorous hand on the tiller, someone unafraid to crack down unmercifully on Vice, someone untainted by corruption. In other words, himself.

Matson stabbed the offending page with a thick forefinger. "Well?"

The *Argus* editorial for Tuesday, November 4, 1845, entitled, *The New Police*, ended on a bombastic note:

> *A bloated and incipient mass of corruption presides over the command of the new police, burdening the taxpayer with the needless expenditure of $1,500 per annum for his service. Doubtless there are a few decent men apart from loafers, ward heelers, and blackguards, to whom the prosecution of justice is now entrusted, but the unceasing assaults and depredations upon our citizenry prove incontestably that the Municipal Police are wholly inadequate to the task of maintaining order.*

The Inspector of Hacks and Cabs, who counted himself among the aforementioned "few decent men," tugged at his beard, a habit he had when he was thinking. Ever since the department's inception that summer, J. Phineas Brunton, crusading publisher of the *Daily Argus*, had hurled a stream of invective at the chief—and Harrington had privately cheered him on. He longed to suggest deploying a hundred men on a bold raid on all forms of waterfront vice, mass arrests leading to massive headlines, but knew this was not the answer the chief was waiting for. As long as gamblers and whorehouse keepers filled aldermen's coffers, such raids would be limited to a few paltry hold-outs.

"I heard Captain Carson's hauled in a suspect for questioning in that Cuyler's Alley business," he threw out. "Seems this cove's dead to rights. Your police protectors at work. If we can get the other papers to go with that, Brunton'll look like a jackass."

"Some drunken sailor pinked in a whorehouse brawl? Are you joking? Two inches on the fourth page. We play that kind of thing up, we're playing Brunton's game."

"There's more to it than that, Chief. The victim's not been identified, but from the looks of him he's no sailor. Bit of a nob, I'd say."

"You've seen him?"

"He's laid out at the morgue. A pretty sight. Face pounded into raw meat. Stripped to his silk drawers, with a motley cravat round his neck. Coroner said he'd not seen anything as vicious in twenty years on the job."

The Chief sighed. "Another jinglebrains from somewhere up the river, coaxed by a friendly stranger to his demise in some dreary house of ill fame and robbed blind. A lamb to the slaughter. What can we do, Harrington? Are we clergymen, supposed to help them suppress their baser instincts?"

Matson's scowl settled on his paperweight, a leaden hand of King George III, remnant of a statue pulled down by rebels in '76. In the ensuing silence, Harrington watched his boss's gaze turn inward and knew better than to interrupt. For the thousandth time he wondered at the two separate people that seemed to inhabit that rock-ribbed carcass. On the one hand the wily, street-smart politician, as unscrupulous and coarse as a jail-house turn-key, on the other the philosopher, the reformer, the father-confessor.

The Chief leaned over conspiratorially. "I'll tell you what, Harrington. Stir the pot. Have that young reporter from the *Post* look the body over. Play to his vanity. Drop a few hints about the victim's background: wayward son of the upper ten, with a taste for the low life. An appeal to members of the public with missing sons to come forward, to maidens who've mislaid their beaux ... Working round the clock to hunt down the killer ... Get it in tomorrow's paper. That'll put egg on Brunton's face. Who's Irontop hauled in, anyway?"

"Some Irish bruiser from a sailor's brothel near where they found the body."

"As I feared. Keep the thug out of sight for now, Harrington. We'll have to keep the papers guessing. 'Following several avenues of investigation ... Closely guarded information.' That sort of thing. Leg it over to Captain Carson's place at once. Tell him to hush up the arrest for the time being. Better still, have him along to show off the body—he'll have 'em hanging on his every word. Get moving. I want Carson here now!"

Startled by his chief's unexpected eruption, Harrington made for the door. He was halfway down the hall when he heard his name called and doubled back to see what fresh instruction his boss might have for him. But Matson merely pointed up at the window, smiled and gestured for Harrington to resume his seat. After four months of basement occupancy the chief had learned to decipher with reasonable accuracy certain of the footsteps pounding the paving stones above his head. Though he felt as though he were constantly under foot, the discovery did serve as an early warning system—as the confident, loping gait now approaching in the hall attested.

Seth "Irontop" Carson, Captain of First Ward Police, Democratic pol in good standing, saloon-keeper and fabled volunteer fireman, beat a quiet tattoo on the chief's door then entered discreetly, as though not to disturb anyone. Though discreet was hardly the word one would have used to describe this blond-maned specimen in his street fighting days, when the anvil-like set of his shoulders and his apparent imperviousness to pain had earned him his *nom de guerre*.

Chief Matson lost no time in apprising the captain of his plan, and Harrington handed him the offending editorial. As Carson read, his lips silently formed the words—until he came to Brunton's assault on the chief. Matson stared unblinking. "So who is this paragon you have in custody, Captain?"

"Name's McGlone. Age twenty-seven. Bouncer at a whore-house run by a pimp named Johnson at 65 Front. Record of assaults a mile long. Only a matter of time till he graduated to murder. This one has all the hallmarks."

"Such as?"

"Cuyler's Alley, where the dear departed was found. That's the usual depository for Johnson's guests."

"There's nothing I detest worse than poor hospitality," the chief put in acidly.

"McGlone ain't content to leave a man senseless, Chief. He likes to dress his victims up—or down, I suppose." Carson

14

eased back and offered a wicked grin. "A few weeks ago we found one in a plug hat and suspenders, nothing but. Before that it was a truss, white gloves and hob-nailed boots, with a cracked monocle to grow on. This time, just a pair of silk drawers and a fancy plaid cravat round the old gutter-lane. Simple but elegant, eh?"

"I trust we'll be securing a tie of our own round this black-guard's neck," sneered Harrington.

"He'll ketch alright, Frank, don't you worry. We're tuning him up right now. It's only a matter of time."

"Go easy on him," the chief interjected. "As I say, I want him out of sight for the time being. Let him confess in a day or two. By then—if the *Post* goes with the story, and I think they will—we may know more of the victim. But keep 'em guessing all the way. Keep 'em guessing." He sat back with an air of satiation. "Good day to you both."

The sunlight was gone from the window. As he followed Carson through the door, Harrington looked back at the chief sitting in semidarkness like a vast, stone sphinx, two little glass frames all that was left of his stare. What would it take to move him? he wondered.

CHAPTER 3

Mrs. Fitzgerald was in a "frippery dippery" as her late unlamented husband was wont to call her rare moments of panic. She had contravened one of her most firmly held principles, one that any self-respecting landlady in the crazy metropolis of New York (and she counted herself among that number) ignored at her peril. She had failed to nail down the references of a lodger before admitting him to the hallowed precincts of her Greenwich Street boarding house. And the consequences were staring her in the face like a spreading gravy stain on her best lace tablecloth, the one her mother—God rest her dear soul—had crocheted for her own dowry back in the old country.

It was getting on for nine of a Thursday evening, and from her vantage point at the foot of the stairs Mrs. Fitzgerald heard the low thud of the attic door closing and, straining her ears, listened to the footsteps descending the four flights. A policeman, he said he was, an inspector of something or other, gave the Chief of Police as a reference, no less. He'd seemed well-spoken, tall, not unpleasant-looking, well cut suit of clothes. Come from Cincinnati, he said. Customs and Excise there for a number of years. Happy to take the always-hard-to-rent attic (to the right sort, that is). No complaints about the roof leak, slight as it was. Single.

Ah! There's the rub. And her with two young daughters, Eliza of marriageable age, and already making eyes at the young man. That was it. Not that he'd taken advantage, she'd give him that.

A couple of weeks ago, it started. Mrs. Jensen, one of the regulars at Mrs. Fitzgerald's weekly game of whist, swore that she'd seen Mr. DeShays before, though she couldn't say where,

16

even after agonizing over it to everyone's irritation. Then just this afternoon, on his way in, Mr. DeShays had put his head round the parlor door to say he'd be going out and wouldn't be requiring dinner, and Mrs. Jensen nearly spat out her scone upon recalling, as he walked upstairs, it was in a play she'd seen him! At the Chatham Theater, several years ago! Against a chorus of doubts she asserted that the play, *Rob Roy*, had been very exciting, and that the young man had cut a fine figure in his kilt.

A policeman was one thing—reassuring in a way to have the Law under your roof, particularly with this River Mauler on the prowl—an actor quite another. Mrs. Fitzgerald told herself she had her daughter's best interests to consider, not to mention her own reputation. Word would get out in no time that she was running a theatrical boarding house, and everybody knew what that meant. Mrs. Jensen, with her tongue, had probably told ten people already. Was Mr. DeShays with the police at all? On reflection, he didn't seem the type. Too—what was the word? Cultured? Oh why hadn't she checked! Still, she had to find out, take steps. She couldn't live with herself another moment. And these encounters were best done in a public place. Tenants could get nasty. Why, one time …

"Ah, Mr. DeShays, a moment please, sir." The parlor was mercifully empty and she ushered him in and shut the door.

"Is anything the matter, Mrs. F?"

She winced at the familiarity, heretofore encouraged. "I'm not a person who beats about the bush, Mr. DeShays. I'll come right out and say it."

"Say what?" he asked, apparently genuinely perturbed, when she didn't go on. (But these actors could fool anybody, wasn't it their job?)

"Were you ever in *Rob Roy*?" she blurted, adding, "which I believe is a theatrical play of some sort," as the thought of his nice legs in a kilt made her suddenly blush.

"Is this some kind of interrogation?" he challenged.

"It's just that Mrs. Jensen, one of my whist regulars, swears she saw you on the stage."

"Charmed, I'm sure, Mrs. F, but I'm just a policeman. No doubt you've checked my references. In fact," he brightened, "I'm off this very minute to celebrate with my colleagues the latest triumph of the Law. You'll have read the papers. I'd be flattered if you'd consent to accompany me and make out of what promises to be a boorish evening something rather special."

This was too much for Mrs. Fitzgerald. "Oh, Mr. DeShays," she cried, backing through the door, "forgive me, I'm so sorry to have doubted you."

"On the contrary, Mrs. F," he shot back. "In this life you can never be too sure." Stepping into the street DeShays shuddered and drew up the collar of his coat. Not from the cold—it was a balmy evening for the time of year—but from the memory of himself prancing around the stage of the Chatham in a kilt. Was it only three years ago? It seemed a lifetime.

The rough sawing of an Irish fiddle, the earnest clanking of glasses and the hubbub of a spirited free-and-easy filled the confines of Spider Murphy's Opera Saloon and spilled out onto the balmy night air. An Indian summer's eve was drawing a full house to the Bowery barroom, where men thronged over a sawdust-covered floor everywhere matted with clots of tobacco juice.

An array of bottles, beer glasses, tumblers and decanters lined up with a few cigar boxes along a counter behind the bar, above which a pair of worn boxing gloves hung from the frame of a tarnished mirror. On the wall opposite, a row of camphene-lamps formed a string of pale haloes which mediated a thick gauze of stagnant cigar smoke tinged with the stale odor of spilt beer. The walls were adorned with prints of race horses and doughty pugilists in game-cock poses, all barely discernible in the enveloping murk.

Miles DeShays, Inspector of Junk Shops and Second Hand Dealers in the City of New York, leaned his lanky frame against the end of the bar and regretted the day—not so long ago—that he'd given up cigars. For sheer self protection from the nauseating stench of this hell-hole, a cigar was almost an

18

essential. Near him smoke-eaters from the local firehouse vied for space with a smattering of low level municipal functionaries and workingmen. While the regulars hunkered over the bar, nursing their tumblers and talking of the day's events, a second tier of men crowded in behind them. DeShays watched as one hard case demonstrated just how close to a knot of delinquents he could spit the juice from his quid, without actually hitting them.

Down the far end of the bar the proprietor, Spider Murphy, a famed boxer, plied a customer with a steady stream of watered-down liquor in exchange for a little private entertainment; a customer well known to DeShays in his thespian days. In his heyday, T.J. Winchell, a comic impersonator known professionally as Winchell the Drollerist, had pulled in the crowds at some of the East's most fashionable houses. Strange to see him rubbing elbows in such company.

Down the length of the room ran two rows of scarred wooden tables, the rear ones, near a makeshift stage, occupied by flashily attired rakes and gamblers, showmen, a judge or two, and an alderman holding court with several sluggers from a local Democratic club. All were gathered to celebrate victory in the recent election.

All drinks were on Carson, the hero of the hour, who—along with Frank Harrington and a select coterie of officers—seemed to be having himself a grand old time. Irontop's name had figured prominently across the day's front pages. Following the *Post*'s exclusive the other papers had lapped up the River Mauler story, vying with each other to reveal the identity of the corpse in Cuyler's Alley. Some declared him a well-known actor from the London stage, others a wealthy scion of the top ten thousand, a foreign spy, a procurer who'd met a richly deserved fate, a missing banker suspected of embezzlement. As for the killer, he assumed the proportions of a monster, a Caliban of the waterfront who mauled his victims before decking himself out in their togs. Dubbed the River Mauler, the news of his arrest by Carson had, in the words of one scribe, "produced a collective sigh of relief from the Battery to Harlem." Even Brunton's *Argus* had offered grudging praise, though, to be sure, the chief's name had gone unmentioned.

DeShays picked his way through the crowd towards his fellow policemen. Given his druthers, he'd have chosen almost any other group in the room to associate with. But the occasion was, he recognized, something of a command performance, and he didn't want to alienate his new colleagues unnecessarily. Galling enough having someone thrust upon them whose sole qualification for the job was a politically well-connected uncle. (Not that politics wasn't mother's milk to the lot of them.) Worse, to install someone as obviously ill-suited to police work as DeShays smack under the chief's nose.

Pausing at the end of the bar he slapped his old friend, Winchell, on the back. "What? Not only do you monopolize the talent," he shouted to Spider Murphy, "you corrupt with your liquid poison the fairest flower of our stage! Yield, I command you, to the long arm of the law. Come sit with us, TJ," he appealed to the comedian, "and help celebrate the latest triumph of the angels of light over the powers of darkness."

"As a good Christian, now, would I serve His Lordship anything that ain't been baptized?" the Spider protested loudly, to the guffaws of those nearby. To which the Drollerist responded by raising his glass, downing its contents at a gulp and falling back in a theatrical faint into the arms of DeShays, to further hoots and catcalls.

Arm in arm the two men—tall and sturdy, drooping and thin—made their way towards the back of the room. "I'm ashamed to be seen associating with the likes of you," murmured Winchell, who indeed seemed not as drunk as DeShays had feared. "A disgrace to the profession, that's what you are. How could you do it, son, and hope to hold up your head in decent company again?"

"Do what, TJ?"

"Join the pigs, what else?"

"I am fleeing from pigs. There are more pigs per square foot in Cincinnati than any other place in America, as you'd know if you had spent the past three years in exile in that porkopolis, as I have."

A welcoming bellow from Carson, whose attention had been drawn to their approach, ended the exchange. Space was made at the table and another round called for. Harrington, scattering cigar ash, leaned across to shake the Drollerist's hand. "Delighted to make your acquaintance, Mr. Winchell. My wife is a great admirer of yours. Indeed we plan to attend your forthcoming performance at Barnum's Monday night."

"'is wife's the Feejee Mermaid!" blurted an inebriated wag.

Harrington ignored the sally. A teetotaler, he ascribed all such rudery to the scourge of drink. "She's particularly partial to your Scotch and Irish impersonations. I trust you will not disappoint her."

"Winchell for Chief!" came another wisecrack.

"Why not?" yelled a voice, "The whole bloody outfit is a bunch of goddamn comedians!"

DeShays strained to get a look at the speaker, a ferret-faced little fellow with an ugly goiter. He felt Carson's rough hand clasp the back of his neck in a friendly grip and was grateful. "Drink up, lad. Don't bother with those dildos." Carson was alright. It was Harrington and the chief and some of the others who'd be only too happy to see the back of him.

"Win-chell! Win-chell!" The fiddle had ceased its scraping and from somewhere in the crowd the chant grew and grew. Moments later scores of glasses were pounding the tables in unison. The Drollerist scowled at DeShays as if it was his doing, then shrugged helplessly. Harrington leaned over and gestured towards the little stage. Winchell started to get to his feet, then sat down again. Oh Lord, thought DeShays, he's not going to make it.

But no, the man was up again. He tripped on the edge of the crude wooden platform, but turned it into a joke which the crowd cheered. Even without his makeup the Drollerist, with his rubbery features and pasty complexion, appeared the very model of a clown. His eyebrows were faint, and his small dark eyes stood in sharp contrast to his pallid skin. With a bold gesture he tossed his coat to one side, revealing loose-fitting red trousers, a buff-colored waistcoat and a large black cravat, which he tugged at before rolling up his sleeves and adjusting his top hat to a level plane.

"Farmer Ryan," he began, "had been making love to his pig for some years past. One day his conscience got the best of him, and he says to Father O'Connor, 'I can stand it no more, Father, for I've made love to me pig.'

"'Tell me now, was it a bo'rr a girl, me son?'

"'Why surely a girl, Father. D'ya think me some kind of a mollie?'"

Winchell's opener met with hearty shouts of approval and the loud rapping of knuckles. As the applause subsided, the comedian fixed the gathering with an arch stare. He stood stock still for a moment, then began to stroke his beardless chin in mock reprimand. A half minute passed, but still the man, now seemingly sober, said nothing. A few nervous twitters erupted as the otherwise silent gathering awaited a punch line. In the back, curious heads craned for a better look.

Winchell's aging but oddly boyish face assumed the expression of a leering satyr. Harrington began to shift uncomfortably in his chair. Carson offered a wry smile as he returned the stare, braced perhaps for an act he thought he'd seen before. Finally, after what seemed an eternity, the Drollerist's thin, reedy voice filled the room.

"'Twas the Second of November, I still can remember
A sad fool did breathe his last sigh
A stiff in the alley, a swell's grand finale
Little pigs, whole hog or die!"

As Winchell launched into a refrain, DeShays became aware of a certain restlessness among his fellow officers.

"Little pigs lie on very good straw
Straw, straw, sham diddle daw!"

From the bar area came a few corroborating guffaws. While Harrington and his party exchanged angry glances, Carson, DeShays noted, kept his eyes glued on the singer as if encouraging him to go on.

"If an innocent man, a poor son of Erin
Must hang by the neck, we ask why

'Twas all in the plan, of a sly perliceman
Little pigs, whole hog or die!"

Now the men around DeShays had heard enough. Half of them were on their feet. Scattered boos and whistles and a few cheers swelled into a chorus of disapproval. Winchell's thin wail was all but drowned in the din as he struggled on.

"And where will it end, o my little song?
Song, song, dan diddle dong!
And where wi——"

A fusillade of cigar stubs and a couple of tumblers found their mark, and before Carson could stop him, a young officer rose and shoved the comedian back. He fell hard, amidst peals of derisive laughter, but, affecting the air of a martyred hero, collected himself with the greatest deliberation.

DeShays's first impulse was to flatten the man who had shoved his friend. Instead, he sprang forward and offered his arm to Winchell who angrily brushed him off. Winchell's progress towards the door was slow and unsteady, but determined. As he moved, a way opened before him through the crowd whose taunts and jibes gradually dwindled to a few self-conscious asides and even a smattering of applause. DeShays, unsure whether to follow him out and risk another rebuff or stay and risk despising himself, caught Spider Murphy's eye at the bar. With a wink and an incline of his ram-like head, the Spider indicated the door.

Out in the fresh air, DeShays searched for the Drollerist among a sea of shifty faces on the lookout for a good time.

He was nowhere in sight. Everywhere loud young men were venturing to and from billiard rooms, saloons, dance halls and bowling alleys. Outside an oyster cellar a lad was vomiting up his brandy and oysters while his friends looked on. The night was still young. But of Winchell there was not a trace.

CHAPTER 4

Four inspectors occupied a chamber adjacent to that of the chief. The morning found them catching up on the week's paperwork. Harrington customarily approached the task with the relish of a frustrated novelist and Friday was no exception. Steadfastly ignoring DeShays at the next desk, he scribbled industriously, punctuating the end of each paragraph with an exaggerated and unmistakably dismissive flourish of his quill, as if to emphasize his disapproval of his new colleague.

When DeShays attempted to exculpate himself from the previous night's fiasco and explain that Winchell was soused out of his mind and didn't know what he was saying, the silence only thickened. Nor did the other inspectors or a resident scrivener make the slightest effort to smooth things over. Besides Harrington there was Daniel Hewison, Inspector of Omnibuses, an overweight dullard who was the chief's brother-in-law, and A.C. Speight, mustachioed Inspector of Pawnbrokers, a steely-eyed grifter with a dozen years of police work behind him. The scrivener was Willoughby, a sallow-complexioned youth who aped their terse mannerisms. The knowing glances and whispered comments which passed among this impenetrable circle told DeShays he was a marked man. Not one of them would look him in the eye.

Just when it seemed to DeShays that the temperature had hit bottom and if he stayed one more minute in that cold company he couldn't be held responsible for the consequences, in walked the chief. The next thing he knew a giant hand gripped the back of his neck and he felt the glint from those square spectacles burning a hole clear through him into the papers on his desk.

As the chief turned on his heel, it seemed to DeShays that

he had been visited by Death, had felt its touch and under-stood its call. He stood up and, too, made for the door. It had been his intention, he supposed, to then and there tender his resignation. Hot-headed though he was, the sniggers that accompanied his exit served to bring him to his senses. Besides, there was Uncle Allaire, his mother's brother, to con-sider. A prosperous foundry man, Alderman for the Eighth Ward, Morgan K. Allaire was among the mayor's most gen-erous supporters, and DeShays owed his post to his considerable pull. He couldn't disgrace himself by quitting over the silent treatment.

Still, he ruminated, as fifteen minutes later he prepared to make his first inspection of the day, this is no kind of life. Winchell was right. He'd have to find something else, and soon.

It was dark when he walked down City Hall's basement stairs and along the passage which led to the office. Turning the knob on one of the large double doors, he was relieved to see he had the place to himself. Or almost to himself. Only the night man, Zebulon Honan, remained, slumped and asleep in an armchair by the gurgling pot-bellied stove. The wall-mounted gasoliers flamed low.

Old Honan, as he was familiarly known, was something of a mystery to DeShays. Well past retirement age, the chief gave out that he'd kept Honan on from the old watch system out of charity towards a formerly distinguished officer. Indeed, the two went back a ways in law enforcement, and DeShays had heard whispers that Honan's too accurate memories of certain incidents would keep his job secure for as long as Mat-son was Chief. Though it was hard to reconcile this doddering old toper with the man who had foiled the great City Bank robbery of 1817, the year DeShays was born.

Perhaps the old man sensed himself the subject of these thoughts because as DeShays passed by he fancied that Honan peered at him momentarily with a dull eye. He logged in, locked his little black book in his desk, and was soft footing it towards the door when behind him he heard a voice. "Will you slip away without so much as a salutation to a fellow suf-ferer of the genus humanus?"

25

DeShays turned. "I was trying not to wake you, sir."

"Many's the man that thought Old Honan's eyes were closed who lived to rue the day. Come now," he coaxed, "and join me in a little toast—to the end of a working day for yourself, the beginning of one for me. Or is it the embrace of a young wife you're heading out to, a chicken in the pot, a fire in the grate? No, I think not. You've not the married look about you. Sit you down, sit you down. Take the load off those feet." As he spoke he polished with a none too clean looking rag two glasses, into each of which went a finger of brandy.

Honan's innocent reference to his marital status, coming out of the blue like that, got DeShays right in the gut. He was grateful at the prospect of a bit of cheer to see him out into the raw night.

"Here's to fame and fortune." Honan raised his glass, drained it at a gulp, and administered a refill. "A profitable day, has it been then?" DeShays grimaced, at both the harsh tang of the booze and the memory of his day. "Don't let them get you down," Honan waved a disparaging hand in the direction of the desks. "They're nervous, you see. Can't blame them. Don't know who you are, do they?"

"It's not exactly a secret."

"A spy, that's what they're saying. They have their interests to protect."

"Oh sure I'm a spy. For my uncle."

"Or the chief, perhaps?"

"A spy for the chief. That's rich. I like that."

"Perhaps our chief suspects someone of holding onto purloined property. He has a fondness for items whose prior ownership is unclear, you see. A regular treasure trove, that safe in his office."

"You mean—?"

Honan nodded. "An expensive proposition, that house he's built himself uptown, if you get my drift. Furniture from France, they say. Marble from Italy. The wonder is, they say, that you don't take more of a private interest in matters yourself, with so many opportunities."

How many pay-offs from how many second hand dealers would it take, DeShays surmised as the brandy pleasantly explored every tributary of his body, to build such a place. Rummaging in his pockets Honan came up with a damp looking cigar butt and offered it to his companion who declined. Repeated attempts to light up having failed, he set it near the furnace to dry. Meanwhile the headline on a newspaper lying on the floor caught DeShays's eye: "BLOOD-SOAKED HAND STAYED. RIVER MAULER INCARCERATED."

"I've seen the body." Honan splashed brandy into both glasses. "Most sickening thing I've encountered in all my born days."

"Who was he, do you think?"

"Whoever he was, something don't smell right. Perhaps it is just a botched robbery. Then why leave him lying in your own back yard? And with the river just yards away?"

"Are you saying they arrested the wrong man?"

"Between you and me, sonny, there is no River Mauler. The Chief dreamed him up. The *Argus* has him on the defensive see, so he reckoned that a bit of well-timed public hysteria might help his cause. McGlone was in the Tombs within minutes of them finding the body. Very convenient, if you get my drift.

"Another odd thing: earlier I heard Speight tell Harrington that that watchman redeemed his gold watch from a Chatham Street pawnbroker right after the coroner's inquest. Wonder where he got the chink to do that all of a sudden?"

The rain had tapered off by the time DeShays emerged from City Hall. Scents of wet horsehair and manure clung in the night air as he passed the Park Theatre, where a row of coachmen vied half-heartedly for his attention. Soon the theater would let out and reward them with richer pickings. His objective: a basement tavern. As he bent to peer through its window a beggar, who crept up from nowhere, pushed the door open for him. DeShays scanned the long, low-ceilinged room to the realization that old times were dead times. The newspaper men, artists, musicians, actors and sycophants that he might have recognized from years ago were nowhere to be seen. No face seemed familiar. They looked younger, over-dressed, artificial—poor imitations of the characters he remembered.

Amid the scores of playbills and yellowing newspaper clippings clinging to the walls, a miniature of Junius Brutus Booth in the role of Macbeth caught his eye and kindled fond memories. It portrayed the great man at his zenith, clad in armor forged from strips of colored tinsel. As DeShays eyed the portrait, firm hands gripped his elbows from behind. "Impersonating a police officer is a very serious offence, young man."

The stentorian voice could only belong to his old friend Jonas Phillips, proprietor of "Number 11," as the tavern was familiarly known. DeShays, in his soggy pea coat and lumpy cap, formed a sad contrast to the dandified middle-aged man who now embraced him. "But I suppose we'll let it go this time," concluded Phillips good-naturedly, ushering DeShays towards the booth at the back where each night he held court as confidant to the great and would-be great, who valued his warmth, Scottish wit, and extended lines of credit.

Over beers and a plate of oysters the two settled in to talk of old times and toast old friends. It was nice to blend with a familiar atmosphere, like settling into a favorite chair and a soft pair of slippers. Opposite the booth a fireplace crackled comfortingly. Many months had passed since such a warm glow had spread across DeShays's face. He felt a renewed craving for a good cigar as Phillips lamented the deteriorating state of the fare offered these days at the Park. "It's getting so an actor's no more than a zookeeper, what with heroic wonder dogs and equestrian extravaganzas trailing dung across the stage."

DeShays remarked that business seemed unaffected, as he watched waiters bustling from booth to booth setting down piping hot bowls of chowder, hot mutton pies and mugs overflowing with porter. "Don't let appearances deceive you," Phillips leaned across the table, "It's not the same crowd as you and I remember. Something is rotten in Gotham."

"Which reminds me, you haven't seen Thomas J. Winchell lately?"

"Winchell? Is that why you've come? Admitted, the man is a garrulous old bore, but that's hardly cause for arrest, is it? Though let me guess—he's wanted for the crime of extortion. It's got to where one buys him a drink just to shut him up. His credit's dried up in this establishment, but there are still some who'll stand him a round. He's not been here tonight."

"I had a curious encounter with him yesterday. You've read of the Cuyler's Alley murder by now."

"Don't tell me Winchell's the River Mauler!" Silently Phillips signaled another round, then narrowed his gaze. "Though come to think of it, the way they hauled in that Irish thickwit was a trifle too—convenient, shall we say?"

"That's it. There was a free-and-easy over at Spider Murphy's for Irontop Carson. Half the department was there. Winchell was drowning himself at the bar. We hadn't seen each other since I got back. First thing he does—like certain other people, Jonas—is to take me to task over my new job. Fair enough. But what happened next defies belief."

"He paid the bill?"

"I brought him over to where we were sitting. An inspector named Harrington professed to be a great admirer, or at least said his wife was. So Winchell gets up and sings a song effectively accusing the police of purposely hauling in a dupe in the Cuyler's Alley case."

"Obviously the man's off his head."

"They thrashed him soundly before he escaped. I chased after him, but he vanished."

"A classic ploy for attention, if you ask me. Winchell's desperate for it."

"So now, as his friend, I'm a pariah around the office." DeShays described his reception that morning and the chief's behavior.

Phillips was curious. "I've heard a slew of rumors about that murder. From your privileged perch, can you shed any light?"

"Can you keep a confidence?"

"I'm grossly insulted you should ask."

"The whole River Mauler affair was a charade for the press

29

cooked up by Matson to get back at the *Argus*. They attack him every chance they get. McGlone was in custody days before his so-called arrest."

"That fat bastard. Perhaps Winchell was onto something?" Seconds later Phillips burst out laughing.

"Care to share the joke?"

"Tell me, who was Winchell drinking with?"

"Spider Murphy kept topping him up."

"No. It must be La Rue! I know it. He often drinks here with Winchell. The man puts a wild rumor into TJ's head, then watches the old buzzard run with it. A few bumpers and Winchell's a prophet without honor. It a great source of amusement around here."

"Who's La Rue?"

"An impersonator—famous actors mainly. Macready, Booth, Kemble. So sorry to disappoint you, inspector, but Winchell's just a mimic, after all."

"I don't know, Jonas. TJ may be past it, but I can't believe he's become such a fool as that. It would be interesting to know what this La Rue told him, if anything."

"Well, to satisfy your raging curiosity, next time he comes in I'll pump him. That way you'll have an excuse to look in again, old boy!"

"The Law will repay you for the drinks; Matson keeps a treasure trove in his safe within arm's reach."

The two men rose, drained their tankards and wiped the foam from their lips. Phillips eyed his friend quizzically. "By the by, Miles, how serious are you about this police business?"

"It's a living, if not an honest one."

"A word in your ear, friend to friend, if I may. Many's the actor I've known come to a sticky end because he crossed the line from make-believe to the real thing. From illusion to delusion, so to speak. It never works."

CHAPTER 5

It was with surprise that DeShays, late to the office, encountered the stocky figure who lingered beneath the portico that gloomy Saturday. Yet there the old timer stood, a racing sheet tucked under his arm, sucking on a cigar stub, possibly the self-same stub he'd had about his person the night before.

"Mornin', Chief," grunted Honan as DeShays reached the top step. This title he applied to nearly everyone, with the notable exception of Chief Matson himself.

"Likewise to you, sir," replied DeShays, perceiving that the other was not entirely sober.

The old man maneuvered the damp stub to one corner of his mouth. "Read a newspaper yet, son?"

DeShays figured on a little sporting chat. "Had a wager on the ponies, did you, sir? I'm told that Pilgrim's Progress outpaced Young America by five lengths over at Union Course. A bit suspicious, if you ask me. Glad I'm not a betting man."

"Too bad," croaked Honan, "Not a reading man either, I see. Well, it so happens the Father is mad as all hell."

"Matson?"

"It's that Brunton from the *Argus* again. Got the men downstairs fairly buzzing. Seems the Father will be wanting a word with you on the subject."

"What a newspaper may write can be no concern of mine, I can assure you of that."

A look of amused skepticism entered the old man's eye. "Then never you mind. Ignorance is probably your best defense. But a word of advice. When you're in with the Father, don't say a blessed goddam thing else you'll be confessing to murder before long. Remember our little talk last night, son. Godspeed." Pocketing his cigar butt, Honan touched the peak

31

of his cap and ambled off into the thick of Park Row traffic.

Descending the stairs, inchoate notions as to what might be afoot struggled to the fore of DeShays's mind. At the turn of the brass doorknob the patter of conversation within ceased abruptly. Harrington, Speight, Hewison and Willoughby, huddling conspiratorially around the stove, returned his questioning glance with defiant stares. "The Chief will be having a word with you now," Harrington snapped.

"May I enquire as to why?"

"You'll find out soon enough." Speight's look of malicious enjoyment rendered DeShays doubly uneasy. His faint knock on the chief's door was answered with a curt, "Enter!"

The room was in almost total darkness. As DeShays pulled the door to he sensed the approach of someone behind it, doubtless eager to hear all that transpired. As though he'd been waiting for the moment all night, Matson got up and reached for the Venetian blinds, which rose in a snarl.

DeShays blinked against the sudden light. No pictures graced the chief's walls, no haven where a victim's gaze could snatch a moment's respite from the unwavering, inscrutable countenance which filled the room. On the desk: just an inkstand, a newspaper, and the disembodied lead hand resting before its master like a loyal pet. But there would be no interrogation other than that which DeShays must perform on himself. Instead Matson spread out a copy of that morning's *Argus*. Without preamble, in a voice drenched in disgust, he began to read.

"'It was learned last night from a source exclusive to this journal'"—here the chief took a moment to gaze dispassionately at his audience—"'that the municipal police department conspired, at the highest level and from motives of base self-aggrandizement, to deceive the public into believing that the so-called River Mauler was still at large and a menace to our citizenry. In truth an arrest had already been made, and the suspect, a brothel bully well known to First Ward police, was already in custody. The object of this farce? To enlist public support for a police mired in lethargy and corruption, by transforming a simple matter of justice into a desperate hunt for a ruthless predator.'

32

"'We can only conclude that the new police, while display-ing a veneer of dutiful vigilance, are in truth chiefly involved in maintaining their own private interests, however dubious and depraved, at the public's expense. The next time our Chief of Police reaches into his safe for a fistful of the treasure trove he keeps therein, let him recall on whose backs that money was raised. The widow struggling to feed her children, the humble pensioner, the honest merchant, the bone-tired laborer.'

"'In the name of justice, in the name of mercy, in the name of our republican institutions of government, we say, It Is Time to Go.'"

Right up to the last few sentences DeShays refused to believe what the chief was insinuating, but with the mention of the safe came the memory of the previous evening at the "11": good food, strong drink, easy gossip with an old friend. A painful silence stretched out as guilt and defiance fought for supremacy in his mind.

"It is time to go," reiterated Matson at long last. This time it sounded like a sentence.

DeShays had difficulty reconstructing what happened next. That he was on the far side of the chief's door and that his star was on the chief's desk was clear enough. That no further words had been exchanged was also clear. In effect, therefore, he'd resigned. No feeling of relief greeted this realization, only the yawning awareness of his own stupidity. Passing the open door of the office he fancied he heard the derisive laughter of his erstwhile colleagues. Jackals, he thought, sniffing a fresh carcass. The ring of his boots down the marble corridor sig-nified his response.

Flushed with anger and humiliation, DeShays strode north at a rapid clip. Instead of turning west towards his lodgings he continued up Broadway, threading his way through bustling sidewalks and a score of building sites, beneath can-vas awnings and timber scaffoldings, past modest brick buildings adorned with bright green shutters, past fashionable shop fronts flanked by tall granite pillars, past the Olympic Theatre and Tattershall's horse and carriage mart, past unfinished Grace Church, stark, white and windowless.

Within twenty-five minutes he'd reached Union Square. Soon Broadway became a rutted dirt path that wound into Bloomingdale Road. As the country opened up DeShays passed shantytowns, small farms, isolated shacks, the estates of the wealthy. It felt good to walk, to stretch his limbs and get the stench of the city out of his nostrils. He meant to exhaust himself, emotionally and physically, to numb himself completely until rid of his anger.

The rain of the previous night had given way to gray skies and soft breezes befitting the "season of mists." As DeShays picked his way around the puddles and stood aside to let the occasional carriage jolt by, his brain began to clear. He considered how best to break the news to his uncle, whose trap he'd stumbled into without a glimmer of suspicion. That he'd been suckered into becoming an inspector of junk shops had him laughing out loud to the trees and bushes. Why had he gone along? He needed a job, that was the short answer, the alternative too bleak to contemplate.

DeShays's father, a Frenchman, vanished before he was born, leaving it to his mother's brother, Morgan K. Allaire, who had made a small fortune in the foundry business, to help raise him. He'd counted on his only son taking over the reins in the course of time, but just last month an accident at the smelter had reduced the lad to a cinder and denied that dream. In the clannish world of the East River foundry men, Allaire felt he had no choice but to look to his nephew, flesh of his flesh, to be his heir.

The prospect so appalled DeShays that when the police post came up he grabbed it. How craftily his uncle, knowing him better than he knew himself, had foreseen the outcome. He had only to wait. More than ever, reflected DeShays as he plodded northward, he was in Uncle Allaire's pocket.

On he walked, scarcely conscious of the magnificent decay around him, the autumn foliage, muted and sparse, nature hunkering down for another winter. Beyond the hamlet of Manhattanville he turned back. A chill wind had got up and was furrowing the surface of the river into tiny whitecaps. On the far bank the cliffs were already dark with shadow. If he kept up his pace he'd be home before nightfall.

Eventually, dog tired, buffeted by a maelstrom of dead leaves and dirt, he hailed a passing stage which left him not far from his lodgings. With just enough energy to climb up to his attic room, he stretched out on his bed and slept.

DeShays awakened to pitch darkness and the realization that supper had long passed downstairs. By now he was thoroughly famished. A proper anodyne was needed in the shape of a good meal while he could still afford one. Drunk with sleep, he cracked his neck, outstretched his arms then arose to light the oil lamp on his table.

On an impulse he pulled his best clothes from the wardrobe and tossed them on the bed. He put on a white shirt with a raised collar, around which he crafted an elegant cravat of red patterned silk. He smoothed and parted his dark hair, then donned grey trousers with black stripes, a silk waistcoat, narrow, square-toed shoes, his overcoat, gloves and flat-brimmed top hat. Satisfied with what he saw in the cheval glass, DeShays bounded down the stairs and hit the street. His destination: Pelham's, an elegant eatery about a half-mile south, of which his friend Billy Holmes was part owner. They'd known each other since—as stage-struck teenagers—they'd found employment doing odd jobs around the Park, graduating eventually to a succession of minor roles. DeShays entered the bustling eatery and took a place in the front room. Here the tables were set across from a Gothic-looking fireplace, the larger back room being given to a row of private booths.

As much as the food, he liked the atmosphere; the smell of pipe tobacco, the walls covered with oil paintings by young artists. Settling into a corner by a grandfather clock, he was greeted in a friendly West Indian lilt by a waiter named Sebastian, a handsome young mulatto who served him a choice cut of veal and a glass of porter as Holmes attended to the clientele in the back.

When the crowd thinned Holmes, whose angular features and long dark swept-back hair lent him a dramatic air, took the chair opposite unfolding a copy of the *Spirit of the Times*, a paper which carried the latest theatrical news. DeShays assumed the role of captive audience as Holmes launched into his customary state-of-the-theater monologue, while Sebastian cleared the table.

"I'll expect you've heard that Humphrey Bland will be putting on *Henry VIII* over at the Park. And that none other than Mrs. Bland shall take the part of Anne Boleyn, with Mrs. Shaw as Queen Catherine. Miles, I predict that history is about to be re-written."

"How so?"

"Reliable sources indicate that Henry is on the verge of abandoning Anne for Queen Catherine. Alas, I fear that Henry's reign shall be but brief this time."

"Do I detect a touch of the green-eyed monster?"

"That tart? He's welcome to her. We can't all be 'stars' now, can we, Officer?"

"Ah, but I retired mine this afternoon."

Holmes extended a fervent handshake. "You've come to your senses. Sebastian!" he called out, gesturing for him to top up DeShays's porter. "The man has a conscience after all!"

"If I claimed it was a question of high moral principle, I'd be lying. It was sheer stupidity."

Sebastian poured the drinks and Holmes thrust his ceiling-wards. "Then here's to sheer stupidity!" They clashed glasses. "But what will you do?"

"There's the rub. If I don't find something soon I succumb to the vice-like clutches of my uncle Allaire. But what am I good for? I'm doomed."

For a long moment Holmes regarded his friend over the rim of his glass. Then he laughed. "Just how desperate are you, old sod?"

DeShays took note of the dare-devil gleam in the other's eyes. "What did you have in mind?" he asked guardedly. Memories of madcap schemes dreamed up by a young Billy Holmes flooded back.

"Come with me." Holmes led the way through the steamy kitchen, snatching a butter cake off a tray. Outside he hoisted an eyebrow and looked at DeShays squarely, his molars attending to the cake as he spoke. "Your policial experience may be of use to me, dear Miles ... I meant to tell you, but the right situation didn't present itself. It so happens I maintain an interest in an exclusive and very private club for discriminating gentlemen. The police are, so far, unaware of this venture, which helps keep expenses low. A doorman with your expertise may prove invaluable. Midnight to the wee hours, three days a week. Interested?"

DeShays was uneasy, but with no other prospects and a bit of prodding he assented. Terms were agreed upon, free meals being the clincher, and the two stepped back into the restaurant to seal the deal with a bottle of port, brought over by Sebastian with what seemed to DeShays a look of knowing satisfaction.

The very next evening DeShays made for the address his friend had inscribed for him on an otherwise blank card.

CHAPTER 6

At first DeShays was puzzled. The address was the one given on the card, he was on time, yet he saw no signs of life. Rather the opposite: the yard before him was filled with blank gravestones and memorial sculptures. Beyond stood a wide two-story brick building surmounted by a solemn-looking stone Cupid.

Leaning on an iron railing just outside the arc of a corner street lamp, DeShays wondered what to do. No one came from within the darkened structure and no one passed. A strong wind pushed through the street, causing a newspaper to cling to the back of his leg. He brushed it away then tried the gate. It opened soundlessly. At the front door he knocked and waited, again no one. He tried the handle to no avail. A movement over to his left made him start. DeShays peered into the gloom. A man was beckoning, from his dress, a clergyman. For a brief instant a lantern illuminated his face. It was Billy Holmes.

DeShays followed Holmes through a door at the far end of the building and found himself in a dark passage that went on for longer than he would have thought possible. They crossed a small courtyard and entered a low wood-frame construction. At the top of a flight of stairs Holmes rapped on a door. Eyes appeared behind a sliding panel and they were admitted to a spacious, dimly lit room by the self-same Sebastian whom Holmes now introduced as his partner in crime.

DeShays looked over the spacious room. Camphene lamps clung to unplastered walls and the windows were thickly cloaked in black. At the far end a small stage was draped in purple velvet and flanked by two tall braziers. Onstage, Holmes explained, voluptuous models undraped themselves in tableaux such as "Venus at her Toilet" and "Bathsheba in the Bath."

"Dear Miles," he continued, pointing towards a tall stool near the door, "your role is to sit right there and watch for the presence of philistines, policemen or otherwise. Should you detect an undesirable, I am to be alerted at once. And of course you are to collect the price of admission, which is a half dollar."

Soon the models arrived and patrons began to filter in. Upright-looking grey-haired men, young professional types and loudly dressed rakes. It wasn't long before the first sign of danger showed itself. DeShays slid open the panel to find that there was indeed a policeman come calling. There on the landing stood a familiar figure, a tubby man with a forlorn expression, like that of a dog locked out of his rightful abode. Daniel Hewison, husband to Chief Matson's sister. In an instant the club was transformed into a gathering of the Christian American Bible and Tract Society as Sebastian frantically replaced brandy with Bibles.

Holmes peered out. "I had no idea he was a policeman, but not to worry. He's among our most valued clients." Hewison was admitted and brushed past DeShays without a glimmer of recognition, not that he'd ever offered one before. The club reverted to form.

DeShays trained his eyes on Hewison during the next tableau in which the curtain opened on "Odalisque, the Harem Slave," featuring a buxom quadroon. Sprawled on the couch in a pose of naked abandon, her head tilted and her eyes half shut, she dangled a fan of peacock feathers between her legs. The crowd leaned forward as one as the fan wavered slightly but didn't drop. Later DeShays was amused to see Odalisque visit Hewison's table and subject herself to his greedy inspection. As they left together he fancied the inspector noted his presence, but couldn't be sure.

In the wee hours, after the place wrapped up, DeShays sat with Holmes and Sebastian counting jars full of coins and downing brandy. Grateful as he was to his friend for the job offer, he realized it wasn't for him. Sooner or later word was bound to get about and, keen as he was to distance himself from Uncle Allaire, there was no point in embarrassing him. In vain Holmes tried to convince him to stay on as DeShays struggled to stay awake. Even when they upped his share of the take to one third he shook his head. About eight in the morning he returned to his lodgings to sleep the sleep of the dead.

DeShays awoke to repeated knocking at his door. For one awful moment he imagined he was back at the Park and had missed his cue. But it was only his landlady asking if she should keep supper for him. Staggering in that morning he muttered some lie about being transferred to night duty. Not to worry, he yelled, he'd snatch a bite somewhere later. He'd slept for nearly twelve hours. As he lay in bed watching shadows play across the sloping ceiling an uneasy feeling, as of a thing forgotten, crept upon him.

In the throes of a pounding hangover, he rolled onto his stomach and stared blankly at the near wall. Minutes passed before he realized what was bothering him: it was Monday night, the night of Winchell's promised performance at Barnum's. Perhaps because—being off the force—he had nothing to lose by it, perhaps out of sheer curiosity to see what further mischief Winchell might wreak, perhaps even in a last ditch effort to save the old Drollerist from himself, DeShays knew he had to be there. Already he might be too late.

At the corner of Greenwich and Canal he looked for an omnibus but there was none in sight and anyway omnibuses were too slow. He reached Broadway fast enough, but Broadway was jammed with traffic and thronged with crowds strolling at a leisurely pace. Small parties came and went from fancy restaurants and saloons, crowds milled about or stood three deep to gawk at brightly lighted window displays. Everywhere people moved with agonizing slowness. Men encumbered by sandwich-board advertisements seemed as though placed to bar his path—he'd never seen so many at one time. And only in New York did people stand stock still at the curb, engrossed in conversation as if around the fireplace at some social gathering.

DeShays shouldered his way through the crowd like a man possessed. He was panting and drenched with perspiration by the time he entered Barnum's. Reaching into his pocket, he asked the clerk if he was in time for Winchell.

"Save your money friend. He just left. And he won't be back in a hurry."

"Why?"

"He's paid to do impersonations, not blather on about the damn River Mauler."

"Oh God."

"The police got the wrong man, he says. In two seconds, if they ask him, he'll show them the River Mauler. Then he called on any policeman in the audience to come forward while he waved around a bloody great mirror. I wouldn't want to be in Winchell's shoes tonight."

DeShays stood for a minute on Broadway pondering his next move. Crossing Park Row he turned east into Ann Street away from the crowds, making for an oyster bar he knew on Fulton. Near Phillips's place he briefly fantasized about giving the bastard a sound thrashing, but decided it could wait.

Theatre Alley ran between Ann and Beekman. As DeShays neared the mouth of the alley disturbing sounds reached him—the scuffing of heels on paving stones, the dull thud of boots sinking into soft matter, muffled groans, the sickening smack of hard blows hitting home. Somewhere near the rear of the Park Theater a violent struggle was under way.

"Police!" cried DeShays. Dim as the light was, he discerned red trouser legs writhing on the ground beneath two burly bruisers, one of whom turned to fix him with a defiant sneer. Where had he seen the man before? That night at Spider Murphy's? After a parting kick to his victim's ribs the brute loped off while his accomplice, a hulking lad with a great plug hat, hurled a bottle which missed DeShays's head by a foot and smashed to pieces on a wall.

Kneeling on the cobbles, DeShays groaned as he recognized his battered friend. Pulling loose the old man's scarf, he wound it around Winchell's head to staunch the blood from an ugly gash, then ran to find a cab.

He found one on Park Row and with the driver's help lifted Winchell aboard. Putting the whip to his nag, the cabman set his sights for City Hospital, careening into Centre Street, turning west on Duane, and turning DeShays's insides out as he clung to the limp form alongside him.

Near the hospital DeShays changed his mind. Leaving Winchell there meant delivering him into the hands of his persecutors. Winchell must disappear for a while. Leaning out the window he yelled his own address to the driver.

DeShays had hoped to arrive at 488 Greenwich undetected by his landlady, but it was the rare coach stopped at her door. Glancing up as he struggled with the Drollerist's uncooperative limbs, he saw the night-capped visage at the window. She was at the door before he could get out his key.

"It's my cousin, poor man. Found him lying face down in the gutter. I fear that demon rum has finally bested him."

"Good heavens, Mr. DeShays. I pray it's not too late for a cure to put him right."

"I pray that your prayers will be answered, Mrs. Fitzgerald."

When they reached the attic the driver, a Scotsman named Stewart who refused all offers of payment, helped remove Winchell's boots and overclothes and get him onto DeShays's bed. As the night wore on Mrs. Fitzgerald and her daughter, Eliza, dressed his wounds and applied healing compresses, and not until the patient was breathing peacefully did they retire. Later DeShays crept downstairs to the kitchen. The remains of a leg of mutton and a hunk of stale bread somewhat assuaged the gnawing in his gut.

His vigil lasted into the early hours. When Winchell at last stirred and opened his eyes, DeShays administered a little brandy from a bottle he kept in his trunk. "Am I in heaven, after all?" Winchell asked, licking his lips. "If so, what is your business here, Miles? How come they let you in?"

In as few words as possible, DeShays recounted what had happened.

"So you've quit the porcine precincts, my boy? You don't know the good that does me."

As the fallen impersonator lapsed into a deep sleep, DeShays mused on the descent of his star. Time was when the name of Winchell echoed through fashionable parlors, but the fad for one man shows was a brief one. As his popularity waned his drinking grew worse and his act became increasingly abrasive, if always brutally honest. Winchell lashed out at his public as the mood struck him, oftentimes stepping out of character to engage in direct mockery, so that audiences began to feel as though they were seated above a trap door.

The smudge of brown hair dye on Winchell's pillow spoke volumes. The man was a squeezed-out lemon. If DeShays hadn't chanced upon him, he reckoned that Winchell might have met a fitting end, killed for having spoken his mind once too often. Perhaps that was what he was really after. When he was stronger and ready to talk DeShays would find out more.

Dawn peered over the skyline as DeShays lay on the floor to catch a bit of sleep, but with Winchell snoring like an ox and the adrenaline still flowing he couldn't go under. Each time he began to doze events of the past week presented themselves in tantalizing fragments until at last he pulled himself up. Rummaging through a drawer for a sheet of paper, he sat down at the table. For a while he was still, thinking out the words, assuming the character he knew so well; then he inked his quill and began to write:

The Honorable Oliver W. Matson
Chief of Municipal Police of the City of New-York

November 11, 1845

Dear Matson,

Recently, through the good offices of His Honor the Mayor, my nephew, Mr. Miles DeShays, lately of Cincinnati, was employed by the newly re-organized Police Department in the capacity of Inspector of Junk Shops and Second Hand Dealers. It has come to my notice that, on the 8th of November instant, Mr. DeShays tendered to you his resignation on grounds that he was

43

suspected of disloyalty to the department and that you accepted the aforesaid resignation.

Enquiries instigated by myself have revealed that my nephew's actions, far from any taint of disloyalty, served to alert the public to certain irregularities in the operation of the department which will doubtless now be rectified. I therefore request that he be reinstated in his duties forthwith. Surely our police are in need of men who are not afraid to speak out for honesty and truth.

Should you fail to act on this matter within a reasonable period of time, rest assured that I will not hesitate to set in motion a full inquiry in Council as to the shortcomings of the present department and the remedies that might be taken to correct them.

I remain, as always, yours respectfully,

Morgan K. Allaire, Alderman for the 8th Ward City of New-York

Meanwhile, DeShays mused as he carefully blotted the page, there was one man he might be able to talk to.

CHAPTER 7

Irontop Carson wasn't what might be called a policeman's policeman. He hadn't the bureaucratic instincts of a Harrington or the practiced expertise of a Speight. His name conjured up the image of a volunteer fireman-hero, the rabble-rousing foreman of "Red Ghost" Engine Company No. 5. But Irontop's flair for rallying the vote from his Iron Mug Saloon had won him friends in high places, and a copper star was his reward. It suited him as oddly as his new headquarters.

Carson's First Ward station house was situated incongruously atop the Franklin Market which sat between Front and South Streets at the center of Old Slip. At eight o'clock in the morning its aisles were jammed with commerce. DeShays, heading for the stairs, picked his way between bins of cabbages and cages brimming with baby chicks as men stood at counters downing quick breakfasts and a top-hatted butcher importuned him from a stall festooned with choice cuts.

Upstairs, under a pitched roof, a stark white room boasted several rows of benches. At its far end, past a waist-high wooden partition, stood a raised counter. At the counter sat a stocky, swarthy man poring over some papers like a schoolmaster in an empty classroom at recess: First Assistant Captain Dick Poole.

It was Poole who really ran things day to day in the First, and DeShays guessed that his men had just turned in the watch reports he was reading, and that the dregs of the night had recently graced those benches. When at last he glanced up, his look induced in DeShays the feeling of a victim of leprosy violating quarantine.

"Captain Carson, please."

"Anything in particular it's about, DeShays?"

45

The clock on the wall behind the counter gave DeShays his cue. "I guess you could say it's about Time. I'm ten minutes late."

Poole hesitated, caught off guard, then grudgingly stepped down off the platform. "Wait right there." DeShays could scarcely see the man's lower lip when he spoke, so thick was his mustache. Ambling into Carson's office, Poole shut the door behind him. Minutes passed before he stuck his head out and beckoned DeShays to enter. Awkwardly, he then showed no signs of leaving.

"Hello Miles. Surprised to see you at this hour." In the dark office, behind a big desk, Carson seemed unusually remote. His deep drawl—or was DeShays imagining?—held an undertone of mockery. The two policemen exchanged glances, Carson nodded and Poole left.

The handshake Irontop offered felt like the grip of a vise. DeShays took a seat and took in the long blond hair and strapping build of a man pushing forty and in the prime of life. He noted with wry approval the diamond stickpin twinkling from a crimson necktie and the paisley patterned silk vest, an ironic backcloth to his policeman's star.

A noise, something between a wheeze and a groan, came from the neighborhood of Carson's feet. Craning his neck, DeShays saw a white bull-terrier lying, panting and half asleep, by the brass spittoon to the right of the desk. "That's Caesar." Carson reached over and tugged one of Caesar's ears. "That's all right boy, there there." The dog rolled onto its back as he rubbed its stomach then playfully stuck his hand between its slobbery jaws.

"That must be him." DeShays nodded towards a framed lithograph on the wall. "A beautiful terrier."

"Yea, a real champion in his day. But you didn't come to pay homage to Caesar, my man. What can be done for you? You look as though you haven't slept for a week. Been enjoying yourself since you quit?"

DeShays felt cool grey eyes scanning him as though he was an intriguing hand of cards. "A couple of bruisers nearly killed T.J. Winchell last night. They well might have if I hadn't come along."

Carson's gaze hardened. "Where'd it happen?"

"In the alley behind the Park Theatre."

"That's not my territory. Why come to me?"

"I know it's not in the First—but Cuyler's Alley is."

"What's your meaning?"

"I recognized one of the assailants. Saw him that night at Spider Murphy's. Winchell was on at the American Museum last night. Had more to say about the police and the River Mauler."

"I see. Well, free speech does pose its risks. I'd like to help, Miles, but the Fourth is Captain McGillicuty's territory. You'll need to go see him on this. Where's Winchell now?"

"Asleep in my room. I thought it safer than the hospital."

"Then why not wait till he comes round, find out just what happened and see McGillicuty? Why the long face? What's on your mind? Out with it."

"It's the Mauler affair. Just maybe Winchell had a hold of something. For instance, why doesn't anyone claim to have known the victim?"

"Bodies wash up here every couple of days, Miles. Most of 'em aren't ever identified. That's how it is."

"This was no vagrant or petty thief. And why did this McGlone leave the corpse right there where he worked? He could at least have dumped it in the water. Is he that stupid?"

Carson leaned his elbows on the desk, his hands forming a little temple as he cracked his knuckles one by one. He seemed to dip into a reserve of patience. "McGlone's about sung it, you know. It's only a matter of time."

"What about the watchman who found the body? Eli Miller? Seems like he redeemed a gold watch from his pawnbroker soon after testifying before the coroner's jury."

"Listen Miles, if you'd like to know where Miller got the money to do that, just ask the man yourself," Carson responded wearily. "He didn't pilfer the body, if that's what you're driving at. We're well satisfied of his honesty." Jerking a leg onto the desk Carson leaned back, hands clasped behind his head. For a moment DeShays fancied there was more to the action than physical comfort, that perhaps Carson was blocking something.

"My advice to you is this, Miles." DeShays felt the weight of his steady gaze. "You're out of the Department. For your own good, stay clear. Listen, I understand how you feel about your friend. If it turns out there's anything I can do, just ask." Carson seemed almost apologetic as he rose to offer another bone-grinding handshake.

Poole remained buried in his papers as DeShays asked to see a city directory. Feigning indifference, he reached into a drawer and came up with a thick volume on which he clamped a hairy hand. "A little lost, are we? Need help finding the way?"

DeShays stifled an urge to tweak the man's nose. "I think I can manage, thank you." With the task ahead, it wouldn't do to rile Carson's prime minister. Holding the directory out of Poole's line of vision, he thumbed through the pages. Miller's address was less than a mile away. "Good day to you, Assistant Captain."

Plopping the volume back on the desk, DeShays made for the door. He was just past the benches when he heard Poole's reply: "Good riddance to you, fool." He hadn't counted on a fond farewell.

Exiting the market by the fishmongers' stalls, DeShays was overcome by the aching need for sleep. But sleep would have to be postponed. A good thing that Rose Street was practically on the way home.

CHAPTER 8

Rose Street sloped gently towards the East River, the stepped fronts of its meager dwellings giving an impression of a row of dominoes set at a slight angle one to the other. DeShays could scarcely recall his last sight of this now forlorn corner of the metropolis. A good twenty years ago it must have been on a visit with his mother to one of her several maiden aunts. Time had not been kind to Rose Street.

In one of these oddly set houses lived Eli Miller, or so the directory said. Yet, on first perusal, no such number as 26½ presented itself. Number 26, yes, but not 26½. The most likely candidate was a low brick structure next door that proclaimed itself a printer's, though a rap on the shuttered window raised no response. Between the printer and a corset factory on the corner ran a narrow alley into which DeShays ventured. A thin tabby straddling a wall to his left observed his approach then dropped from sight. Visible above the wall was the top half of a two-storey structure somewhat overgrown with vines. Finding no entrance to the place on the alley, DeShays doubled back to Number 26 to investigate.

More than likely the night watchman was home asleep at this hour of the morning and wouldn't take kindly to prying strangers; a policeman though, even a masquerading one, was hard to ignore. The door, opening to his knock with startling alacrity, revealed a long-visaged, wary-eyed woman with hollow cheeks, thin lips and a high forehead. The greasy silver bun and faded brown dress left little room for doubt: this was a landlady, albeit a few notches down from his own.

"Good morning, ma'am. I'm Officer Bostwick. Here to inquire after Mr. Miller."

"I'm glad you've come, Officer, we're terribly concerned."

The words sounded rehearsed, as though his appearance had been expected. "He's never been gone this long before. But where is my husband? Is he still at the station house?"

"I expect he'll be along presently." DeShays pushed his luck: "I've been sent ahead to search the premises."

The woman retrieved a key from a small table in the hall. "Follow me."

Relieved that she hadn't asked for his star, he followed her past the parlor, catching a glimpse of himself in a mirror above the mantle. As an actor he'd once played an inspector, then he'd been one; now, he mused ironically, the circle was joined.

At the end of the narrow hallway they came to a damp, dingy yard. Mortar and moss oozed from the wall on the alley, which was abutted by the privy, a rude wooden hut. To DeShays's left washing hung from a low clothesline extended between the two buildings, so that he couldn't see much over the picket fence separating the next yard. In front of the rear house the landlady pointed up at a window between peeling green shutters and pronounced it Miller's.

Trailing behind his guide up the creaking staircase DeShays wondered how to go about a search with no idea what he was looking for. At the second landing they came to a squat white door facing the stairs which the woman unlocked, standing aside as if showing the room to a potential boarder.

Stepping into the cold interior, DeShays felt like an intruder. The place was drab and depressing, with a reek of stale tobacco and unwashed linen, the private odor of an old man. While the landlady drew the thin calico curtains and opened the window his eyes fell on a tall wardrobe, a small chest of drawers, a worktable and a wall-mounted cabinet. The job shouldn't take long, and just as well, for the husband was likely to return soon.

He began with the wardrobe. Baggy cotton trousers, thin flannel shirts, their warmth long washed away, a woolen sweater, a frayed muffler. From the top shelf he plucked an old fire helmet of varnished black leather, hard as iron, with a leather shield that bore the number "22," the company name "Phenix" and the initials "E.M."

"At the table he never stops telling everyone about the great fires of old," said the landlady. "A veritable Vulcan, my husband calls him."

Beneath the bed a white canvas valise with color printed designs held yet more rumpled clothes. The chest of drawers disclosed stockings and yellowing underclothes. The cabinet contained a bowl, shaving brush, razor, toothbrush and a few patent medicine bottles. There was nothing beneath the mattress. DeShays felt the landlady hang on his every move and had a hunch she was waiting for the right moment to ask him something.

From the worktable DeShays picked up a half-finished wooden rattle such as watchmen carry on their rounds. Scraps of soft pine and wood shavings littered the floor. Miller, apparently, was a whittler. On the mantle over the fireplace a group of dusty figurines—firemen, sailors, Indian chiefs, all with oversized heads and feet—smiled the same eerie smile, as though mute witnesses to a shared secret.

A small toy horse lay on its side with one of its wheels missing. "That would be the Tompkins child's, one of my other boarders. Mr. Miller is rather like a big child himself. Never married, you know."

"Any living relatives?"

"There was a niece, but yellow fever got her a few summers back."

"How long did you say since you last saw him?"

"Been three or four days now, it has. Not that he isn't paid to the end of the month. Always punctual, he was."

"Any unusual visitors? Strangers calling?"

"Not as I recall. Kept very much to himself, he did. Just the officer about the Cuyler's Alley business."

Had Carson come himself? DeShays wondered. He opened the left-hand drawer of the worktable. A few carving tools were all it contained. The right-hand drawer wouldn't budge; something was wedging it shut. He picked up an end of the table and shook it.

The drawer opened to reveal a long-stemmed pipe, a magnifying glass, some newspaper clippings and a pair of scissors.

Evidently Miller had clipped out all mention of his name from the newspapers. "Mr. Miller was quite tickled by all the attention he got," she offered over DeShays's shoulder. "After his grisly find, he was out quite a lot, probably sharing his ghastly tale with all his drinking friends, whoever they were."

DeShays turned around. "Or are, as the case may be."

"Officer, if you don't mind my asking, how long is it before Mr. Miller is considered legally dead?"

So that's what was eating the old crone. In her mind she had the walls whitewashed already. Sifting through the clippings, he murmured absently, "It could be a long time indeed."

"Well, I'd best leave you to your own devices," she said with dull cheer. "I'll be down in the kitchen. Let me know if there are any clues, or what we may expect to happen from here."

"Thank you, ma'am. I'll call on the way out." He heard the stairs sag and moan beneath her. Though there seemed nothing more to see, he felt unable to leave. A fly droned and buzzed around his head. From the warehouse across the alley he heard porters swear and shout. Again he went through the wardrobe and the chest of drawers. The pockets of Miller's clothes yielded nothing more than a brass button and enough lint to fill a mattress. In the cabinet all was as before. Only the valise was left. He pulled it from under the bed and this time emptied out its contents.

As DeShays straightened out the rumpled clothes, he was amazed to see what they were. That soiled woolen something he'd passed over turned out to be an expensive black pilot coat with slanted pockets and huge buttons. Looking inside the coat, he found the remaining shards of a label which had been roughly cut out.

From the coat tumbled a pair of narrowly cut trousers, green wool with gaiter bottoms and striped with a black grid, along with a brocaded silk waistcoat of top quality. Articles unlikely to belong to one such as Eli Miller. On closer inspection the coat, and particularly the waistcoat, were smeared with brownish stains that had to be blood. The trousers might have fit himself. He compared them with the trousers in the wardrobe. Miller's were shorter and wider round the waist. Then the dull drumming of the door knocker from across the yard told him that he'd overstayed his welcome.

He stuffed the clothes back in the valise, suspecting that Miller was not likely to complain about missing them, whatever his fate. Valise in hand, he darted down the stairs, but too late: a muffled stampede sounded from the front house. More than the husband was heading his way.

His only chance of avoiding the latecomers was to hide. He glanced towards the space behind the staircase but a bucket and mop were in the way and the landlady was sure to notice their displacement. His only hope was the privy, if he could get to it in time. A couple of rapid strides and he flattened himself against the side of the wooden shed. That instant the back door of the front house burst open.

From his sidelong vantage point the profile moving past the hanging wash was all too familiar. The landlady and a bespectacled codger in an old brown tailcoat, wisps of white hair flying in all directions, followed.

DeShays listened to the steps on the stairs until he judged A.C.Speight, for he it was, to be at Miller's door, then tossed the valise over the wall. "That's him, Inspector!" shrieked the landlady as DeShays vaulted into the alley, narrowly missing a wheelbarrow and scraping his palm on some pebbles.

"Halt, police!" Speight's harsh voice rang out. Grabbing the bag, and keeping low to the wall so as to remain unseen from the windows above, DeShays rounded the corner past the factory. Duane Street was empty, save a tinker walking towards him whacking on a tin pan, "Pots an' pans! Mend yer pots an' pans!" Taking no chances, DeShays sprinted down Rose towards Pearl.

Rounding onto Pearl he cursed his luck. The pavements were dense with crates stacked high outside the tall red counting houses, their huge shutters spread overhead like iron ears. Husky porters in wide brimmed hats and baggy shirts sweated and shoved while young clerks idled on granite loading docks and smoked, and carts and dray horses rendered the cobbled street impassable. Slowed to a tortoise's pace, dodging skids, barrels, bales and boxes, DeShays kept glancing over his shoulder.

Beyond the counting houses the pavement cleared. Catching sight of a northbound omnibus boarding at the corner, DeShays ran for it as though for the last boat out of hell, managing to catch the driver's attention just in time.

Taking a seat by the door in back, he put the bag on the floor, conscious of looks from his ten or so fellow passengers. As the coach rumbled through Chatham Square, he scanned the horizon. Yellow 'buses lumbered towards Harlem or Manhattanville, carriages steered an uncertain course in the opposite direction, while barrow boys dodged in and out of traffic. At length the sight of the new branch post office on the corner of East Broadway reminded him of the letter in his coat pocket.

Wiping his forehead with a handkerchief, DeShays felt eyes on him from across the 'bus. "Pardon me, sir, but where did you get that bag?" A pretty woman in a lilac bonnet with a toddler on her lap was smiling at him. In his nervous state of mind, Miller's valise seemed to stick out like a sore thumb with its printed pattern of intertwining red, blue and yellow. He imagined its description in the newspapers. A mistake, boarding a stage where people had time enough to remember things.

"It was my father's," he mumbled.

"Thank you. It's quite attractive. My husband could use something just like it."

The stage rolled into the Bowery past Spider Murphy's. Craning left, DeShays watched the Bowery Theatre's colonnaded facade fill the grid of windowpanes like pieces of a moving puzzle. By the Branch, a small hotel next door, he caught sight of a street porter who sometimes delivered letters for his uncle. Clopping hooves and rattling panes came to a decrescendo as he pulled the leather strap running along the ceiling connecting to a pedal beneath the driver's foot.

"Bin on vacation, Mr. DeShays?" The lad loitering in the doorway of the hotel saloon grinned as DeShays, bag in hand, gingerly negotiated the steep rear steps to the street.

"No Mose, just running a few errands." Clad in a black frock coat, his black trousers stuffed inside heavy work boots, his dyed and greased black locks tumbling out from his stovepipe hat, Mose Humphreys looked about nineteen to DeShays.

"How's de uncle?" Mose asked gruffly. "Bin awhile since I had a job from Mr. Allaire."

"So happens I have one from him now. It's of great importance; that's why you're the man for it, Mose." Reaching into the inside pocket of his pea coat DeShays withdrew the letter he'd sealed with wax, handing it over as though a document of state. "On no account did you receive this from anyone other than my uncle. Is that clear?" he asked, reaching into his pocket for a silver half dollar.

"As a summer sky of deep a-zure," grinned Mose, as DeShays pressed the coin into his palm. He whistled as he read the address.

"Don't hand it to anyone but Chief Matson, no matter what," instructed DeShays. "If he's not in, go back later."

"Le grand fromage, eh? Must be some pumpkins goin' down." Mose looked around surreptitiously as he stashed the letter inside his coat. "It'll be there yesterday. Rely on me, friend."

CHAPTER 9

As DeShays, lugging Miller's bag, ascended the stairs to his attic chamber, he imagined the chief seated in his gloomy office at that very moment, scowling at both message and messenger; it was his way to leave people standing in a state of uncertainty long after they might have been dismissed. He thought, too, of Winchell, by now perhaps in a condition to reveal whether there was indeed more behind last night's assault than an insulted policeman or two.

He'd about reached the third floor landing when he found his way barred. It was Millie Fitzgerald, the landlady's six-year-old daughter, who'd been lying in wait for him in a doorway. The game that unfolded had become all too familiar. "That'll be five cents, Mr. DeShays." A giggle exposed the gap in the little teeth while Millie tilted her head daintily, her brown curls falling to one side as she extended her out-stretched palm. Lately her demands had become exorbitant, the rate rising from the half cent DeShays had volunteered to the cost of an omnibus ride or a glass of beer.

DeShays had learned the outcome of refusing these demands; soon Mrs. Fitzgerald would ask him what the poor child had done to arouse his displeasure. DeShays gained the landing, put down the bag and reached into his pocket for a cent, knowing that Millie would grudgingly accept this after at first proclaiming it too little, as she now did. DeShays ended negotiations with a playful but sharp tug of the child's ear. "Run along now Millie. I must see about my cousin without delay." The girl let out another giggle and scurried downstairs.

DeShays opened the door to his room and didn't like what he saw. The spot where Winchell should have been resting was simply a shallow hollow in the bedclothes. Neither his boots nor his outer garments were in sight. The bird had evidently flown. DeShays shoved the bag under the bed, stamped around the room impotently for an instant then shouted for Mrs. Fitzgerald to come up at once.

She answered DeShays's red-faced questioning in a tone both defiant and beseeching. "Why surely I must go to market now and then, or we'll have no supper at all. I told Eliza to keep a firm eye on your cousin while I was away, and that I suppose she did, isn't that right Millie?" The child nodded nervously and disappeared behind her mother's skirt. Clearly Eliza had at some point set her sights elsewhere.

DeShays pressed on, his voice modulating lower and lower as it did when he became angry. "This is most irresponsible. Where is Eliza? I demand a word with her this instant, Mrs. Fitzgerald." A slight tremble in the woman's hands alerted him to his menacing tone. Softening it, he asked, "Perhaps my cousin left a note of some kind?"

A hapless look froze on Mrs. Fitzgerald's face and an awkward standstill prevailed as DeShays realized he'd been harsh with the poor widow. Millie, from the safety of her mother's skirt, stared up at him the same greedy gap-toothed smile that had greeted him upon the stairs. So that was it—Eliza had left Winchell under Millie's watch for a short while, just long enough. Winchell, roused and tortured by the child, had paid the exit toll gladly.

DeShays sat in the space where Winchell had recently been and buried his face in his hands. Easier to stuff a genie back in its bottle than catch up with the man. "You may go now Mrs. Fitzgerald," came the resigned voice from between the hands. "I'm very sorry to have been cross with you."

She responded with a solicitous hug from above. "I understand, Mr. DeShays. It's your own flesh and blood. I can imagine how I would feel if one of my own was lost, God forbid."

Before he knew it mother and daughter were gone and unseen hands, as if from ocean depths, pulled him down to the mattress into a sleep that lasted through the afternoon. In dreams he cowered in the corner of the staircase of Eli Miller's boarding house wearing a dandy's blood-soaked togs, as the landlady pointed at him, screaming, and Speight closed in, sporting a cracked monocle and smacking a truncheon in his palm. Next, he was running barefoot in his nightgown along South Street in the dead of night, pursued by policemen brandishing torches and Dick Poole twirling a watchman's rattle. Then came blackness and the sound of a distant fortepiano, on which played curious music. First a strange waltz, followed by a Turkish march, a Hungarian dance, then a gallop, through all of which ran strains of Yankee Doodle. From beyond, little Millie yelled his name.

DeShays awoke in a sweat, but the effort to sift dream from reality defeated him and he sank back to semi-consciousness. Someone was knocking at his door.

"Good heavens Mr. DeShays!" Mrs. Fitzgerald burst in, chortling with excitement. "Wake up and come downstairs! You've a highly distinguished visitor indeed!" Coyly neglecting to mention who the visitor might be, she rushed off. DeShays sat up woozily, surprised that night had already fallen. He lit the oil lamp on the table by the bed then took out his pocket watch—it was five-thirty. After a minute the warm fog in his head cleared, yet the strange music resumed. No one in the household was capable of coaxing such virtuosity from Mrs. Fitzgerald's small upright. True, Eliza was a budding amateur, yet this couldn't be her. Visitor? What visitor? DeShays arranged himself in the cheval glass and made his way downstairs, very much on his guard.

Entering the front parlor he saw in the corner by the window the back of a thin man clad in tight-fitting black, a silver tonsure framing his shining dome, arms poised high above the keyboard like the wings of a feasting vulture. A closer inspection confirmed that here was a complete stranger, whose gaze seemed to encompass some otherworldly vista as a gondolier's love song unfolded beneath supple fingers. Unable to imagine what such a man could possibly want with him, DeShays joined Mrs. Fitzgerald and her daughters in a semi-circle behind the piano stool.

Warily he looked on as Mrs. Fitzgerald beamed, her hands

clasped against her chest in a gesture of pride and satisfaction, while Eliza wore a beatific smile, her oval face absorbing the fireplace's warm glow. Millie stood back a little and chewed her thumb, not sure what to make of things. It all seemed innocent enough, which puzzled DeShays even more.

As the playing grew in pounding intensity Mrs. Fitzgerald caught DeShays's eye, fearful perhaps that her pianino might soon be reduced to firewood under the flurry of fists, forearms and elbows which assaulted the keyboard. Miraculously, as if for young Millie, the sound modulated into a gentle cradle song, a chorus of ethereal harps and chiming bells, cascading cadences and glistening flourishes singing out as though the humble upright was a glorious Pleyel in the hands of Chopin, and Mrs. Fitzgerald yielded once again to the spell.

Then the tune decreased in volume yet further, until the pianist sadly dragged his finger the length of the keyboard in a plaintive glissando, as if the time for dreaming had come to an end.

The small group, including the cook whose head appeared in the doorway, burst out in applause as DeShays remembered a performance he'd read about in which an Austrian virtuoso, whose name slipped his mind, had thrilled a packed house at the Broadway Tabernacle, playing variations such as he'd just heard. As if reading his mind, the pianist turned and fixed his glistening blue eyes on DeShays, speaking in a thick accent. "Leopold De Meyer at your service, Mr. DeShays."

DeShays stepped forward and De Meyer rose quickly to clasp hands. "I wish to thank you for saving the life of a great actor fallen on hard times, an artist sadly neglected in his own country. That is, my dear friend, Thomas J. Winchell."

Mrs. Fitzgerald let out an astonished gasp. "I'd no idea who your cousin was, Mr. DeShays. Mr. Winchell, indeed?"

"You've seen Winchell?" DeShays demanded, incredulously. "Is he all right? Where is he?"

"He came to my hotel after his fortunate stay at this splendid home. I learned of the beauty of your daughters, Madame, and of your selfless heroism, Monsieur. Sadly, however, his condition remains critical. His life is hanging by a thread. At present he can see no one. And so I wish to repay you in a small way with a ticket to my upcoming recital at the Park Theatre, after which I hope we shall dine, sir."

The visitor reached into his pocket and withdrew a small envelope, bending over ceremoniously as he handed it to DeShays. "And now I must take my leave." He kissed the hands of Mrs. Fitzgerald, stooping to do the same to Millie, then lingered long over Eliza, milking her soft fingers and casting a dewy look into her star struck eyes. Mrs. Fitzgerald handed him his topcoat and hat bidding him return before leaving town. DeShays followed Eliza and Millie into the vestibule. "Good evening to you all, and may you long live, Mr. DeShays," said the Austrian as he doffed his top hat in parting salutation. Fixing DeShays with an amused little smile, he ventured into the night.

Scarcely had the door closed than Mrs. Fitzgerald and Eliza hugged, all giggles and smiles in their excitement, while Millie plunked out a few random notes on the keyboard. Turning on his heels DeShays started upstairs. "Mr. DeShays, have you nothing to say?" asked Mrs. Fitzgerald, astonished at his suddenly distant demeanor. "I gather Mr. DeShays is still sour over this morning," offered Eliza, loudly to be sure he heard it.

In his dim room DeShays sat by the small table by the window and carefully withdrew the contents of the envelope. There was no ticket, only a note. DeShays unfolded it, and by the flickering light read the neatly printed capitals:

LOVERS FOR LOAN
APPLY AT THE TEMPLE OF THE MUSES THIS
VERY MIDNIGHT LITTLE PIGS LIE ON VERY
GOOD STRAW LA RUE

Only one man could he think of who might guess what the strange words signified.

Pelham's had not yet filled up when DeShays arrived to find Billy Holmes leaning against the bar, immersed in a copy of *The New-York Flash*, a rag catering to the tastes of "discriminating gentlemen."

"Holmes, I have a puzzle for you. A secret message, if you will."

"Nothing is secret, that shall not be made manifest," intoned Holmes, motioning towards the waiter's table. "Join me in my office, friend, and we'll know more."

Placing La Rue's note on the checkered tablecloth, Holmes sat down to examine it as a general might study a map detailing enemy positions on the eve of battle. DeShays, opposite, refrained from hazarding any guesses of his own, not wishing to break his friend's concentration. Soon Holmes began mouthing words and nodding to himself. "What does it all mean?" DeShays implored.

"On one level it's pretty clear, old fellow. I'm surprised you don't see."

"For God's sake, man, spout."

"If memory serves, it relates to a high point in your thespian endeavors." Holmes was not about to deprive his friend of the chance to play Tantalus. "Whoever penned this clearly had some knowledge of your brilliant career."

"Flattery will get you nowhere."

Holmes poked an accusing finger in DeShays's face. "Did you not play the male lead in that unfortunate farce, *The Loan of a Lover?*"

"Slap on the cuffs. But that was years ago!"

"And who played the fair Gertrude, your leading lady?"

"Pauline Dowling."

"Voila!" Holmes exclaimed smacking his hands together in triumph as DeShays regarded him blankly. "Dear me, Miles. Must I spell it out? Those years in Cincinnati have taken a toll. Let's see ... The ravishing Miss Dowling, hearing of your return to civilization and recalling the blissful hours spent in your company, has summoned you, O Fortunate One, to her boudoir this very night, the midnight slot having doubtless become available ..."

"Wrong," DeShays snatched up the note and re-examined it. "Pauline? We couldn't stand one another. It was all we could do to have to kiss on stage."

"Dear Miles, *semper modestus*. Of course, you won't have

heard of this summer's sensation, our floating theater. A theater on a boat. The Temple of the Muses, no less. Bearing culture to the Philistines up and down the Hudson. Currently berthed for the winter in the East River at the foot of Moore Street. And the scene, so I hear, of some rather unusual revelry."

"The Temple of the Muses?" DeShays rolled his eyes.

"And muse in residence, if you will, none other than your very resistible, if you say so, Miles—and who am I to quibble?—Miss D. Gone on to fame and fortune, the toast of every stage-door Romeo from Peekskill to Poughkeepsie. Talent, as we so well know, will out. In one way or another."

"Let's say you're right, though I don't believe it for a second. What's La Rue got to do with it? I must say, he fooled me completely. Do you know the man?"

"By repute a slippery devil. Engaged no doubt in supplying fresh meat to the reputedly ravenous Miss D. If I were you, Miles, I'd take him up. Might be diverting. Let's see, 'Little pigs lie on very good straw.' Little pigs: that's you I'm afraid. Very good straw: her?"

"Wait a minute, that was Winchell's line—in his song at Spider Murphy's!"

A steak and kidney pie later, when DeShays left Pelham's, he was as mystified as ever as to the meaning of La Rue's cryptic message.

CHAPTER 10

The maid had come to his room in DeShays's absence and got a log burning in the small grate, for the evening was cold and damp with the promise of a bitter winter to come. Reaching into the standing wardrobe, he withdrew a battered leather valise. From beneath his bed he pulled Miller's bag and by the flickering firelight emptied its contents into his own.

It was nearly half past nine when DeShays, avoiding the scrutiny of his landlady, ducked beneath the lintel of 488 Greenwich clutching the handles of both bags. Walking towards Canal the only sound he heard was the trickle of rain-water in the gutter. Near the corner he stuffed Miller's bag in a bin of rubbish then headed east on Canal. A few minutes later the clatter of an approaching omnibus came as welcome relief from the wet: he'd forgotten his umbrella.

Pellets of rain flattened against the windows of the 'bus and wriggled slowly downward as it rattled along Canal and turned south on Broadway. Inside the coach an effluvia of stale breath, wet wool and damp wood mingled in a fusty aroma, the sniffles of DeShays's half-dozen or so fellow passengers adding to a prevalent aura of misery.

By the time they reached Wall Street the rain had tapered to a fine drizzle. Stepping off, he walked east along a deserted stretch of wet stone facades and shuttered office windows. It seemed no place for living things. Peering down dim side streets towards lonely warehouses, he thought of the missing watchman and wondered if he'd truly met his end. He'd surely be easy prey on his early morning rounds.

Already he could see the pinpoint gleam of deck lanterns and the looming outline of masts at water's edge. By the hazy sheen of a street lamp, halfway down Coffee House Slip he spotted a sign carved in the shape of a black tankard swinging above a barroom door. Drawing closer, he heard muted shouts and stray laughs.

Nobody paid attention as he stepped inside the Iron Mug. Irontop Carson was nowhere to be seen, though his dog, Caesar, was keeping a close eye on things, padding about in the sawdust like a policeman on his rounds. Most of the fifteen or so men present, who had the look of sailors, fishermen or dockworkers, were gathered around a center table whooping it up as a man with long dark sideburns rolled up his right sleeve to show a burly tattooed forearm. He was grinning defiantly at a lean, balding redhead who stepped from behind the bar to take the opposite chair.

The redhead rolled up his own right sleeve to reveal the wiry forearm of a blacksmith, and from nowhere shot DeShays a glance. "If you will be so good, sir, to please call time ."

Suddenly all eyes were on him, and with Caesar sniffing the bag at his feet, he quickly gave the word. Shouts of encouragement for the arm wrestlers erupted as they grimaced and struggled, their chairs creaking beneath their shifting weight. Just then he felt a friendly arm fall around his shoulders. Seth Carson, in shirtsleeves, had come down to see what the hubbub was about. As DeShays started to explain himself, Carson directed his attention back towards the contest. All of a sudden the bartender maneuvered his adversary's arm to a forty-five degree angle, then lowered it to the table as though shutting the lid of a cigar box.

Carson had slipped behind the bar and was working one of a half-dozen kegs ranged along a shelf, filling two jars of porter. Handing one to DeShays, they clinked. "To Jack 'Hammer' Lang," was his ironic toast, which the bartender overheard, and turned to acknowledge with a little nod.

So that was it. The victor was none other than the winner of a much ballyhooed prize fight recently staged on Staten Island, lasting nearly three hours. Who would have guessed, from the man's unmarked features and well-spoken address? Grinning wryly at DeShays's unstated realization, Carson appeared a changed man from the morning, when the oppressive atmosphere of the station house had seemed to weigh on him. "Once in a while he actually pours somebody a drink," he drawled. "But why the baggage, Miles? Leaving town under cover of night?"

"Can we have some privacy?"

Carson lifted his eyebrows in surprise. "Certainly. C'mon."

Glass in one hand and valise in the other, he followed Irontop towards a back room, aware of the inquiring glances of some of those present. Leaving DeShays to stand in the doorway Carson put a match to an oil lamp mounted on the walls. "Shut the door," he said. From above there came the sound of an infant crying, then faint footsteps. "My wife, Sarah," he explained. "And there's another one on the way."

DeShays offered congratulations—he hadn't known that Carson was a father.

"There'll be no sleep for the weary. You're unusually quiet, young man. Show your hand."

"It's Eli Miller. I went to his house. He's been missing for days."

Carson seemed surprised. "First I heard of it."

"According to his landlady, he was basking in the notoriety. Toast of the town."

"So maybe the drink got the better of him?"

"She's convinced he's dead. Wants to rent out his room."

"Why didn't anyone report this?"

"They did. The landlady dispatched her old man. When I arrived she took me for a policeman. I was looking through Miller's things when Speight showed up. The husband must have gone to City Hall."

"Speight?" Carson swore. "Even if Rose Street is outside my ward, whose investigation is this?"

"You weren't told?"

"Like hell." Carson leaned his weight on a billiard table, the main feature of the room.

"I hid in the yard till he got upstairs, then jumped over the wall. But I didn't escape empty-handed." DeShays bent over his battered case, fingers nervously plucking at the straps.

"What have we here?"

Onto the green baize surface of the table, piece by piece, DeShays laid out the clothes, as if a tailor, arranging them lengthwise to describe the flat shape of a man. Carson watched in silence, his face a mask of stone. "These were stashed beneath his bed."

Carson reached up to a lighting fixture suspended from the ceiling over the table and lit its twin oil lamps, then leaned forward to peel open the coat's lapels. Finding no label, he muttered something to himself. "Pockets?" he asked, turning to DeShays.

"Nothing."

After testing the fabric here and there, Carson ran his fingers lightly over the blood stains. For a moment he stood there, shaking his head. Then he extended his hand. "Put her there, Miles," he said. "I'd say the best detective in New York is unemployed. At least officially."

DeShays had scarcely thanked him for the compliment when there came a loud rapping on the door.

"Put those duds away," Carson said in a voice hushed yet sharp. DeShays stuffed them back in the bag, shoving it beneath the billiard table. "Yea, what is it?"

"Open up, Seth." It was Hammer Lang. "Poole's here. He wants a word with you."

The two men looked at one another. "Don't say a word about what you've found."

As the door opened DeShays felt the weight of Poole's stony glower. "Well what is it, Poole?" Carson sounded in no mood for nonsense.

Poole paused a moment, as if reluctant to switch his gaze from DeShays. "They found Eli Miller. He washed up by the DePeyster Street pier a little while ago."

"Good God. Who found him?"

"The crew of a sloop moored there, the Victorine. They hooked him in."

"Sounds like the tobby coves."

"Miller's knowledge-box is split wide open. A tobby only stuns his man, then dunks him after he's fleeced him. A nice accidental drowning. Ten to one this was over before Miller hit the water."

"I'll get my coat."

"And boss—" Poole dropped his voice to a growl as if to exclude DeShays. "Speight's there. And Harrington." He turned and disappeared into the barroom. Carson shut the door. "Damned vultures." He pointed under the table. "I'll take that upstairs for now. We'll talk later. You coming?"

The question came as a surprise. "Is that wise?"

"Maybe you're right."

Emerging from the back room with Carson, DeShays felt all eyes upon them. Watching Carson and Poole disappear into darkness towards DePeyster he recalled his strange dream in which Poole and his torch bearing mob had chased him down the very street they were now on. Buttoning his coat to the collar and adjusting his muffler, he set his face to the south.

CHAPTER 11

From his vantage point at the window of a seedy grogshop DeShays watched the man. He stood huge and wooden as a totem pole some hundred yards off on the deck, his bulk a deeper black against the black of the night sky.

After leaving the Iron Mug, DeShays had walked a dozen blocks south along the waterfront. It had not really been his intention to pursue the matter of the midnight rendezvous, but the news of Miller's death hard on the heels of the discovery of the clothes conspired to shift his thinking. At the very least, just to satisfy his curiosity, he would venture a look at this so-called floating Temple of the Muses, so graphically described by Holmes.

Sure enough, docked alongside the pier at the foot of Moore, there it was: the solid grey bulk of a converted man-of-war steamship, a relic, according to Holmes, towed up from Virginia, refitted in New York, some thirty yards long at a guess. The bow-slits of light edging the tightly curtained cabin windows signaled that somebody might be home. As DeShays drew abreast of the vessel, intending to amble nonchalantly on, faint sounds of merriment from within reached his ears and caused him to stop, turn and listen. It was then that he noticed the virtual Goliath rise up from the darkness of the deck to stand at the head of the gangplank as if daring DeShays to advance another step.

Normally he might have accepted the challenge, but with the hour barely gone eleven decided to bide his time and walk on. And the grogshop across the way was proving an excellent observatory.

Its proprietress, a hag of enormous girth swathed in a purple shawl from which only her nose protruded, seemed delighted to take him under her wing once he'd explained himself as a French tourist collecting anecdotes for a book about the city. She called off a couple of decrepit tarts who'd been tipsily attempting to pick his pockets, doubtless reserving the foreign greenhorn for some more fruitful plucking.

"What an extraordinary—comment on dit?—phenomenon, Madame, the floating theater," DeShays laid on the accent with a trowel. "But to attend a performance, is it possible?"

"You must wait till the spring for that, young man. They say it'll reach Chicago next year and travel down as far as New Orleans."

"Are there people on board? I heard music just now as I passed."

"They come and go in their fancy carriages," the woman sniffed, "you'll see." Clearly no business from the boat came her way. Indeed, DeShays appeared the place's only customer.

"That watchman at the gangway, would he stop me going aboard for a look?"

"Mangle you soon as look at you. Sent many an innocent to the sick-house, that one. They say he comes on at Barnum's now and again. Freaks and stage people, that's what they are. Good-for-nothings."

Two men entered carrying a heavy box between them and made straight for a back room. Invoking the mother of God and all the angels and devils, the woman hurried after them. Fence: so that was her game. Gingerly he sipped the beer she'd pressed on him and, noticing how the tarts—collapsed together in a corner—eyed him with fresh intent, wondered if it was spiked.

Out on the quay the giant still stood sentry though, as predicted, carriages were beginning to arrive; smart two-wheel broughams, fancy barouches, spacious four-wheelers. When he glanced out again, the view of the sentry and the boat was obscured. Interesting about Barnum's. Winchell, La Rue, and now— He turned it over in his mind. Peering at his watch in the dim light he saw he still had several minutes in hand till the appointed hour.

Abandoning his drink and bundling up against the cold,

69

DeShays stepped out of the grogshop for a better view of the proceedings. People were hurrying in twos and threes down the gangplank, men and women, searching out their various means of transport. People of substance, he reckoned, middle-aged, respectably—even fashionably—dressed. The sort who could afford to keep a carriage or two, calling out their good-byes amidst the yelling and cursing of the drivers and the snorted responses of the horses whose cloudy breath and sweating flanks tinged the night air. Almost a school-letting-out-for-the-day feeling. A release of good fellowship.

Then DeShays was alone again on the dark street, a few pungently steaming mounds lingering evidence of the recent commotion. Light still seeped from the cabin windows, and as the clock on some nearby church chimed the midnight hour he realized that his mind was made up. Approaching the quay, he looked in vain for the sentry. Having withdrawn the gangplank with a great clanking and scraping (a detail overlooked in La Rue's instructions) he seemed to have withdrawn himself too. Perhaps his shift was over for the night.

DeShays contemplated the gap at his feet—a not unmanageable half fathom—as water lapped gently against the vessel's side. A sign attached to the railing read: DRESS CIRCLE, 50 CENTS, PARQUETTE, 25 CENTS, PRIVATE BOXES, $3. Just then a shaft of light darted out from his left to illuminate the spot on the deck on which he would have to land. For an instant the silhouette of a woman was framed in the opening before the door closed and she was gone. Here goes, he thought, and jumped.

Scrambling to steady himself, DeShays set his back to the engine room and tensed for the onslaught of the giant. Only the dull creak of the boat and familiar jostle and tap in nearby rigging disturbed the night. Then the light reached out again and seemed to haul him towards itself till he was through the door, enveloped by it.

"Pauline."

The arms, already eagerly clutching to receive his outer garments, stiffened. DeShays looked down into a face numbed in sudden horror, a face he had once known well. Those eyes,

70

captive-making saucers of liquid green, the auburn hair in tight unfamiliar ringlets, the porcelain skin, the once luscious lips.

"You? Someone's idea of a joke, is this?" And yes, the voice, always the give-away, the clue to the demon within. It was Pauline all right. Her bare arms and long red nails struggled now to push his coat back on. He didn't try to help.

"Pauline, Pauline— Who were you expecting?"

"Why are you here?" The arms relaxed a bit.

"I was told you sent for me."

"Even had I known you were back," her words dripped scorn, "why would I want to see you?"

"For old times sake?"

The sarcasm was lost on her. "Who? Who told you?"

"La Rue." It didn't seem to register. "The impersonator."

"Well, whoever it was, perhaps you'll be good enough to leave. I'm not alone, you know."

He looked beyond her into an elegantly furnished state-room with a marble-topped table and lampshades of cut ground glass. "So, doing pretty well. Good parts, great reviews, I hear. Congratulations."

"Why, thank you." The change was instantaneous. How like clockwork flattery works in our profession, he thought.

"And you?"

"Out of the business, I'm ashamed to say."

"You never showed much promise."

He let it go. "Trying my hand at law and order."

"Not the new police? You? I don't believe it."

"Nor do I, really. One has to do something."

"I mean the coincidence. You don't by any chance know— ? No, silly me, what am I thinking of!"

"Who?"

"It doesn't matter." She turned away.

"Know who?"

Pauline sat down at the table and fanned herself with a handkerchief. She seemed flushed and breathless. "Oh dear me, I must have rather overdone it." She sipped from a half-full wine glass and DeShays wondered if she wasn't a bit tipsy.

71

He sat across from her. "The crowd that was here tonight—"

"Friends," she waved away the question. "Friends of the Floating Theater. I'd give you a tour only I'm expecting someone at any moment." She gazed at him, her lips curled in an unfriendly smile. "Poor Miles. The years have not been kind. So what exactly is it that you do?"

"Ah, the usual: pocket bribes, evict widows and orphans, get out the vote. Why?"

She giggled unconvincingly. "It might come in handy, that's all, knowing a policeman."

"Your servant, I'm sure."

"And now, dear Miles, I must ask that you leave at once."

He heard the key turn in the lock behind him, and groped his way to the gangplank, feeling like an utter idiot. He was about to make the leap when what appeared in the gloom as a bundle of freight developed hands and feet. As the giant heaved himself up beside him, all DeShays could think of to say was a somewhat defensive, "Good evening, friend."

The man must have been seven feet tall since DeShays himself stood at six. He was swathed in what appeared to be an enormous bearskin from which his head stuck out, a head which, incongruously, was completely bald. And to DeShays's great relief, he was smiling sweetly.

"I beg your pardon." DeShays cupped his ear for he couldn't understand a word the man was saying. It sounded like gibberish, a string of throaty gurgles repeated over and over. Then it occurred to him that it was gibberish, that the man was mute.

He walked away along the waterfront every now and again looking back to where the giant still stood. Till at last the darkness swallowed him up. Already running in DeShays's mind was Billy Holmes's gleeful response to this all around tale of woe. Poor Pauline, imagine the shock she must have felt at his precipitous reappearance in her life. For he'd not been wholly truthful in telling Holmes that as her paramour in *Loan of a Lover* he'd hardly been able to stomach even a stage kiss.

CHAPTER 12

"But what good is a man after he's hanged, Mr. Jenkins?" inquired young Evans of his neighbor across the breakfast table.

To which Mr. James Jenkins, a well-fed Englishman of fifty-two years and a tailor by trade, replied: "What good's anybody after 'e's gone and snuffed it? Only good that'll come of this 'ere River Mauler business is a firm example in the form of public retribution, I say."

"In fact, there is no evidence whatsoever to support the view that such gruesome spectacles serve in any way to prevent the commission of crime," persisted Evans, adjusting his own spectacles, which never seemed to sit well. "Quite the contrary. A public execution is nothing more than a field day for pickpockets and a holiday for drunken ruffians."

"Now don't let's forget the landlords and ladies, sir, ain't that right Mrs. F?" replied Jenkins, who usually got the best of the high-strung Evans by letting him work himself into a snit. "The papers said they'd have fifty cents a head for the privilege of a bird's-eye view of the gibbet, such as may be had from the rooftops overlooking the yard of the Tombs. But I'd wager that one of us'd have no problem gaining admission, eh, Mr. Inspector?"

DeShays himself had just assumed his place at the table. Not having taken in the conversation he merely smiled at Jenkins, wishing to have his bacon and eggs without engaging Evans, an apothecary some five years his junior, whose huge orange side-whiskers reminded him of an orangutan he'd seen in the Cincinnati zoo.

"To witness a hanging is doubtless a perquisite of office," interjected Evans, scarcely allowing DeShays his first gulp of coffee. "But perhaps matters of life and death do not concern an inspector of junk shops." In the presence of Eliza Fitzgerald he lost no opportunity to contrast his perceived exemplary station in the firm of Henry B. Quackinbush, Chemists, with that of his assumed rival. Though Eliza's frown and the way she fixed her eyes on her plate might have given a less self-impressed person pause for thought.

DeShays chewed his bacon and stared fixedly through the window into the blackness of the yard, leaving Eliza's mother gently to chide Evans for his provocative comments, careful as she always was not to alienate the young man. If Eliza was unimpressed with Evans's prospects her mother was not.

Evans was not long silent. "Though in the light of this morning's *Argus* the subject may become moot." As though laying down a gauntlet, he produced the newspaper from his lap and spread it over his empty plate. "I quote from the editorial, *Where are the Stars?*"

As Evans continued, DeShays laid down his knife and fork to listen.

"'The new police, in their investigation of the horrible murder in Cuyler's Alley, have floundered from the start. With the apparent murder of the watchman Eli Miller, it is clear that their work has been at best negligent. Would they now have us believe that the suspect McGlone can be in two places at once? Fie! There is, in fact, no River Mauler, that mythical beast being merely a cynical invention of Chief Oliver W. Matson—'"

Someone was knocking at the front door. Mrs. Fitzgerald and Eliza seemed equally anxious to escape, but it was the maid who went to receive the caller as Evans finished declaiming and folded his paper with an air of deep satisfaction.

The acne-plagued face that appeared in the doorway was among the last DeShays had expected to see. "Good morning, Willoughby," he said, seeing the boy's evident discomfort, for he'd behaved rudely towards DeShays and now found himself as it were in enemy territory. Indeed, the police office scrivener and factotum acted like a hostage being put to task by an unseen gunman, so wooden was his stance. "Shall we have a word in private?"

"Chief wants to see you now," he blurted. "That's all I was told."

Hiding his surprise, "Tell him I'll be along presently," replied DeShays. With a nod the lad turned and fled towards the street.

"I had no idea your work was so important," said Mrs. Fitzgerald, who was becoming more impressed with DeShays with each new visitor.

"You tell that chief of yours we say he's all right," added Jenkins good-naturedly. "Who cares a whit what the *Argus* says—I say he's on the side of right and order."

Climbing the steps of City Hall then descending to its basement DeShays experienced corresponding ups and downs. Even had Matson guessed that his letter was forged, surely he wouldn't be so impolitic as to broach the issue with DeShays's uncle. Better for him if DeShays had forged the letter, for the wrath of a leading alderman might have repercussions at a time when Matson could ill afford enemies in powerful places.

Still, the closer DeShays got to the dread door the more he felt like a left-back student about to repeat a grade. He was surprised and relieved to see, seated at his usual table, Zebulon Honan, the night man, inexplicably on the day shift. A sporting paper was spread before him as he fed himself from a bag of peanuts.

Old Honan raised a quizzical eyebrow at the sight of DeShays. "Timing is not your forte, sonny," he said, tossing an empty shell into a pail several feet away. "No wonder you didn't last in the theater."

Somewhat dismayed at the implication, DeShays played along. "Missed my cue again, did I? Late for the tearful reunion scene?" Putting his head round the door of the inspectors' room he was surprised to find only the scrivener, at the far end, scrawling away. Seeing who it was, Willoughby smirked as he wouldn't have dared an hour before.

Muffled voices sounded from within the chief's office, unintelligible to DeShays, though the anger in the chief's voice was clear enough. He looked to Honan for an explanation.

"Things have changed around here," said the old man cryptically, gazing up at DeShays with the look of a witness about to relate the details of a terrible accident. Reaching into the bag he cracked open a nut with his teeth as a sudden eruption was heard within. Then the door opened and the inspectors filed out, looking more like inmates than policemen.

First came Speight, with the guilty grin of a boy chewed out for a naughty prank. Seeing DeShays he flashed a bitter smile, the glint of a dagger in sunlight. Next was Harrington, ashen-faced, narrowing his eyes at DeShays as though warning a leper to stay away. The two hurried off. Hewison stumbled after them, looking dazed. The sight of DeShays seemed to panic him. He made straight for his desk. A moment later Carson strode by. As his footsteps rang down the hallway DeShays could have sworn that Irontop flashed him a knowing wink.

At Honan's nod, feeling like a zookeeper entering the cage of a starved bear, DeShays crossed the threshold of the chief's inner sanctum. The great man was seated behind his desk, a look defiant yet resigned etched across his craggy features; a sea captain at the prow of his sinking ship. He scarcely regarded DeShays at all, his thoughts apparently on distant horizons far beyond the insignificant young man before him.

After an eternity without comment he pulled open a drawer and foraged around as if searching for a seldom used key. At last, finding what he was looking for, he slapped it down on the desk as if to say, "There!" For a while the copper star sat between them, till DeShays leaned over and cautiously picked it up and, the chief offering no objection, put it in his pocket.

Was he expected simply to disappear, DeShays wondered, to creep from the room into a world of ambiguity and backstairs infighting? What were his duties to be? He needed to know, but, given the timing, it wouldn't do to ask questions, just as it somehow wouldn't do to leave at that point either.

Matson glared at him curiously, his mouth slowly opening into a mirthless smile revealing a line of crooked teeth. "Perhaps your, er, *sabbatical* has given you pause to think seriously about our purpose," he said, hands clasped over his massive belly. "Though given your family connections, perhaps you lack the hunger to succeed here."

"I'm grateful for the opportunity to try again, sir."

"I need hardly remind you that you've been of precious little use thus far," reminded the chief. "It puzzles me that you seem so bent on rejoining us."

"I'm here to be of service, any way I can," protested DeShays.

"Any way?" the chief paused, removing his spectacles as though preparing for a heart-to-heart with a wayward son. "It seems I'm surrounded by knaves and backstabbers," he sighed, eyeing the door through which they had just left. "Perhaps you can be useful, after all: the eyes and ears of the chief."

Thrusting his weight forward in his chair, so that DeShays involuntarily jerked back, he added, "Because an attack on the chief is an attack on the entire police force of the City of New York. We are one and the same, indivisible. Understand?"

"Yes, sir."

Matson relapsed, replaced his glasses and sat for a few moments staring either at his visitor or through him to some dark recess; because of the refraction of the light, DeShays couldn't tell. "I seem to recall that you had once some thespian inclination. If I from time to time choose to enquire about it, you will know what we are talking about. Meanwhile let's see if we can find employment for idle hands."

From a bottom drawer Matson withdrew a cardboard box filled with papers. Reaching in he grabbed a stack, cursorily sorted through it, and thrust it across the desk. "Each day this office receives at least fifty items of so-called intelligence about the late affair in Cuyler's Alley. There have been at least a half-dozen such incidents since then, yet thanks to the newspapers we are continuously flooded with more such nonsense every day. Take a look. It's probably worthless, but it'll keep you busy."

DeShays rose, tucking the papers under his arm. He could hardly believe how well the interview had gone. "Am I also to resume my duties as an inspector?" he ventured to ask.

"All in good time," said the chief, "all in good time. Let's see how productive a member of the force you can be. Pro-ductive, from the Latin, *producere*, 'to bring forth, to generate.'" He patted his belly. "And DeShays,"—DeShays had his hand on the doorknob—"I'll be seeing your uncle tonight at the mayor's reception. I'm sure he'll be delighted that you decided to rejoin us."

CHAPTER 13

Passing Honan in the hall as he left Matson's office, DeShays couldn't resist giving the old geezer thumbs up as he flashed his star. His luck seemed suddenly to have turned. Not only was he back in the department—and with the chief's ear to boot—but was officially assigned to the case he had determined willy-nilly to pursue. For the time being, at least, he didn't need to work through Carson.

Yet by the following Saturday much of the wind had gone from his sails. The murder had, it seemed, inspired anyone with any sort of grudge to put pen to paper. Complaints about tenants, neighbors and in-laws abounded. DeShays sat in well-appointed parlors on furniture decades old, and in dingy boarding houses amid peeling wallpaper, listening to suspicious old spinsters and widows reporting the nocturnal habits of servants, neighbors and boarders.

Nor in the ensuing days did the chief make any pointed theatrical references or mention the mayor's reception, though there was nothing in his manner to indicate suspicion of DeShays's forged letter. Indeed, he seemed inclined to leave DeShays be, at least for now.

That Saturday's interviews were proving even more unpromising than those of previous days. A senile old man who claimed to be a veteran of the revolution had information about a British spy. In a German enclave on the southern end of Greenwich Street, the wife of an ice vendor was eager to turn in her husband who was out at work. And, as every day since Wednesday, there were visits to false addresses whether supplied out of mischief, malice or real suspicion he couldn't know.

Towards three o'clock DeShays made his way up towards

Chatham Square. The afternoon sun cast long shadows around the square, and with the work week winding down the sense of a promising Saturday night hung in the air. Skies were clear, the weather turned mild for late November. Apprentices, shopkeepers and clerks stood in conversation beneath the awnings, passing the time. One Kate Felton had asked merely that someone call at her business, nothing more. As he crossed from Chatham Street towards the northern end of the square a stray pig trotted by, bent on urgent business. Looking up he read the words, DAGUERREOTYPE ROOM, painted in black beneath the upper story of a small south-facing building.

Ducking beneath the canvas awning which stretched to the sidewalk's edge, DeShays entered the building through a doorway to the right of a hatter's shop which occupied the ground floor. A dark stairwell led past a paint store on the second floor and a lithographer on the third. On the fourth, light flooded from an open door.

The room he entered was spacious, with tall windows. A sitting was underway. An old woman, dressed in her proud best, glanced kindly at him from a chair while a much younger woman in a light blue dress tilted a cheval glass to throw light on the sitter. In front of the chair at a distance of several feet stood a black camera box mounted on a tripod.

The young woman, apparently satisfied with the adjustment she'd made, greeted the newcomer as she walked towards the camera, but advised him that the light might not last long enough to take his portrait. DeShays thought better of announcing his purpose before the sitter and said that he would wait anyway.

Walking to the window, he looked out on the square below, then busied himself examining the numerous daguerreotypes framed on the walls. Within each frame were several portraits, three or four inches high. Ordinary people: a fire captain in his helmet and red flannel shirt holding a ceremonial trumpet, a mother with her infant son, young couples of humble means dressed up for a keepsake of their courtship.

A larger image—of Chatham Square taken from the studio—looked as the square below just had, albeit in reverse and eerily emptied of life. Just the ghostly outline of a carriage. He knew the camera was too slow to capture life in anything other than a posed portrait, yet for all that the portraits on the walls struck him as unusually natural.

The sitting concluded, the daguerreotypist withdrew the copper plate from the camera box and disappeared into an area to the right of the entrance, presumably the darkroom. Watching her, DeShays put her age at about twenty-six, a couple of years younger than himself. An attractive woman, a little over five foot, well-formed and with brown hair gathered in a bun.

"If you sit perfectly still, your picture will smile on the plate," the old woman offered with a chuckle as DeShays joined her at a table on which lay a scattering of journals and newspapers.

In the *Tribune* there was talk of America going to war with Great Britain over the disputed Oregon territory. On the Cuyler's Alley murder, it was reported that the reappearance of Eli Miller, dead, gave rise to renewed speculation that the River Mauler, or his accomplice, was still at large. On the front page of the *Argus* a virtuoso pianist named Leopold DeMeyer was said to have "thrilled audiences at the Park Theatre." The engraving, to DeShays amusement, looked nothing like La Rue, and he thought of the explaining he was in for if the Fitzgeralds saw it.

After a time the daguerreotypist returned and the old woman viewed her likeness, with which she declared herself delighted, as also with its handsome case. She paid two dollars and left, bidding everyone a cheerful good night. Her sitter gone, the woman turned apologetically to DeShays. In the waning light it would be difficult to take his portrait, she said. Sensing her dismay at his fruitless wait, DeShays quickly announced that he was from the police, producing his copper star.

"I wondered when you'd come." She was obviously relieved.

"I take it you are Miss Kate Felton?"

She nodded. "I won't waste more of your time. It's about a customer who came in the day before that horrible murder."

"Please continue."

"It was Saturday afternoon, a little earlier than this. Mind you he wasn't the type of person I usually see here. A young man of means, by the looks of him. I gathered he was passing through the square and decided on a whim to have his portrait taken."

"Is that what he said?"

"No, I guessed as much from his clothing."

"What was he wearing?" DeShays suppressed his excitement, as though asking too quickly might result in the wrong answer.

"You shall soon see. I assumed he was well-to-do because he looked used to the type of clothes he wore. It wasn't as though he'd dressed just for a portrait." She appraised him frankly. There was a direct quality about Miss Felton that appealed to DeShays. "I gathered it was for a lady friend—unless he was in love with himself. He asked that it be colored in oils, you see, and selected the most expensive case. And only after seeing the finished portrait. He offered a generous amount if the picture could be ready by Monday, and I accepted. Only he hasn't returned."

"I take it he paid in advance?"

"Oh, yes. That's why I didn't come to you right away. I didn't want to part with the portrait in case the man came back. But let me get it for you."

It was odd to find a young woman in such an occupation, DeShays reflected, a pursuit that to him seemed almost necromantic, with its glass lenses, darkrooms and strange chemical procedures designed to capture life on a copper plate. Perhaps it was her father's business.

Miss Felton returned holding a palm-sized case and motioned DeShays to follow her towards the windows where the light was best. She carefully watched his reaction as he viewed the face captured on the mirror-like plate.

If the picture was small there was no mistaking the silk brocaded vest worn by the seated figure, the green trousers striped with black, and least of all the plaid cravat. It was fortunate that the man had wanted his portrait colored. Miss Felton had done excellent work.

"I take it that the colors are true to life?"

"I took notes."

"Did he leave his name?"

"He did." She seemed to relish the moment. "His name was E. Rutherford Bewly."

"Address?"

She shook her head.

"Any clues as to where he was from? Accent? Englishman, perhaps?"

"American. Easterner. But not a city person."

"Height?"

"About your height. A little stouter though. There was a softness about him."

DeShays turned his gaze back to the picture, as though it had been too much to absorb all at once. The din of an omnibus rolling through the square below hardly reached him. The young man was blond, in his mid-twenties, with hair parted almost directly above his right ear, just as DeShays parted his. The smooth features were those of one whose path in life was well-paved. A sense of satisfaction stamped itself on his expression. The left corner of his mouth was slightly upturned, whether by dint of a smile or the natural set of his lips DeShays couldn't say. He asked Miss Felton about it.

"I'd say it was just the way his mouth was formed by nature."

DeShays gently closed the red velvet-lined case as if shutting a casket by proxy. "May I take this with me?" he asked, almost forgetting that he was a policeman with the right to do so.

"Of course. But Officer, I won't let you leave here without telling me anything! Do you recognize Mr. Bewly? You seem fascinated by his portrait. Is it true that the poor soul you found had almost no clothes excepting his cravat? I find this all hard to believe!"

"It's much too soon to make a judgment."

Kate Felton's expression turned matter-of-fact. "I understand—a policeman can't reveal his hand too soon. But if Mr. Bewly's portrait should be of use, or even if it isn't, I'd like to know. Do come back and tell me."

DeShays promised that he would, and made his way downstairs. For a while he stood by the curb beneath the awning, staring into the darkening street, too overwhelmed to plot his course. He felt as though a ghost, occupying a place outside the dimensions of everyday life, observant, apart. On the corner of Oliver Street a lamplighter on his ladder ignited the last of the gas lamps to go on around the square.

After a time DeShays tightened his muffler and headed south, just to move, with no particular destination in mind. Suddenly everything had changed and he hadn't the faintest idea what to do about it. Carson had the clothes he'd taken from Miller's room which, matched up with the likeness he had in his pocket, would prove to even a casual observer the identity of the murdered man. Yet it was now the chief to whom he was supposed to report. Wasn't there a third way, an interim solution? Abruptly turning on his heel, he doubled back the way he had come.

From across the street DeShays saw that the studio's curtains had been drawn. The stairwell to the Daguerreotype Room was in gloom, the only light coming from the half-open doorways on the lower floors. On the fourth floor all was dark, the door to the studio closed. He heard the bustle of footsteps inside and knocked. The footsteps stopped. After a pause, a wary voice—Miss Felton's—asked who was there. DeShays announced himself.

"Just a moment, please." Was there irritation in her voice? When she opened the door, he asked to come in. The room was dim, lit only by a single wall sconce. Smelling iodine, he knew she'd been in the darkroom.

Sensing her discomfort, he decided to speak at once. "Miss Felton, I've been thinking ... I'm here to ask for your assistance, and that what I ask remain confidential between us."

She turned and looked at him. "How dramatic you policemen are! I feel rather as though I'm in a play!" Part of DeShays felt the same way—it seemed an occupational hazard.

"Your encounter with Mr. Bewly may be of the greatest importance. But we won't know more until we find out who knew him. There's the question of his next of kin, and so on."

"Or knows him, perhaps?" asked Miss Felton with a clever smile, as if to say that confidentiality would have to extend both ways.

DeShays asked if he might sit for a minute. He studied the notices printed on the back pages of the newspapers strewn across the table and, pencil in hand, jotted down some lines: *Wanted: Information concerning E. Rutherford Bewly, last heard from about the 31st of October last, will be thankfully received by Katherine Felton, the Daguerreotype Room, 1 Chatham sq., 4th floor.*

Ripping the sheet of ruled paper from his little black book he handed it to the daguerreotypist who nodded and passed it back. "I imagine this will appear on Monday?"

"In the *Tribune*, I think. Maybe the *Herald* too."

"And what am I to do with the hoped-for influx? What of mysterious souls who may stop in? What am I to tell them?"

"Take their portrait if you like. Say you're acting for a friend from out of town who'll be by at five. With your kind permission, I'll be here at five every day."

DeShays scribbled his home address, adding a word of caution. "If you need to contact me do so at my home. The fewer people who know of this, the better—for now." As an afterthought, he added, "That goes for the police, too. I'm acting for the chief, and the chief alone."

"How foreboding it all sounds, Officer DeShays. If you don't mind my saying, it's an unusual name—DeShays. Would it be French, by any chance?"

"That's for another day," he smiled.

"Mind yourself on the stairs," she called, as he groped his way down.

CHAPTER 14

In a smoky Canal Street cellar DeShays partook of his long-awaited oysters in silent celebration, chasing them with a strong brandy which sizzled pleasantly in his gut. Back at home he made his way straight upstairs, in no mood for Evans's blathering or Mendelssohn's *Songs without Words* as rendered by Eliza on the piano.

Into the wee hours, in nightcap, slippers and flannel nightshirt, with sleep far from his thoughts, he paced his threadbare rug or sat at the table before the dormer window staring at Bewly's portrait without really seeing it. After a few swigs of brandy from the bottle he kept locked in his trunk his jumbled emotions began to sort themselves out and a certain disappointment crept in. Did brandy make him objective or simply morose?

It was as though he'd discovered a painting in one of the curiosity shops he policed on his rounds, and taken it home only to find he didn't like it anymore. The more he looked at the face of E. Rutherford Bewly the less sympathy it engendered. DeShays reached back, trying to picture the sitter as a child surrounded by the trappings of boyhood, the apple of a mother's eye. But Bewly's self-indulgent mien evoked nothing. The man seemed about as human as a pig's head in a butcher shop window.

A hog in togs, that's what well-dressed loafers were called around the office, with a nod to the jargon of thieves. A cold pig was a victim whose clothes had been stolen. A smirk was a superficial fellow. Settled, that meant murdered.

Whether or not the enigmatic set of Bewly's mouth was or was not a smirk seemed a moot point—it looked like a smirk. Why had he not been missed by now? Had no hotel or place of lodging with an unpaid bill sought him out? No relative or friend inquired of the police? No missing person notice put in the paper? And what of the lady friend, the presumed recipient of the likeness? Was she not expecting him? And why had his face been bashed beyond all recognition? What secret was his that only murder and disfiguration could safekeep?

DeShays sank into bed and pulled the covers over his face. Tomorrow, first thing, he would lodge the notice with the papers. On Monday, with any luck, the city would offer up one of its secrets.

When, on Monday morning, DeShays arrived at the office, Old Honan was again at the door in place of Davis the usual day man, his customary sporting paper spread before him on the table. "It's about time you got here," the old man grunted as if he'd been waiting awhile, though glancing at the clock DeShays saw he was punctual to the minute. "I've got something to tell you." Honan rubbed his hands together in anticipation. "Ah, but such knowledge as I have to offer doesn't come cheap."

"Name your price," said DeShays, just as, from his office, the chief called out Honan's name.

"One minute, sonny. The supreme being beckons."

As Honan disappeared, DeShays picked up the paper, marveling at the detailed notations with which he'd peppered the schedule of races. Clearly Honan studied matters of the turf scientifically, weighing probabilities and making calculations with the precision of an astronomer. The third race, which was to take place at Union Course next day, seemed particularly to have engrossed him. He'd appeared to struggle between two horses before penciling in one, Tom Cribb, for the winner's circle.

"It's the day shift for me from now on," Honan announced, re-emerging.

"What about Davis?"

Honan raised his hand to his throat executing a neat slice. "Working two jobs on top of this, all he does is sleep. The Father says his snoring's enough to wake the dead. And we wouldn't want that, would we? Not with all the skelingtons in these here cupboards. Comes of having seven kids." He wagged an admonitory finger.

"Talking of skeletons, you said you had something for me."

"Ah, that would depend." Honan leaned back as if holding out for the main chance. "What's it worth to you?"

"I have it on good authority that Black Joke will place first in the third race at Union Course tomorrow." Black Joke was not among Honan's picks.

"In the reign of Queen Dick," declared Honan.

"In the words of Spider Murphy," countered DeShays.

Honan squinted suspiciously. "A friend of Spider's are we?" For it was understood among the cognoscenti that the Spider exercised some influence over matters of the turf. Yet as DeShays spoke he felt a tinge of guilt, for he hadn't seen Spider Murphy since the night of Carson's fete. "Time will tell," Honan concluded, beckoning DeShays closer. "The fact is since Saturday everyone around here's been taking a keen interest in your career. Made me kind of wonder myself."

"Oh yes?"

"Hewison asked first. Wanted to know what you were doing back in the office. Breathing a little heavy too, he was. Seemed pretty upset about something."

DeShays smiled. "So the chief doesn't confide in his brother-in-law."

"Then Harrington: solicitous for my well being all of a sudden. Brought a tear to my eye. Asked after my daughter, first time ever. Told him I haven't seen her in five years. Hasn't written me in two."

"I'm sorry."

"Not your fault, is it? Well what could I tell him about you? You're on special assignment? Why not ask the boss?"

"Who else?"

"Speight, very quietly. Wanted a word in the hall. 'A.C.,' I told him, 'if you don't know, who does?' Regular pack rat that one. Hoards knowledge like he hoards gold. And him without so much as a family to spend it on."

"Well, I'm flattered."

"So what exactly are you doing?"

"What's it worth to you?"

Honan let out a faint chuckle. DeShays was nearly at his desk when he heard his name called and doubled back.

"I almost forgot. Dick Poole was here Friday delivering ward returns. Wanted a word with"—he jerked his chin at the chief's door—"but he was with the mayor, as it happened. Asked after you, too. Wanted to know what the deuce the sonofabitch was doing here. 'Ask the sonofabitch yourself,' I said. Don't much care for his manner, but I'll tell you gratis: he'll go far, that one. Mark my words."

"The further the better, as far as I'm concerned." DeShays recalled Carson's look as he emerged from the chief's office the last time they'd seen each other. No doubt Irontop was behind Poole's inquiry. Perhaps he'd been wrong in not including Carson right away in his discovery of the daguerreotype, risking his ire. He might have some fence mending to do.

One by one the inspectors trooped in. Hewison made straight for his desk near the stove (there were perks in being the chief's brother-in-law) and pretended that DeShays didn't exist. Speight and Harrington followed, exchanging perfunctory nods before taking their seats to read and scribble. The feigned indifference with which they regarded him now struck DeShays as amusing, even pathetic. That they were reduced to quizzing Old Honan about him tickled him. Interesting that Harrington and Speight had asked separately. Perhaps the two weren't quite the Castor and Pollux he imagined and the chief's principle of divide and rule had taken hold. Indeed, things were so quiet that DeShays felt as though he were sitting amongst a mime troupe.

He spent the day fruitlessly following up the last of the leads the chief had given him and reached Chatham Square shortly before five. Darkness had descended. Looking up at the Daguerreotype Room he saw that the curtains were drawn. With the possible moment of truth at hand, he ran up the stairs two steps at a time and hadn't completely recovered his breath when he rapped on the studio door.

Kate answered at once, wearing the same blue dress as Saturday and holding a candle, the studio being cast in darkness.

"The hour is upon us, Inspector. Follow me and we'll know more of the dead." Evidently the woman had a healthy sense of gallows humor; DeShays followed her to the waiting area used by her clients, where a candelabrum sat on the table between them.

"No table tapping please, Kate. It's the living we're after. Has anyone been by?"

"Unfortunately, yes. An awful man was here this afternoon."

"My condolences and apologies," said DeShays, feeling more anxious than sorry. "Tell me about this awful man."

"A sitting was underway when he arrived. I watched him mope around looking at the pictures on the wall without much interest. I sensed something malevolent about him. But even the bad want their portrait taken. After my sitting concluded I asked if he had any props in mind. But instead he asked for a picture case, as though that idea had just occurred to him. He had a stare which would stop a clock, as though he was sure the worst about you was true and he was just waiting to hear about it.

"I told him I don't sell cases separately. He said, 'What a pity,' and just kept staring at me, as though expecting me to confess to something. The man didn't blink the whole time he was here. The sitter was waiting and I wondered how I might be rid of him. I asked if there was anything else he wanted. 'Oh yes,' he said, horribly facetious, the very soul of contempt. I'm afraid I lost my nerve at that point. I had to be rid of him at once. I asked if he was here about the advertisement in the paper. 'Yes, that's why I've come,' he said. But why didn't he mention it before? 'Then you'll have to come back at five,' I told him."

"Did he leave a name?"

"I asked. He said, 'That's all right,' nothing more. Then he looked over the place as if to see how it might accord with some hidden idea. It was as though he were a pirate after concealed treasure. A pirate, that's just what he looked like." DeShays asked for a fuller description.

"He was several inches shorter than yourself. Built like a

bull. A thick mustache covered most of his mouth. Brown eyes. Extremely hairy hands." Kate feigned a shiver of disgust.

DeShays was transported back to his visit to the First Ward station house. The unblinking stare, the mustache thick as a shoe brush, the hand which had held the directory. Dick Poole? Or Speight perhaps? Or, more likely, a total stranger. Most men shaved their upper lips these days. It was just on five o'clock. The next few moments might tell. Twice they listened to approaching steps in heightened anticipation only to hear them stop at the lithographer's below.

By candlelight DeShays checked his pocket watch from time to time. After forty minutes he pronounced their vigil at an end, advising Kate to leave with him. Kate let out a deep breath on reaching the street. "Well, that was fun," she said beneath the awning, extending a gloved hand. "Shall we do this again tomorrow?"

"The last thing I want is to put you at risk. I'll try to look in once or twice during the day, just in case. May I see you home?"

As it happened Kate lived on St. John's Square, a few blocks from where DeShays boarded. As they walked west, he learned that she shared the house with her widowed father, a dry goods merchant, and that, like himself, she had been born in the city, having learned daguerreotyping in a prominent Broadway studio and set up her modest business with her father's backing.

On a quiet street west of Broadway DeShays became aware of footsteps closely in step with their own, sounding from a steady distance, as when listening to music he might hear a motif rise to the fore as the rest faded away. Twice he quickly turned his head yet saw no one. Kate seemed to share his discomfort. Lest he alarm her, DeShays didn't look back again and instead gently slipped his arm in hers.

St. John's Park, its dark precincts feebly lit by oil lamps, stood in sharp contrast to the working-class hurly-burly of nearby Greenwich Street. A majestic chapel towered over a park enclosed by a tall iron fence, surrounded by elegantly timeworn brick homes. Scarcely could DeShays wait to deliver

Kate to her door, so anxious was he to know who was behind them. Like dripping water, the steps seemed to increase in volume the longer he listened. Perhaps his somewhat hasty manner in bidding her goodnight left her puzzled, or perhaps she put it down to sudden shyness.

Standing half-hidden in the well beside the stoop of the house, DeShays heard the steps quickening. Shortly two figures emerged from the gloom, arm in arm, a man and a woman walking in lockstep as if late for a rendezvous. As they passed, seeing DeShays, the man lifted his hat in a gesture that spoke almost of mockery. The man was middle-aged, soberly dressed in a velvet-collared black overcoat buttoned to the neck. The woman, in a hooded green cloak, was considerably younger as far as DeShays could discern. He'd not seen either one of them before, and, as their footsteps faded in the gloom, almost laughed aloud at the foolishness of his concern.

CHAPTER 15

At eight a.m. on a Tuesday morning the Iron Mug presented an air of sleepy indifference, its front door propped open with a metal pail. Inside, the chairs lay upended on the tables, glasses were shelved in a neat row behind the bar and on the floor the grooves in the sawdust suggested a recent sweeping. Nothing moved save the dust floating in the light cast through the street-facing windows.

Tempted as DeShays was to stop in at Kate Felton's studio when he set out that morning, another more pressing—if not as welcome—call demanded his attention. Though DeShays now answered to the chief, Irontop was the man he'd turned to after handing back his badge. He needed to square things with Carson (away from the station house) before his lack of contact came to look like deliberate avoidance. After all, Carson was the man in whose ward the murder had occurred, and DeShays knew he would need to keep him as an ally as he pursued the matter.

DeShays rapped against the inside of the door. His hopeful "Halloo!" echoed through the empty barroom; a testament to Carson's reputation, that his place could be left unattended like this. From somewhere upstairs came the wail of an infant and the patter of light footsteps across the floorboards. He called out again. If memory served, a door on the right-hand side, just beyond the bar, led up to Carson's quarters. He found it unlocked.

The door opened on a bare hallway cast in the gauzy light admitted through a skylight. Feeling uneasily like a prowler, DeShays started towards the stairs and was about to call out again to make himself known when the sudden creak of a floorboard startled him. Before he could turn, his left arm was wrenched behind him and a sweaty hand clamped itself over his mouth. His heart seemed to double its beat and rise towards his throat.

"Lost our way, have we?" came a baleful voice, the texture of sandpaper. The words were whispered straight into DeShays's ear by a creature whose breath made him want to puke. "It's your lucky day—know where you are, hickjop?" DeShays's arm was yanked still harder. The pain was excruciating but with the hand smothering his mouth he could neither speak nor groan. Short of breath, he began flailing his free arm like a drowning man.

"Sneak thieves—I hate 'em," continued his assailant as if addressing an unseen third party, giving a tug on the arm so sharp that DeShays feared it might part from its socket. "No dancin' permitted here. What's your name, gip?" The words came rapidly and DeShays knew he was at a lunatic's mercy. Struggling to answer through the suffocating grid of fingers, he finally managed to blurt it out.

"Let's see yer stinkin' mazzard, dearie." DeShays felt like a rag doll as his assailant turned him, slamming his back against the wall by the foot of the stairs. Cauliflower ears and a bushy brow that didn't stop for the bridge of the man's nose, which might have been flattened by a trip-hammer, proclaimed the battered features of a boxer. But it wasn't the battle-scars but the uncanny discord between the man's deep eyes which most inspired fear.

Pressed to the wall by an arm against his chest stiff as a wooden beam, DeShays saw recognition flicker in those crazed eyes. Upstairs Caesar began to bark and at the sound he felt the man's hold relax ever so slightly. At once the barking grew louder as the door at the top of the stairs swung open and both men cast their eyes upward. In his white nightshirt, his long hair unkempt, obscuring his face and falling to his shoulders, Carson appeared like some wild prophet of old.

"What the devil, Izzy!" he thundered. "Let that man go at once, you understand?" As though he were obeying the command of a hypnotist, to DeShays's amazement his tormentor dropped his arms to his sides. Like a scolded child, he gazed

94

at the floor, as Carson continued in a voice that wasn't harsh but rather reasonable. "Be a good man and say you're sorry. He's my guest, not an intruder. In fact he's a policeman."

Despite Izzy's outward obedience, DeShays sensed the confusion he felt in being told to apologize by the very man he was trying to protect. "Okay, boss." The words came slowly, grudgingly. "Sorry. No offense meant. I thought you was a prowler. Try announcing yerself next time." Izzy offered his hand, and DeShays gave his, albeit gingerly, looking into those uneven eyes. Honor was for the moment satisfied.

As Izzy withdrew to the barroom, gently closing the door behind him as if to show himself a respecter of privacy, DeShays saw past where he'd been standing to the dark hole of the cellar steps which is where he must have sprung from. Carson meantime had retreated. DeShays heard him quiet Caesar, then came the sound of an infant crying and a woman calling out, wanting to know what the fuss was about. Again Caesar began barking and Carson reappeared at the top of the stairs. "Sorry about that Miles. Let me restore the peace and I'll be with you. Why not go down to the kitchen and we'll talk there. Izzy should've stoked up the stove. Coffee's in the cupboard."

Just make yourself right at home, thought DeShays, rubbing his left shoulder and flexing his twisted left arm, which felt as though it might never function properly again. He heard Carson moving about upstairs and raised voices though, with the door closed, the words were muffled. Reaching for his cap, which had fallen in the tussle, he made for the cellar stairs.

The kitchen ceiling was low, with so little room to spare that DeShays had to stoop. Thus far, he reflected, everything had gone wrong. Never had he felt more out of place than in this cramped room with its flagstone floor and wide brick hearth. He found a copper pot already filled with water, poured in a quantity of coffee grounds and set it to boil. Minutes passed and he waited, with only the stove's roar for company.

The wait and the familiar smell served to calm his nerves. After letting the pot come three times to the boil DeShays filled two mugs with a brew strong enough to make an elephant dance and set them on the table. Leaning on his good elbow, he let the steam from his mug drift deliciously past his face and stared up through the squat kitchen windows at the feet of the occasional passer-by in the street.

At last the sound of a descending tread announced the appearance of Carson, tired-eyed, clad in slippers and a maroon silk robe. "That's not the way we usually greet our guests, Miles." He paused in the doorway as if to be sure of DeShays's forgiveness. "Izzy was a prize fighter. Sometimes he forgets himself. Someday he'll probably forget his own name. That's Izzy Mendoza. Heard of him?"

"I've seen a litho done a while back, now that you mention it. One would scarcely know him." Indeed, it seemed to DeShays that Irontop's patronage must be the only thing keeping him from an asylum.

"A good man at heart, believe it or not," said Carson, assuming the seat closest to DeShays. "He comes here every morning, cleans up and looks after the bar for me. As you can see he's as loyal as Caesar."

As if on cue, a tiny quartet of steps was heard on the stairs and Caesar crawled in, nosing his way under the table. Carson leaned down to pet him, took a long sip of coffee, then to DeShays's surprise pulled a cigar from the pocket of his robe. He bit off the paper tip, walked over to the stove to light it and sat down again, ready to hold court. It was as if the business upstairs had never happened.

"I was wondering when you'd come around again." After savoring a few puffs he set the cigar down in a small pewter tray. "I see the Father forgave, eh? Tell me how that came to pass."

"Wisdom was received from a higher authority."

"The same that got you with the department to begin with, eh? So to what do I owe the pleasure of your company this fine morning?"

"Here's how it all stands," DeShays reported. "The Chief dumped a bundle of odds and ends on me out of his desk drawer. Stuff relating to the Mauler case, for want of a better term. Worthless, most of it. People with bones to pick, senile old codgers and crones, landladies after uncollected rent, and so forth."

"Privy collection."

"There was a diamond in the night soil. A lady daguerreo-typist wrote to say that a man paid for his to be colored and hadn't picked it up. To cut the story short, I have in my possession the likeness of the man found in Cuyler's Alley. I've yet to tell the chief. I thought I'd tell you first."

Wordlessly, Carson stretched out his hand.

"Not here. It's under lock and key."

"How, then, did you reach this conclusion?"

"In the portrait the man is wearing the self-same garments I found under Miller's bed."

Carson smiled, as if at some private joke. "Eli Miller," he said with a blend of cynicism and wonder. "Well, very good indeed, you're a sly one. Looks like you'll make a policeman after all—a better one than me." He savored a long sip of coffee. "I wouldn't have thought that Miller had it in him, would you? I guess that bloke was three sheets to the wind when they found him."

They. The word, spoken so nonchalantly, jarred on DeShays. He wondered if Carson too had been holding his cards close to his chest since they'd last spoken. "Who are *they*?"

"Why the surprise? Whoever killed Miller was covering his tracks. You're with me on that? Why would he need to do that, unless he was involved all along? Miller was what we call a crow—someone who keeps watch while someone else does the dirty work. He was a watchman, after all. So we need to know who Miller knew, and that's what I've been investigating. I can't do much with an empty suit."

"And what have you found thus far?"

"He's never attended state prison. The Chief has a list of everyone who's been there since time began. We've examined police court records, but his name doesn't turn up. Either this was a first offense, or he's covered his tracks pretty well. So we're looking at his recent associations."

It was clear to DeShays that Miller had plundered the dead man, but that didn't necessarily make him an accomplice to murder. This was a man who'd pulled people from burning buildings for no pay, who'd earned for his pains a lonely existence in a dingy room. DeShays thought back to the crude figures he'd carved, the toy being repaired for a child he must have known and the niece felled by yellow fever. If he'd lapsed in taking the clothes, an old man with no criminal record was an unlikely accomplice to murder. Nor did Carson's theory account for the degree of violence done to Bewly.

"Miller may have acted like a vulture, but the damage done to the dead man's face hardly tallies with robbery. Surely a robber would stop when his victim was helpless."

"In my brief time with the police, one axiom has held true, Miles; the shortest distance between two points is a straight line. And since Miller stole the man's duds ... say, what was his name again?"

"Bewly—I haven't discovered an address yet."

"Since this Bewly's duds were found in Miller's room, we can only conclude that Miller is implicated in his death. I'd wager anything on it. I can feel it in my bones."

"So McGlone's off the hook?"

"Not so fast. I reckon there were three of them."

DeShays was skeptical. "We won't really understand what happened till we find out who Bewly was. Only then are matters settled."

"What difference does it make? Some fancy greenhorn in the wrong place at the wrong time." Carson stubbed out his cigar with a vengeance. "You know, I think you like the process too much to want it to end!" Then, seeming to pull back from the point of anger, his next words were spoken as those of an elder sibling.

"Listen, I had the same feeling a few months ago, when we finally nabbed the man who killed that old spinster on Henry Street, remember? You never forget your first murder. But you have your fun—I'm the one sitting on the fire. The Chief wants results, and yesterday. You heard him. Miller's damn death has opened the whole thing up."

"Understood," said DeShays. "But give me time to discover more about Bewly while you look into Miller's connections. Could be it'll help us find that third man."

Carson reached across and clasped his hand on DeShays's shoulder, shaking him gently to and fro. "Now you're talking, brother. Don't be so glum. I've never seen anyone so disappointed by success!"

In the doorway appeared a handsome lass not more than twenty-five, with long, wavy brown hair and a considerable bust draped by an Indigo shawl. In DeShays's eyes she might have been the model for any number of ships' figureheads. Carson, with his back to the stairs, hadn't heard her come in and seemed annoyed for some reason. Nevertheless, he introduced her as his wife, Sarah, and DeShays rose to take her hand. She was off with the baby to see her parents, she announced, before retreating.

Carson explained that he'd been married less than a year, and that Sarah was the daughter of an innkeeper across the river in New Jersey. "Her old man says I've done him out of several hundred a year by taking her out from behind the bar," he joked, accompanying DeShays upstairs. It seemed like a line he'd used before.

Leaving through the front door, it occurred to DeShays that he might have saved himself a good scare had he come in that way. Despite the rocky start things hadn't worked out so badly. At the door Irontop again placed his hand on DeShays's shoulder, the gesture and the look in his eyes seeming as much to offer congratulations as to indicate the trust he placed in him.

On the street outside the Iron Mug sat a dray from a local brewery. The driver and the man Izzy were unloading beer barrels and rolling them across the sidewalk. Disinclined to cross the fighter's path again, DeShays, intending to head west, instead walked towards the water.

CHAPTER 16

Though the day had begun fine, clouds were moving in from the west as DeShays hurried across the square and took the stairs to Kate's top-floor studio two at a time. A sense of worry, of something not right somewhere, had dogged him since leaving the Iron Mug. Was it Carson, he asked himself, with his out of hand insistence on Miller's guilt, or was it perhaps Kate? Since walking her home the night before he'd reproached himself for putting her in the way of anyone with an interest in Bewly. A madman like Poole, for instance, or that couple last night. Wasn't there something odd in the way the man raised his hat to him in passing? A challenge almost, or an invitation, like an arched eyebrow?

His worst fears seemed confirmed when, panting from the climb, he tapped on the studio door and, instead of Kate's light footfall, heard the approaching tread of a much heavier boot.

Instinctively DeShays pulled back a pace as unseen hands fumbled with the lock. Someone not used to the place, he surmised, as a strange voice barked out, "Who's there?"

"Police!" He tried to sound tough, but felt ridiculous. What would a real policeman do now in his shoes? He had no club, no gun, no weapon of any kind. The door swung open.

"Mr. DeShays, if I'm not much mistaken." It was the man from last night.

"Where's Miss Felton?"

"In her darkroom. She sent me to let you in." The man stuck out his hand. "Beardmore Paul. We have met—after a fashion."

As DeShays, with considerable misgiving, reciprocated, there came a welcome cry from within. "Oh, Mr. DeShays, I was hoping it was you. Now there'll be no need for Mr. Paul to come back. Mr. Paul has come about Mr. Bewly. "Won't you make yourselves at home, gentlemen, and excuse me for a minute?"

"Well, well," said DeShays, irritated to find the stranger conducting him to a seat in the waiting area as though he owned the place, "so you were not quite the innocent passer-by I took you for last night. Who are you, sir, and what is your interest in Bewly?"

Beardmore Paul lowered his long frame into a chair and stretched his legs languidly towards his interlocutor. "For my sins, sir, I am a lawyer. For my eternal damnation, no doubt, a Philadelphia lawyer. As for my concern with Bewly ..." here he plucked from a waistcoat pocket a small silver box, snapped open the lid, and proffered it to DeShays, who declined, "it is purely professional." Placing a pinch of snuff in the palm of his hand he inhaled through one nostril, repeated the process with the other, and let out a theatrical sigh, "If somewhat delicate."

Bit of a showman, DeShays decided, visualizing the man in court parading back and forth before the Philadelphia jury-men like a conjurer at a children's party, alternately horrifying and titillating his captive audience. What his association might be with Bewly was hard to fathom. "I don't know how much you gleaned from Miss Felton?"

"Damn all. The lady is a paragon of non-communication. But if Bewly's affairs have attracted the attention of the authorities, I assume the lad has not been on his best behavior. Do you, by happy chance, have him under lock and key?"

"In a manner of speaking."

"Ah, the Tombs?"

"Singular, I'm afraid. Potter's field."

"You mean ...?"

DeShays nodded gravely. "But tell me, what's your business with him?"

"My client—the young lady you saw me with last evening, who sat here yesterday, incidentally, for her likeness—has

101

named Bewly respondent in a paternity suit in the Philadelphia courts." He paused. "Dead, you say, sir? Rutherford Bewly, of Albany, New York?"

"Of Albany? That we did not know."

"May I ask how he died?"

"Of course. But first perhaps you'll tell me more about him."

"It was inquiries in Albany led us here to New York. Our man, we were led to believe, was in town on an errand of matrimony, a state of affairs, as you can imagine, my client was anxious to forestall. In scanning the papers we saw the notice in the Tribune and decided—aware of certain traits in Bewly's character—to approach the matter with the utmost circumspection."

"Traits?"

"The fellow had a way with the fair sex, a compulsion, if you like. My client was by no means the first, it seems. His modus operandi is—was—to attract his victim, to propose wedlock on pain of utmost secrecy, to violate her and, lastly, to reject her. Suffice it to say that, on realizing that the address in your notice was that of a daguerreotype studio, my client proposed having her likeness made as a means of spying out the land. When this avenue proved unproductive, we waited for Miss Felton to leave and followed you. Still none the wiser, there seemed little to lose by a straightforward approach. And here I am."

"Tell me about your client?"

"Her name is Augustina Mullins, twenty-three years old, of a worthy if not wealthy Germantown family. Her father is a minister of the church. Over a summer visiting relatives in the Albany area Miss Mullins met, and became quite smitten with, our Mr. Bewly. During her stay upstate Bewly made arrangements for the young lady, her aunt and cousins, to visit him at the sumptuous estate he shares with his elderly parents." The lawyer paused, and DeShays recognized a fellow performer's bit of tradecraft before a key line. "Subsequent invitations were restricted to Augustina and a twelve year old cousin. I should add that the Bewly family owns a glove factory on the edge of town and lives quite comfortably. The parents are well on in years and entrust the management of the business to their elder son. Rutherford, the younger brother, devotes himself to sales, traveling a good deal on business. While in Philadelphia on one such errand, he called upon Augustina. It was at the American Hotel, opposite the State House, that he swore undying love, proposed marriage, and seduced her."

"This was in—?"

"August. Bewly wrote once in response to his presumed fiancée's increasingly desperate entreaties, otherwise silence. The lady's father, my friend, entrusted the vindication of his daughter's honor to me. I can tell you, I don't relish the task of breaking the news to her."

"I surely don't envy you." In DeShays's mind's eye the features—that he had so puzzled over and whose import had so maddeningly eluded him since he'd first set eyes on the daguerreo—at last jelled. Softness yes, as Kate had observed, but not the innocent softness of some indulged mother's pet, as he had imagined. More like the softness of dissipation. Yes, it was in the eyes. Hadn't Bewly's fate very likely to do with this side of the man? A deliberate act of anger or revenge, not an encounter with a desperate predator.

"Was it murder?" The lawyer was staring at him, as if to read his mind.

"You've read perhaps of our so-called River Mauler? The near-naked body found by the East River docks about two weeks ago, bludgeoned out of all recognition?"

"Some such account did reach my ears, though we only yesterday arrived in town."

"Bewly is more than likely that victim. The Saturday he died he came here for his likeness, paid his money, and never returned to pick it up. It's Miss Felton's opinion that a lady was the intended recipient. He was most particular about the frame and the coloring."

"Then may I be so bold as to ask that the likeness be given to Miss Mullins, as if he had intended it for her? We would of course handsomely reward the favor."

"Until the case is closed, we're holding it as evidence. Eventually, I suppose, it could be done—with due deference to the claims of the immediate family. In which regard I must ask you to keep this whole matter under your hat for the time being."

As soon as the lawyer left, Kate Felton emerged from the darkroom. Sensing a suppressed excitement in DeShays's demeanor, she insisted he tell her all that had transpired, and was able to cap it with a story of her own. "Hardly had I unlocked the studio door this morning than a woman burst in. I'd say she was nearly thirty, very fashionably dressed, overly so. An odd bird of paradise, precious stones and silver trinkets everywhere, and a ravishing scarlet cloak. Before giving an account of herself she collapsed into the chair you're sitting in now. She was in a positively hysterical state. I went to the darkroom and brought back a tot of a brandy I keep for emergencies. Only after more would she say why she'd come. It was the notice—I knew it would be, and said 'You must return at five.' She threw an absolute fit, refused to budge. 'If you knew who I was you'd not treat me so cruelly!' she said."

The way Kate trilled the *r* in cruel was amusing; her imitation was stagey, yet her description of the woman did suggest an actress or even an exclusive courtesan. "And she was?"

"She wouldn't say! But something told me that she was the one for whom Bewly's portrait was intended. Only when Mr. Paul arrived did I manage to dislodge her. Or rather did she uproot herself. It's a wonder that you didn't see her leaving—you must have missed her by minutes."

DeShays, after exhorting Kate to be extra careful as to who she admitted, promised to be back in good time. On his way downstairs he looked in at the lithographer's on the floor below and, in his official capacity, requested of a wiry little man in a leather apron that special attention be paid to any unusual activity upstairs.

A little after four that afternoon DeShays found himself again climbing the stairs to Kate Felton's studio. He was anticipating a pleasant hour or so in her company before having to interview anyone who might have shown up about the notice. All day her image had remained with him. Though their conversation hadn't strayed far, he felt he'd known her for longer than just four days, and he'd even begun to wonder how to explain his recent past, and the circumstances of his marriage. For Old Honan had not been entirely accurate in his observation that DeShays had not the married look about him. It was precisely because he was married that he'd left Cincinnati.

Cupid's arrow struck as he played there in a blood-drenched rendition of *Richard III*; though naturally the young lady's father had no intention of abandoning his daughter to an actor. Later, back in New York, came an unexpected summons offering him not only the girl but a job at the Cincinnati Customs House. A premature child was stillborn some six months later, and while DeShays had his suspicions he kept them to himself. Indeed, he tried his best to buckle down to small town life and even learned to hunt Indian style. Till, one morning on the way to work, it dawned on him that the play he was in had run its course. Without a word to anyone he boarded an eastbound boat.

Kate met him at the door, whispering, "She's back," and vanished into her darkroom. Standing with her back to the room, looking out upon the shadowy square, was a woman. In the dim light DeShays saw that she was slender and of medium height. Her hair hung in two braided loops either side her glossy head. A bright shawl reached nearly to the floor. She turned. It was Pauline. If she, in turn, was startled, no movement betrayed it. Neither said a word. The temperature in the room seemed to plummet.

"Shall we sit?" he indicated the chairs. Pauline did not move. "I take it you've come about the Bewly business, that you saw the notice in the papers?" Her lips remained compressed. "Was he a friend? I assure you, you have my word, anything you divulge will not penetrate beyond these walls. This is my work now, Pauline. That's all there is to it."

"He's dead, isn't he?"

DeShays nodded.

With a shriek she rushed past him and threw herself at the door, which somehow she managed to claw open. He heard her clattering down the stairs, but made no effort to follow. His mind churned with the import of what she'd just disclosed. So La Rue, it seemed, had not had him chasing wild geese after all.

"Shouldn't we ...?" He turned at the sound of the voice. Kate had come up behind him. The look on his face seemed to silence her. "What is it?" she asked quietly. DeShays just shook his head. "You knew her, I think?"

He weighed his response carefully. "Pauline Dowling is her name. She's an actress. I met her not long ago. It was on a ship, in fact."

"Oh, I see." Kate frowned, offering a pale smile. Prying was beneath her. "She must have been surprised to find you here."

"As surprised as I was to see her." He moved to the door.

"Do you have to rush off?" she asked. "I'm just putting the finishing touches to a portrait and can't afford to let the paint dry."

DeShays followed her into a room beyond her darkroom where she took a seat at a table. The bright beam of an Argand lamp lit up a trio of portrait daguerreotypes she was evidently working on. On a chair beside her sat a small paint box, on which rested a palette. Kate picked up her brush, daubing it with the flesh tint she'd mixed. The reek of turpentine filled the room.

"A daguerreotype possesses a beauty all its own, don't you think?" she asked as DeShays bent down to inspect her work. "The sitter appears to have entered the magic world of the mirror. Coloring it with oils only brings him back to ours and drains him of life. He dies on the journey."

"On the contrary, you make them uncannily lifelike. I presume those two are twins."

"This work makes me feel as though I'm an undertaker," she sighed, applying the same pale flesh tint to the second girl. "Maybe one day it will be possible to reproduce nature's colors from the inside. Then I'll be done with this task." As she applied the last of the mixed paint to the final portrait she asked, "Would it be forward of me to enquire as to your course of action?"

"It's dark out, and blowing up a storm," he said. "Why don't I see you home, if home is where you want to go?"

"I've been seeing myself home from here at all times, in all weathers, for the past year," she said, to DeShays's ears a trifle mockingly, "I think I can manage. What I meant was, what is your next step in the affair of Rutherford Bewly? Will you pursue the actress?"

"I think I'll leave the actress to pursue me," he replied, "I've a feeling she will."

CHAPTER 17

It was a lucky thing, thought Mrs. Fitzgerald, that she'd reached the door first after her new bell system chimed at eight-thirty that evening. The girls were busy in the front parlor practicing the newest dance craze, the polka, and though Mrs. F had been down in the kitchen she'd beaten them to the door. Not that she was expecting anyone. Mr. Evans and Mr. Jenkins were upstairs—only Mr. DeShays was out. Peering through one of the narrow glass panels to the side of her front door she was surprised to see a strange woman in a scarlet cloak.

Quickly sizing up her visitor, she opened the door and uttered a steely, "Yes?" The woman looked to be in her late twenties, with striking dark eyes, large and moist. It appeared that she'd been crying—some of her makeup had run. Auburn hair spilled from her smart bonnet, and expensive-looking silver bracelets adorned her arms.

It was Mr. DeShays she'd come to see, she explained, apologizing for calling so late. She hoped the directory had listed the right address. Learning that he wasn't in, she asked if he was expected soon. An urgent note in her voice, a slight quaver, worried Mrs. F as she replied she didn't know.

Pauline Dowling, that was her name. Her elocution was fine, too fine for Mrs. F. There was something high-toned and artificial about it, though the quaver sounded real. If Mr. DeShays had indeed been an actor, might she be an actress? She had that sort of name, it rang a bell. Wasn't she precisely the sort for whom the strictest rule of the house was in place, that prohibiting male boarders from entertaining female guests in their rooms?

Seeing Eliza and Millie emerge from the parlor, Miss

Dowling gave Mrs. F a wistful smile, apologized for the intrusion once again and bade her goodnight, turning to go.

Though protective of her daughters Mrs. F was not, by nature, unsympathetic. There was a desperation about this woman, something of the fallen angel, and the landlady was not one to "pass by on the other side." Besides, she was eager to know what her connection to Mr. DeShays was. Might Miss Dowling be his jilted lover? Instinct told Mrs. F otherwise. She told the girls to get back in the parlor, shut the door and mind their business, and asked Miss Dowling in.

A temperamental breed, these actresses. The girl was desperate to see Mr. DeShays one minute, and the next Mrs. F had almost to drag her in to wait, insisting upon taking her cloak and bonnet, which were handed over with some reluctance. Perhaps with reason: fragrant as her perfume was, it couldn't disguise the smell of liquor on her breath.

Once downstairs in the kitchen, seated at the table before a slice of apple pie Mrs. F had gotten from her locked pie safe, Miss Dowling's manner assumed that of a princess. She was unlike anyone Mrs. F had met before, with a way of picking at her pie, taking very small bites, and a delicate way of holding her glass.

While on the one hand she seemed distracted, her eyes roving around the room, she could be gracious, commenting approvingly on Mrs. F.'s new coal-burning stove, asking about the girls, praising their musical talents despite the audible whine of Millie's voice. One day, she said forlornly, she hoped to have beautiful daughters such as Mrs. F's, and a home as nice as hers. She asked after the man of the house, was sorry to hear he'd passed away. Of her own life little was said. Mr. DeShays simply a dear, dear friend. Mrs. F's suspicions upon first glance proved justified: she noticed that Pauline wore neither an engagement nor a wedding ring.

After she finished her lemonade and pie Miss Dowling made a show of feeling better though Mrs. F sensed that she was anxious to go. She asked if it might be possible to leave Mr. DeShays a note, and Mrs. F took her upstairs to the writing table in her bedroom. Ten minutes later she saw her out, wondering what would become of her as she watched the scarlet patch recede down the dark street. Then Pauline looked back and gave a little wave, as if she knew Mrs. F would be watching.

The following day, a Wednesday, found DeShays—holding his cap to his head in the face of a bracing wind—scanning the house numbers along one of the financial district's less traveled side streets. The restaurant, as Pauline's note had indicated, was indeed nameless. The building's peeling white paint set it apart from its red brick neighbors.

The wind pulled the door shut with a bang as he came in from the cold. A waiter, tall, dark-haired, with a high forehead, turned away from the booth he was working to give the intruder—which DeShays immediately felt he was—an abrupt glance. Pauline's dramatic sense was intact—the place was an ideal rendezvous for a shady liaison. A dozen dimly lit booths, above which whorls of smoke hovered as though rising from a volcano, concealed their occupants behind dark green curtains. What a contrast from Pelham's, where he'd dined with Billy Holmes the night before.

Upon coming home somewhat the worse for drink, he'd faced a grilling that would have done the chief proud. Mrs. F, in her nightgown with her hair down, had waited up for him long past her usual bedtime to give him the note.

When DeShays swore to his landlady's disbelieving ears that Miss Dowling's visit was related to a case he was working on, she cautioned him against swearing. Her home was no police station, she told him flatly, reminding him of the rule against having female visitors in rooms. Then she softened up, telling of Pauline's sorry state and handing over the note urgently requesting his attendance at the restaurant at two the next day. He was to present himself as a Mr. Hayes, for whom there would be a dinner reservation.

"One apple pie, one plum pudding!" the waiter called into the kitchen. DeShays watched a male hand adorned with a gold wedding band reach out from inside a booth to snatch shut the curtain to the tinkle of a girlish giggle and recalled the shuttered upstairs windows he'd noticed on his way in.

The waiter approached, walking with a dancer's gait, and asked DeShays if he had a reservation, casting a bleak glance at his cap.

"The name's Hayes," DeShays said, removing the cap and checking the man's eyes to see if he knew it wasn't. With nary a flicked eyelash, DeShays was shown to an empty booth the curtain of which the waiter closed, as though to conceal something unclean. DeShays at once re-opened it and was rewarded with a fleeting smile as the man waltzed off.

Fifteen minutes became twenty-five. At half past the restaurant clock chimed twice. He'd slept badly and the stuffy candlelit booth was confining. Drumming his fingers on the table he re-read Pauline's note and checked his pocket watch. She was chronically late, he recalled, so he went ahead and ordered corned beef and cabbage, and wine. Had she acted on impulse, too embarrassed now to show up? It couldn't have been easy, going to his lodgings like that. Relations had soured between them long ago, and like spoiled milk there was no way of reversing the effects. Perhaps the booze helped. Mrs. F remarked that she'd been drinking.

In a way Pauline's path had mirrored his own. She'd joined the Park's company at seventeen, the scene painter's daughter. As DeShays had moved from utility man all the way to leading man so she moved from utility lady to leading lady. On the way both of them had borne the resentment of tired veterans stuck in a rut. She'd often sought his opinion on acting matters, and adopted some of his pet mannerisms, slowing down towards the end of her sentences as though deep in thought, or turning her back to the audience as though they were eavesdropping on her private world.

Talented though Pauline was, it was her charms which made her a valuable property. No sooner had she walked onstage than gasping old men grabbed their opera glasses, while young blades sat up at attention. "It's a Pauline night," DeShays had heard the bloods say in satisfaction, seeing a poster on which the pointing finger was printed by her name. He remembered the star-gazers of the third tier telling him that, though they found him dashing, business was never bet-

111

ter than on Pauline nights. Nor could he hope to compete with the rich admirers who tossed her flowers after each performance. Pauline was determined to escape the social taint of her station and no one could blame her. Marrying up was the goal. He scarcely foresaw how things would unfold.

His mind wandered back to a Saturday night six years past, to the stage door entrance in the alley behind the Park. He recalled how thin houses had been that week, the bills changing nightly and without notice, and how drained it had left him. Even Pauline wasn't drawing, having been used once too often.

But that night the Park sold out, and with a mixture of fondness and regret DeShays recalled the thrill which had drawn him to the profession. The occasion was the season's closer, a benefit for George Hamilton Powers, lord of the American stage. A night when Powers would glean the entire take after expenses. To guarantee a killing he would perform the lead in *Spartacus*, the sight of his well-muscled and oiled torso guarantee of a full house.

So DeShays readily consented to play the lead in *Vidocq*, the French Police Spy on the same bill opposite Pauline (as his suffering young wife). He'd drawn high praise when he'd stepped in one night for a hopelessly hung-over Powers, playing Macbeth, one of Powers's warhorses. The cognoscenti had taken note—his naturalism was a striking antidote to Powers's bombastic acting. Now Powers, a man given to shows of "true-blue American spirit" as he put it, had declared that the young man merited wider recognition: *Vidocq* would directly precede *Spartacus*. DeShays was grateful, and relieved: he'd heard rumors that Powers had spoken poorly of him.

The memory of the call boy's shrill "Overture on, men!" accompanied by rapping on the dressing room door, even now made him cringe. What should have been a triumph turned to the stuff of nightmares. A group of Powers's adherents were in the audience, primed to give him a dose of "true-blue American spirit." During the first act he heard a hiss coming from the pit, then a catcall or two from the upper galleries. His suspicions grew during the second act, as he played through jeers and more catcalls. By the fifth tomatoes were landing on him. He could still feel the sting of flying nuts.

Checking his watch DeShays saw it was now a quarter to three.

Pauline's fall, as he saw it, had begun that night. As Powers acted the part of Spartacus she'd stood in the wings, her eyes glued to his sculpted torso. Afterwards she and DeShays visited the great man's dressing room. With patent insincerity he apologized for the incidents and vowed to find out who was behind them, then turned to Pauline and bowed. Still in his skimpy toga, he kissed her hand softly, bathing her with charming compliments. DeShays watched her eyes flash when he asked her to sup with him the following night. The moment filled him with infinite disgust. Later Holmes told him that she'd spent that night at Powers's hotel. And the next, and more after that. The two were inseparable at the hip, Holmes liked to say, jabbing DeShays with an elbow.

Pauline grew increasingly hard to take. The following season she took to turning up late at rehearsals, adopted pretentious airs and distanced herself from the secondary players, treating DeShays as though he was a poor substitute for Powers. Her father, normally a joker, kept a lower profile, shunned by his daughter and embarrassed at her behavior. The season concluded, DeShays had no more business with her. The rest was hearsay.

As in the previous year, Pauline joined Powers's touring company, playing across the country in converted barns and breweries, as DeShays would later on. At tour's end they reached the lavish St. Charles in New Orleans where tragedy struck. Powers, waiting in the wings in the part of Othello, was flattened by a counterweight which dropped from the flies, leaving him paralyzed on one side. Despite her father's pleas, the following season Pauline's contract at the Park was not renewed, the manager replacing her with his new mistress.

Pauline became neurasthenic, suffering a breakdown. Though she kept working with touring companies, her looks still a draw, she drank too much and performed erratically, giggling or staring back blankly as the prompter's lines lodged in her throat. By the time her condition improved the major stock companies were unwilling to take the risk. She was fated to tour endlessly. Once, in Cincinnati, DeShays had seen her name on a poster though he hadn't the stomach to go.

The restaurant was emptying out, with veiled women being handed by men twice their age into cabs that materialized as if at some hidden signal. He knew Pauline wouldn't show, that something wasn't right and that now he would have to go and find her. "Does Mr. Hayes come here often?" he asked the waiter as he counted out his tab.

"I couldn't say, I'm sure," the man responded airily.

"Could you say now?" DeShays pushed his copper star under the man's nose. "Does Mr. Hayes come here often?"

The waiter considered. "Every so often, I suppose."

"To meet the same 'certain lady?'"

"You could say so. Excuse my asking, sir," the man dropped his pose, "but is the lady in any trouble?"

"I sincerely hope not," said DeShays. Outside, the daylight had drained away. As the clock chimed four he stepped into the cold pulling his cap down firmly over his brow.

CHAPTER 18

DeShays stood at the corner of Moore narrowing his eyes against the lively breeze blowing in off the river setting the masts clicking and clacking like a standing ovation at the Park. Across the street, in the gathering darkness, loomed the Temple of the Muses, moored where he'd last left her alongside the pier. Yet all was not quite as before. On the ship's bowsprit, high above the cobbles, two deckhands sat securing jibs. Sailors shouldering small trunks or clutching canvas bags drifted up, a pair hauling a sea chest staggering past him. He watched as they maneuvered their load up the gangplank where stood no giant of a watchman on deck to challenge them.

Somehow or other DeShays had to know whether Pauline was on board and, if she was, whether she was there of her own free will. The more he thought about her behavior of the day before the more convinced he was that fear was its driving force, and as he crossed to the foot of the pier he wondered if her nervous manner might have been in response to a danger more immediate than he'd first imagined.

"Top of the evenin' to you, Misseur!" The squawk at his elbow made him jump. The face that leered up at him from the depths of a purple shawl showed itself well-pleased with its effect. "A penny for your thoughts, Misseur," crowed the proprietress of the grogshop, "I'll wager it's a little mademoiselle from old Paree has stolen them away, ey?" In a cackly voice she began to sing:

"Her waist is round and small, her mouth is best of all, for this little virgin, I've got a load o' love."

"En fait, Madame," DeShays interrupted, perceiving one or two of the sailors turn to smirk, "it is ze boat zat intrigues me.

It appears about to depart."

"You shoulda been here last night, Misseur— Say, what's your name, sweetheart?"

"Jacques, Madame."

"'Sans teeth, sans eyes, sans taste, sans everything!' The melancholy one. Oh yes, Misseur. Fair Rosalind, that was me once."

"Last night, Madame, you were saying?"

"A commotion like you've never seen. Carriages piled up on each other. And nobody home but that big mute standin' on deck lookin' for all the world like a hangman, keeping 'em away. Would've got ketched himself if the mob had gotten their hands on him. Theirs were some mighty long faces for all their finery, with the big idiot just standin' there grinnin' away at 'em."

As she spoke DeShays was hard put to ignore the gulls that crowded in on them, wheeling and shrieking like banshees in a tale of Gothic doom. He ducked as one swooped down, grazing his shoulder with a wingtip. "Manners, mes enfants, manners!" screeched his companion, as from the depths of her shawl she flung scraps to the wind.

"But isn't this departure very sudden?" he yelled, in the hubbub abandoning the accents of France.

"Good riddance is what I says, Jacquey." Another volley of scraps rained around them, caught by the luckier birds in midair. "Never a customer among the lot, for all their fancy carriages and finery. And my girls worth any three of 'em."

"So you've no idea—?"

"It ain't too late to slip one of them sailors a doubloon, Jacquey. And for them to spend it with Auntie Mags," she added slyly.

"That's just what I'll do," cried DeShays, escaping amidst ferocious cackling as the gulls circled menacingly.

"You there!" he called to a bearded blond lad in a woolen cap, blue broadcloth coat and striped jersey who'd been lounging over the gunwale of the Temple, watching. "What's your name?"

"What's it to you, sir, if you don't mind my asking?"

DeShays held up his copper star. "Police. Just want a look around."

"This is no pirate ship, sir, but a floating theater."

"Nevertheless," said DeShays, with a stare that invited defiance.

In no particular hurry, the sailor walked towards midships, descended the gangplank and lifted the chains. "May I see your star again, sir?" Again DeShays showed the eight-pointed copper badge. "First time I seen one of these." Satisfied, he stood aside. "Captain's ashore at present, but should be back shortly."

"Where's the boat headed?"

"Baltimore, sir. We sail tonight."

"Has this sailing been long planned?"

"We heard only yesterday. She was set to winter here as we were told. Some of the crew can't be raised. Captain's had to hire extras."

"Been with the Temple long?"

"Just the summer, sir. Joined at Albany."

"Albany, eh? And the company—any of them aboard?"

"No, sir. Disbanded last month. Back in the spring."

"But there've been other—ah—entertainments held here in the meantime?"

"I couldn't say, sir. I only came back aboard this noon."

Entering through a cabin amidships, just beyond the state-room in which he'd stumbled on Pauline, DeShays followed the sailor down some stairs and along a wide gas lit passage with doors on either side. The ship's gas, his guide explained proudly, was manufactured by a portable apparatus housed on board. "Wait here a moment," he told DeShays, "I'll see about lighting up the theater."

So far so good, thought DeShays. Everything seemed open and friendly, perhaps suspiciously so. Sooner or later he would work his inquiries around to Pauline. When the sailor reappeared it was in company of a swarthy bearded fellow of about forty holding a lamp. "Can't light up the theater," he grunted, marching ahead, "Gas not in full production. Give you a look. No harm, I s'pose." He unlocked a door at the passage end.

DeShays stepped into what was, even in semi-darkness, the most incredible auditorium he'd ever seen. From the back of the tier he stared down into a magnificent house decorated in white and pink and gold and crowned by a crystal chandelier. Before him lay row upon steep row. Aft was a stage he guessed to be about forty feet wide, the parquette and boxes together shaping a horseshoe perfectly conforming to the ship's bows.

"Seats a thousand," boasted the sailor.

DeShays asked about the dressing rooms and was told that those for the ladies were behind the stage, those for the men below. A salon was also below, and quarters for the performers. He asked for a look.

"Is there a problem?" demanded the new arrival somewhat testily. "Just what is it you're looking for?"

"I'm sorry," said DeShays. "You are?"

"Second engineer on this vessel. It's just that we are sailing at scant notice. We're shorthanded and not short of work. You're the second officer today to come nosing around. I think you'll find everything is in order. The captain of the First Ward would have seen to that. It's his jurisdiction we're under."

"Captain Carson was here today?"

"His deputy, I believe."

"Pardon me. I'm from headquarters myself. We do tend to trip over each other at times."

The engineer seemed somewhat mollified. "I suppose you're looking for Miss Dowling?"

"Why, yes." DeShays couldn't hide his surprise.

"So was your predecessor. I assure you that unless she's invisible she's not here. The captain had the place ransacked from top to bottom."

"I'm sorry to have bothered you. Perhaps before I go I could see the room where the recent entertainments were held?"

"Show the gentleman the salon," the engineer told the sailor, selecting a key from a bunch at his waist, and with a stiff little bow he disappeared.

The sailor unlocked a polished mahogany door and ventured ahead into the dark, lighting a small table lamp, then a brass chandelier. DeShays set foot in a spacious salon, where

118

long mirrors with opulent gold frames lined the walls, multiplying his reflection and capturing an illusion of endless horizons. At either end of the room stood elegantly carved wooden bars, where bottles and crystal decanters gleamed with colored fluids. Costly lamps with cut-glass shades sat on marble-topped tables. The chairs were richly upholstered in red silk, and there was no shortage of gilt-edged spittoons. He had the impression of being in an expensive brothel.

Walking across a rug of velvet softness, he was struck by the room's curious layout—the tables were on the periphery, the chairs set in a circle and the center of the room was clear, as if perhaps for dancing.

DeShays's curiosity was peaked by a large circular wooden vat, raised a foot or so off the ground. From its lid protruded a number of bent metal rods. Attached to the rods and looped around the vat was a thin velvet rope. Nearby, beneath what at first he'd taken to be a serving table, he noticed a treadle. "May I?" he asked, and meeting no objection lifted the cover.

A series of multicolored glass bowls mounted on a yard-long spindle met his eye, ranging from smallest to largest. A touch of his foot on the treadle set the bowls spinning. Moistening his fingertips, gradually he adjusted his touch until he was able to eke out tones, haunting, celestial or mournful depending on the combinations he chanced upon.

"A rich person's toy, I daresay," said the sailor.

DeShays tinkered a moment longer, then shut the case. His gaze swept the room. "What went on here, I wonder? You've no idea?"

The sailor shrugged. "If I may ask you something, sir, it's about Miss Dowling. Is she lost?"

"What's it to you where Miss Dowling is?"

"I'm sorry, sir," the lad blushed in confusion. "It's just that some of us had a soft spot for her. We wouldn't want anything bad to happen to her."

"I'm sure that Miss Dowling is capable of looking after herself," he said, sounding to his own ears incredibly old and starchy. He was anything but sure.

From the foot of the pier DeShays looked back at the

Temple. The gaudy pennants which had adorned her masts were gone, leaving only a fluttering white ensign bearing the company's name, and the stars and stripes. Soon the big ship would plunge southward through the Atlantic breakers bearing her secrets with her. Glancing at his pocket watch he saw that it was nearly five and fell in step with workers drifting away from a nearby construction site with the onset of darkness.

"His deputy, I believe," the man had said. Poole?

DeShays's inclination was to march over to the First Ward station house and confront Carson. Was Poole acting on his own or behind his boss's back? And how would he happen that very day to be looking for Pauline Dowling at the Temple of the Muses?

On second thoughts a visit to the station was bound to provoke a confrontation, with Poole no doubt sitting behind his desk all glowering innocence. And DeShays didn't want to tip his hand to the man, not till he knew more about what he was up to. No, if he wanted to see Carson he'd have to wait and catch him at the Iron Mug.

Or he might make his way towards Kate Felton's studio. If he hurried he might just catch her. Conceivably Pauline had found her way back there and was waiting.

CHAPTER 19

DeShays rapped on the studio door three times. No sooner had he identified himself than the door creaked open.

"You're late," Kate mock-scolded. "I was about to leave." Indeed, all lights were extinguished save for a small globe lamp set on a table which she held up. "Is anything the matter? You look beat."

"Did the actress return today?" he gasped out, trying to control his breathing after racing up the stairs.

"No encore performance thus far." Shooting him a searching look, Kate retrieved her bonnet from the nearby coat rack.

"It's been a long day, that's all."

"And not over yet, I'm afraid. I'm to deliver a portrait to a gentleman at the Astor House. I promised I'd bring you along in the bargain. His name is Duncan McNight. He works for the hotel," she added, setting the lamp down to tie her bonnet strings.

"Me? Why?"

"He was here about the Bewly notice. Said he'd be on duty at five, but that he'd like his own portrait taken and brought to him tonight at the hotel—along with Bewly's, and whoever was behind the notice. We're to ask for him at the front desk."

"You told him who I was?"

"I did not."

"Good. What's on his mind, do you think?"

"He didn't give much away. But a definite type." She let DeShays place her plain brown cloak upon her shoulders. "Seen it all, kind of a lacquered look, dyed side-whiskers, gold wedding band. Here, see for yourself." She withdrew a small case from her cloak. Opening it, DeShays met the stolid gaze of a man who looked to be in his fifties. "Now, about your actress?"

DeShays closed the case with a snap. "She didn't show."

The night had turned bitterly cold. People with red noses and limbs chilled stiff hurried down Broadway past glittering shop windows, Kate and DeShays among them. By the entrance of the block-long granite pile that was the Astor House carriages mounted with gleaming lamps deposited well-dressed visitors and piles of luggage that uniformed black porters hurried to collect. Kate and DeShays made their way up the steps beneath the lofty portico as young men with uncertain intentions looked on and doormen did their best to keep a hodgepodge of vagrants and street urchins at bay.

From the bustle of a marble-floored vestibule, where cigar and newspaper stands stood like tollgates, they made their way through a spacious hall off which a succession of tall mahogany doors gave glimpses of elegantly appointed parlors, a barroom, a tea-room, and reading and reception rooms. At the main desk new arrivals inscribed their names in leather-bound registers under the indulgent eyes of well-groomed clerks, as men in business attire lounged nearby puffing on cigars, at times peering over blanket-sized newspapers in search of an awaited party.

"Well, hello again, Miss Felton." The genial voice came from beside her, so as not to startle. Duncan McNight offered his hand to Kate then turned keen grey eyes on DeShays who gave his name as they shook.

Trying not to stare at side-whiskers that were indeed dyed a somewhat sudden brown, DeShays saw a man about his own height in a well-tailored if dated black suit. A trace of peppermint hung on his breath. In his portrait, the application of grease affixing the thinning strands of hair to scalp had seemed less obvious.

"If the two of you don't mind, my office is on the second floor. Allow me to lead the way." Following McNight up a wide staircase carpeted in red, they turned left on a quiet corridor paved with squares of blue and white marble past a series of doors paned with thick frosted glass bearing legends in gold: "Hull's Truss Office," "Wm. J. Allen, Hair Restorer," "Benjamin Sherwood, M.D., Magnetic, Optical and Philosophical Instruments."

McNight commented lightly on the weather, asking if either had been to the hotel before, which they had, and if they'd noticed the elder Astor sitting downstairs, which they hadn't. "The old man counts the place among his finest investments. He still derives great pleasure from watching incoming guests. I personally owe him a great debt. My father was for many years his head coachman, and I myself was with the Boston police. When Mr. Astor opened the hotel nine years ago, he appointed me its resident detective."

Towards the end of the hall they came to an unmarked door which McNight, withdrawing a bunch of keys, opened. Turning up the gas fixture, with a courtly gesture he invited his guests to seat themselves in two chairs before his desk.

DeShays eyed a faux-marble inkstand, a supply of quill pens, a pair of opera glasses, an ink-stained red blotter and a periodical, *The New-York Bank Note List and Counterfeit Detector*. To the right of the desk he noted two expensive-looking leather suitcases and a sizeable trunk.

Kate produced the portrait, and McNight opened its little case, nodding in satisfaction. "The subject is certainly no Adonis, but you've done yourself proud nonetheless, Miss Felton. I'm sure Mrs. McNight will be pleased." Opening his desk drawer, he handed her a small envelope. "And you, Mr. DeShays, are related to Mr. Bewly?"

"Police," DeShays said, producing his copper star. "Chief's office."

"Police," McNight repeated with a touch of surprise, leaning forward to hand back the badge. "I rather thought you'd be a relative, or perhaps a lawyer or an insurance man. I take it that you've brought Mr. Bewly's likeness?"

"There wasn't time to retrieve it from safekeeping."

McNight nodded to himself, frowning. "Miss Felton, given that this matter concerns the forces of law and order, I'm afraid that what I have to say to Mr. DeShays must remain confidential. I doubt we'll be long—you might wish to wait in the reading room." McNight rose. "I'd be glad to show you the way."

"I believe I remember," said Kate, valiantly concealing her disappointment.

123

"I won't keep Mr. DeShays more than a few minutes." McNight shut the door gently behind her. "A remarkable woman," he said, reclining in his chair with the air of an older man of the world. "Let me begin by saying that my duties here entail constant vigilance. A hotel with three hundred and eight rooms inevitably attracts rogues of all kinds. At any given time we have between five and eight hundred guests, and there are criminals who would—wrongly I assure you—assume safety in numbers.

"Mr. Bewly's case is unique among those I've encountered, and in my time I've seen all sorts. You see, this hotel is in essence an indoor city. Anything may be had within its walls, and as in any city there are many who would obtain it gratis. Professional thieves stalk the halls, looking to rob the rooms. People register under false names and try to abscond without paying their board. Still others try to obtain meals by impersonating guests. But Mr. Bewly's case fits none of these categories." McNight rose and turned down the gas. "Come to the window for a moment, if you would."

He raised the blinds and the two men looked down onto a paved central courtyard centered around a dormant marble fountain, and across at a vast grid of windows.

"Mr. Bewly was over there, number 152." McNight pointed to a window halfway along the third floor. "He registered on Friday, the last day of October, requesting a quiet room. His stay was to have ended yesterday. Nothing about him aroused the least suspicion. He paid his bill in advance as is customary with first-time visitors. I myself never saw him. He slept here for two nights and dined here on the Saturday with a guest: mutton chops and a bottle of the best hock." He indicated the suitcases DeShays had noticed, "Here are articles of undoubted quality, their worth several times the cost of his stay.

"Understand, I have nothing but the highest opinion of Mr. Matson and the new police," continued McNight, addressing an obvious question, "but the Astor House hardly desires the sort of publicity which you inevitably bring. Besides," with a trace of mischief in his eyes, "I had no evidence of any crime

124

being committed. Admittedly, I have access to certain lines of police intelligence, but my inquiries were for naught: I was unaware of any investigation." He lowered the blind and turned up the gas. "I trust that he's come to no harm. He appears to be employed in his family's glove concern, in Albany. I'll have to write his office about the disposal of his affects."

From a desk drawer McNight handed DeShays an elegantly engraved card with a porcelain-like coating:

J.C. Bewly & Company Glovers & Leather Dressers
396 Broadway, Albany, New-York
(Sign of the Golden Gloves)
Kid gloves, equal to any imported, made to order
E. Rutherford Bewly, representative.

"Mind if I take this?"

"Take anything you need. There's also a letter"—delving again into the drawer—"evidently from a female admirer, posted from this city. Unfortunately, she has not granted posterity her surname. As you will read, gloves are not Mr. Bewly's sole concern."

DeShays pocketed the card and picked up the letter, nodding very slightly as he read the name.

New York, October 17, 1845

Dearest Rutherford,

Again and again I read the letter you sent me from Albany. Although you seem to imply that it will be not long before your hold over my affections is displaced by another, I cannot believe that one such as you, who too well knows how dear you are to me, can possibly entertain so absurd a delusion. You are wrong to imagine that those who would regard me as a mere ornament could possibly usurp your rightful place, and do me wrong to fear as much. In truth, the hollow spectacles in which I daily participate grow more and more unbearable as our time of bliss at last approaches. It is you only who reign o'er my thoughts; the radiance of your glance, the sweet

music of your conversation, the perfection of your form
and luxuriance of your caresses. And when we next
meet, I shall have the most delightful news to tell you.

Your Devoted
Pauline

"Does the name mean anything to you?"

"Nothing," said DeShays, folding the letter and placing it next to the one she'd written him the previous night.

"His dinner companion, perhaps."

DeShays knelt down and piled the contents of Bewly's trunk and suitcases on the floor. The half-dozen medicine bottles suggested a delicate constitution if not a hypochondriac. Opening a small purple bottle, he caught a whiff of patchouli. A fancy case held a silver-handled set of brushes and combs; another, tortoiseshell brushes for tooth and nail. A small tin contained French male safes. Cravats, suspenders, hosiery, undergarments, linen collars, a silk robe took their place by a sample case containing gloves "equal to any imported," and piles of costly shirts and pantaloons.

Bewly's pockets yielded a few small coins, including a five cent piece which McNight pronounced counterfeit, having twelve rather than thirteen stars by its rim. Half-listening, DeShays pulled a folded piece of light blue stationery from a pair of striped trousers at the bottom of the pile.

"A receipt from the firm of Ball, Tompkins & Black, 181 Broadway—for a diamond ring, costing two hundred dollars. Dated the First of November last." The day Bewly had visited Kate's studio.

"Somehow I managed to overlook that," McNight admitted with a touch of embarrassment. "For the mysterious Pauline perhaps."

DeShays folded the receipt, grouping it with the letters in his coat pocket. "I suggest you hold onto his belongings pending word from Albany. You'll appreciate that to keep this from the papers I'll need to exercise the utmost discretion vis-a-vis my colleagues. I don't mean to pry, but it might be helpful if I knew the name of your source."

126

McNight gave a sly smile. "Let's just say it's someone with close personal ties to Chief Matson."

"Good enough," said DeShays. "And if you don't mind, I can be reached at 488 Greenwich Street."

Downstairs again, DeShays put his head round the door of the reading room. Either side of a long, periodical-strewn table elderly gentlemen dozed contentedly in plush chairs. Venturing into their quiet preserve he found Kate sitting in a corner, her face concealed by the Post.

Evidently sensing his approach, abruptly she cast the paper aside a look of warning in her eyes. "What is it?" he asked, provoking an old-timer clutching a magnifying glass to utter a sharp "Hush!"

"He's here, at the hotel," she continued in an undertone, as soon as they regained the lobby.

"Who?"

"The man with the mustache who came to my studio on Monday."

"He saw you?"

"He most certainly did. I was walking down the upstairs corridor and there he was, coming towards me. It was so unexpected, it froze me for a second."

"And?"

"He raised his hat, stone-faced, and just kept going."

"Keep walking," DeShays said, through clenched teeth. "He's bound to be watching."

Her thin arm firmly tucked in his sturdy one, a startled Kate found herself whisked through the crowded rotunda. Once on Broadway she made to free herself but DeShays clung on. "Smile please, Miss Felton. I do believe we're going to the theater."

They crossed Broadway, curving around the southern tip of the park onto Park Row, where a row of hack cabs sat awaiting a fare. DeShays darted ahead of Kate for an instant, snatching a word with a cabbie who abruptly whipped his nag to a trot and wheeled away.

"What's playing anyway?" Kate asked, beginning to enjoy whatever game was afoot.

"*Henry the Eighth*. Humphrey Bland is on the throne."

Stepping with Kate through one of the Park Theatre's narrow entrances DeShays found the gathering strains of a dramatic overture oddly appropriate. The uncarpeted lobby looked plain as ever—not much had changed in three years, though the old statue of Shakespeare above the entrance seemed somehow smaller and walls once dull yellow were now pale blue. As luck would have it, he was greeted warmly by the clerk at the box office, a young man whose name he struggled to recall.

Instead of heading for the parquette DeShays hurried a bewildered but willing Kate to a side corridor, up a staircase leading to a dim lobby with a forgotten-looking bar, then back down another set of stairs which led to a door opening onto the lane behind the theater. As he bundled Kate into the waiting cab and gave the driver her address he saw himself with Winchell on that very spot just eight nights before.

The ticket booth clerk at Barnum's greeted him with a look of weary inevitability. "If it's Winchell you're after he's not shown his ugly mug hereabouts since your last visit and by all accounts won't be welcome if he does."

"Is the Giant on tonight?"

"Which giant? There's Jack the Killer Giant, the Giant Highland Twins, the—"

"He's dumb, I think."

"You mean The Quaker?"

"When's he on?"

"Saturday. The Grand Parade of Giants and Dwarfs."

"La Rue around?"

"On tour. Savannah."

For a moment DeShays considered doubling back to the Iron Mug to give Carson an earful. Perhaps he'd be back by now. But with the bells of St. Paul's chiming the hour he realized how tired and hungry he was and set his course for home.

CHAPTER 20

"Mr. DeShays, I'd like a word with you in the parlor, if you please."

DeShays had the strong feeling that Mrs. Fitzgerald had been lurking behind her front door listening for the sound of his key in the lock. Puzzled, he preceded her into the empty room where she addressed him to the accompaniment of a crackling fire. "I'm afraid there's been an incident." The last word, inflected by her grave brogue, was spoken as if a euphemism for something indescribably indelicate.

"An incident? Of what nature, Mrs. F.?" Was sympathy called for, or alarm? He wasn't sure.

"The privacy of your room has been violated," she burst out, quickly adding, "through no fault of anyone in this home. And I'll trust you not to speak of the matter with anyone else, this being an honest family establishment."

DeShays's first thought was of young Millie. Atop his dresser was a small box containing an assortment of buttons, brass and copper store tokens and cufflinks, which the girl delighted to rifle though in his absence, imagining them to be buried treasure. Once he'd caught her red-handed, though he'd thought it an innocent prank and said nothing. Now he half-expected to be chided for leaving the door to his room open and leading the youngster to temptation.

"Mr. DeShays," went on Mrs. Fitzgerald, her chin aloft, "I do believe that I've told you that this home is not a police station."

"I have always been well aware of that, Mrs. F."

"The trespass was committed by one of your own kind. A Mr. Poole has been to see you. Very polite he was too. The ladies were here for our game of whist and Mrs. Jensen took

129

quite a liking to him. He made quite a show of not wanting to intrude, as he put it—being a wolf in sheep's clothing if ever I did meet one—and suggested that he wait in your room. He showed me his star, and I could see no objection, seeing as he was a friend and colleague, or so he said. And had not my little Millie come upon him in the act, your room might have been turned pretty well inside out. A fine thing for a girl of five to see, I say."

Her last words were almost lost on DeShays as he made for the stairs. Throwing wide his door, he found his mattress halfway off the bed, his trunk with its lock picked, and the contents of his dresser bulging from the drawers. Before he could see what if anything had been taken, a tiny giggle alerted him to a presence in the doorway, and he looked into a child's mischievous brown eyes.

"Leave me be Millie. I've no time for you now."

Again, the giggle. "He didn't find him."

"Whom did he not find Millie? I see your treasure is still here."

"Mr. Willykins—he didn't find him."

It was, he presumed, the name of some imaginary inhabitant of the attic. "Of course, Millie, Mr. Willykins is safe and sound," he said gently. "Run along now, can't you see I'm busy?"

To his amazement the child crawled beneath the basin and, reaching into a hole in the baseboard, removed a small paper-wrapped package, presenting it to DeShays as an altar boy might hand the sacraments to a priest. Kissing the little girl on the forehead, he reached into his trouser pocket for a silver dime, with which she left delighted.

For a moment DeShays stared at the object in his hands, then sat down heavily on the bed. After about a minute during which his mind tried and failed to make sense of what had happened, he unwrapped the little velvet-covered case and opened it to "Mr. Willykins." The nickname rather suited Bewly, capturing the grown-up baby in him that perhaps appealed to Millie's protective instinct. Which gave him an idea. Jumping up, he put his head out the door to call the child back, and found there was no need. She was sitting on the top step of the stairs surrounded by little piles of coins.

"Oh, Millie, there you are. I've been thinking. Perhaps Mr. Willykins would be safest if we put him back where you found him?"

In a trice, it was done. "Shall it be a secret and we're the only ones who know?" Millie asked suggestively.

DeShays saw no way out. "Sure," he said, and forked out another dime.

"Every day?"

"Week." Blackmail indeed, but he could think of no better arrangement. "For as long as he's here."

"Good," she agreed, and, gathering her small fortune, tripped daintily downstairs. In a little while, DeShays followed.

From the vantage point of a table by the back door of Pelham's, where Billy Holmes had found space for him, DeShays nursed his thoughts. On a plate before him a kidney pudding lay almost untouched, thinking and eating being for him largely incompatible pursuits. (At least, the sort of churning aggressive thinking he was currently engaged in.) His first reaction on confronting the havoc wreaked on his room by Poole was to go after the fellow and have it out with him. But the way he announced himself so brazenly prompted circumspection. As consummate a policeman as Poole reputedly was would scarcely act like that without protection or orders from higher up, meaning either Carson, his immediate boss, or, indeed, Chief Matson himself.

Old Honan had mentioned that Poole was nosing about, seemingly interested in his whereabouts. Yet the chief knew nothing of the Bewly daguerreotype, if that was indeed the object of Poole's search. And what else could it be? Carson on the other hand knew of the likeness. But why unleash Poole in this way? If Carson wanted DeShays he'd only to send for him. Was it Poole all along: at Kate's, on the ship, at the Astor, and here at Greenwich Street? But why? It didn't make sense.

In all the excitement he'd forgotten about Pauline's letter to Bewly, still in his pocket. Pushing aside his food, he spread the page out on the table, leaned his chin on his hands, and read again. *"Dearest Rutherford—"*

When he finished reading he kept his hands in position and let his eyes blur the text in front of him. Let's look at things from Bewly's point of view. The letter is dated October 17th. Bewly signed the register at the Astor on October 31st. What was the man's mood? There was the evidence of the purchase of a diamond ring, the receipt dated the day after his arrival in town. And, on the same day, the sitting for his likeness in Kate's studio. A keepsake for a woman friend, Kate had inferred.

Here, surely, was a happy man, a man come to town to present his intended with an expensive ring and claim her hand in marriage. A man who—reading between the lines of her letter—knows that he will not only become a husband, but possibly a father. So he meets his beloved somewhere—over lamb chops at the Astor perhaps—on that day, his first full day in town, and slips the ring onto her finger. The next day, Sunday, they spend together. That very night—or rather early the following morning—a body is discovered by the watchman Miller in Cuyler's Alley, bludgeoned beyond recognition. From the evidence of the clothes: Bewly's. So what was Bewly doing between leaving Pauline and getting himself killed? That he'd spent the time carousing in a sailors' gin den and succumbed to some low-life bruiser—the version put about by the police—just didn't ring true.

Unless, perhaps, he had it wrong and Pauline had spurned him. In that case, where was the diamond? Had Miller taken that too?

And Pauline? How did she fit the scenario? Knowing the lady of old, DeShays sensed something distinctly fishy about her letter. What is she really saying? And what are these "hollow spectacles" in which she "daily participates that grow more and more unbearable"? Presumably whatever is happening at the Temple of the Muses. A suspicion flashed across DeShays's mind, quickly suppressed. He'd show Billy Holmes the letter, see what he made of it.

"Good God, old son, as bad as all that is it?" observed a voice behind him.

"No, it's not the kidneys. If you've a minute, Billy, take a look at that."

Holmes examined Pauline's letter. "Nauseating, I quite agree. Vintage Pauline. Dearest Rutherford is your murderee, I take it?"

DeShays thumb-nailed in the latest developments and Holmes whistled when shown the receipt for the ring. "If you ask me, there's an elementary equation here: diamond safely in hand equals donor instantly expendable. Sic transit Dearest Rutherford. Poor chap, we could have warned him."

"You're not saying—?"

"Oh yes I am. It's not beyond her to have him followed and clubbed. Albany is one thing, New York quite another. The man is an unwanted embarrassment. Our Pauline has bigger fish to fry."

"If you'd seen her face when she came to Miss Felton's studio."

"An actress, and not that bad a one. In her day."

"But why come looking for him? Why respond to the notice at all?"

"Why indeed? The trouble with you, Miles, you're never prepared to face up to the worst in human nature. Not a promising trait in a policeman, I'd have thought."

"In fairness, the faintest suspicion did cross my mind."

"You see!"

"But I don't believe it." DeShays shook his head. "No."

"Oh, before I forget, your arrival was noted by one of our illustrious clients. He wonders if he might trouble you for a private word."

Billy Holmes, claiming to be under strict instructions to reveal no names, lifted the curtain to one of the private dining boxes in the back and closed it behind DeShays. The space was small and stuffy. The lamp burned low. The portly occupant, rising abruptly to greet his guest, caught a leg in the folds of the overhanging tablecloth, setting off an avalanche of crockery. Clutching at DeShays's proffered hand in an attempt to right himself, he lost his balance and they ended up in a clumsy two-step. Behind him, DeShays was aware of the curtain opening and quickly closing.

"I fear I am enormously in your debt, sir," proclaimed Daniel Hewison, the chief's brother-in-law (for he it was) extricating himself from DeShays's embrace and evidently not just referring to his present predicament. "Pray, seat yourself."

The table showed signs of having been set for two. Under the reek of cigar smoke DeShays thought he detected the cloying tang of a woman's perfume. An uneasy feeling that the lady in question might be lurking in the way of his legs caused him to shift his chair sideways.

"Few men in these cut-throat times would have passed up such a—how shall I put it?—such a chance to further their career," Hewison was saying, apparently unfazed by their little contretemps. "I'd be honored to have you join me, sir, in a small refreshment." Sliding open a panel beside his chair he summoned a waiter. It occurred to DeShays that the man had already downed more refreshment than was good for him that evening. Though some years younger than the chief, his bulk seemed to hang on him like a sack of potatoes and his face to convey the unhealthy sheen of the good life gone bad. What it was he was employed to do around the office was, to DeShays, a mystery. As for inspecting omnibuses—his ostensible job—in the few weeks of their acquaintance he'd rarely stirred more than a few feet from the stove. The two men had mutually kept their distance. What could he possibly want of him now?

"For all his worldliness, my esteemed brother-in-law has I fear scant tolerance for the needs of the flesh. The balm that softens the rocky bed that is the lot of us lesser mortals is, in his eyes, akin to the straw on the floor of the pigpen." If the chief's sister is anything like the chief, little wonder—DeShays couldn't help thinking—that this man would seek solace elsewhere. "And while our host has assured me that you, sir, are the very epitome of discretion—" He broke off with the arrival of the wine, putting a wavering finger to his lips and effecting a wink, one rakish rogue to another.

The wine poured and the waiter—who attempted to pick up some of the dishes—waved away, Hewison leaned towards DeShays dropping his voice to a conspiratorial whisper. "His spies are everywhere, you know. Can't be too careful, can't be too careful." They clinked glasses. "But, as I was saying, one assumes the worst, and, after our little encounter the other night, heh-heh, I assumed it of you, Mr. ... I am ashamed to say, sir, I did."

My God, it dawned on DeShays, the poor oaf is thanking me for not blackmailing him. That the thought had not occurred to him would have sent Billy Holmes, had he known, into fits of pitying mirth. Another example, he supposed, of his hopelessly un-policeman-like mentality. But now the chief's brother-in-law was ogling him across the table in his doglike pleading way and he must contribute something to the hitherto one-sided conversation. "DeShays," he said. "The name's DeShays."

"Quite. My point being, Mr. DeShays, that there are wolves out there," Hewison waved his glass in a vaguely warning gesture, spilling wine. "You may not know it, sir, but they're there. And they smell blood, sir. Your blood. As one favor deserves another, it's only fair to warn you."

By the time they had finished one bottle and were well into another, it seemed pretty clear to DeShays who the wolves were, though Hewison drew the line at naming names. Chief suspects were inspectors Harrington and Speight. Wolves, Hewison explained, defend their hunting grounds from marauding newcomers. The imposition of DeShays on the department had caused grave concern in the lairs of wolfdom. DeShays was the thin end of a wedge that would eventually strip them of their livelihoods: an attempt by the mayor and aldermen to horn in on their game by recruiting know-nothings and out-of-work actors—no offense intended—who would tug their forelocks and do their bidding. One way or another, DeShays must go. And, warned Hewison, wolves play rough.

CHAPTER 21

Removing from his eyes the sheet which served as his night mask, DeShays reached for the pocket watch which sat on the table by the bed. It was ten to eight in the morning, and again he'd slept through the bell calling the boarders to breakfast. His stomach growling, he regretted having asked Mrs. F not to knock. The fire had died out, so he launched himself out of bed and into his clothes in a flurry of motion.

Once downstairs he hung his coat and cap on the rack by the front door then entered the dining room, exchanging greetings with Mrs. F, Eliza, the Englishman Jenkins, and young Evans, in whose grasp was a copy of the *Morning Herald*. Not bothering to look up, Evans waved his coffee cup in the air for the maid to refill. "Will they never learn?" he muttered as if to himself.

Jenkins snorted and, looking to DeShays who was carving a tough cut of steak, waved away the question.

"I rather thought we'd concluded our survey of this morning's paper, Mr. Evans," said Mrs. F who, to DeShays's surprise, seemed intent on quieting the obnoxious chemist.

"You're right, Mrs. Fitzgerald. Won't do to be late." Evans folded his paper, rising as the maid returned from the kitchen with the coffee pot. "Thank you, Bridget." He gulped the bitter black fluid. "Congratulations, DeShays, on last night's mingle-mangle. Your colleagues sure met their Waterloo. Or would you say Trafalgar, Mr. Jenkins? After all, this Temple of the Muses was a man-of-war."

DeShays nearly spat out his coffee. In restraining himself it went down the wrong way and he gagged, attracting motherly attention from Mrs. F and a whack on the back from Jenkins in the next chair, who warned Evans to mind his manners.

The latter apologized curtly and stepped towards the door.

"Hold on, Evans." DeShays found his breath. "Let's have a look at that paper."

"Sorry, old man, can't stop now. There's a boy on the corner of Canal who looks as though he could use an extra two cents. The sooner he's out of the cold, the better—the influenza season is here, you know. Good day to you all."

Ignoring Mrs. F's warnings about indigestion, DeShays devoured his breakfast, grabbed his coat, and hurried outdoors, only to find the *Herald*'s newsboy gone, replaced by a red-faced urchin in an old cloth cap and a coat several sizes too large hawking the rival *Argus*. "Bold police raid!" he hollered to no one in particular. DeShays forked over two cents and boarded the Chelsea Line stage bound for Bowling Green, inserting himself between a young oaf with legs akimbo and a well-fed businessman reading the *Commercial Advertiser*. Turning to the front page of the *Argus*, he struggled to focus as the stage rocked to and fro over the cobbles.

The raid in question, as far as he could see, was conducted on the premises of the waterfront grogshop he'd used as a lookout just last week to spy on the Temple of the Muses. Glancing quickly down the page he saw no reference to the Temple or to anything resembling what Evans had gloated over in the *Herald*. On the contrary, the raid was portrayed in glowing colors. Unlike the *Argus* to miss a chance to bash the chief. He checked the masthead to be sure Brunton was still publisher.

The description of the grogshop, "this pestilential den of demons, this nursery of Satan" which "has been permitted to train up a band of burglars, robbers and murderers," bore little resemblance to the place he remembered. Seeing the names of officers Harrington and Speight writ large as they "arrested the notorious 'Aunt Mags' and her debauched inmates, not without considerable risk to their persons," DeShays couldn't repress a smile. That old hag and her listless girls? The whole thing seemed like a publicity stunt pulled off by Harrington with a tame reporter in tow to boost his place in the pecking order and show up Carson, whose ward the place was in.

The stage pulled up on the Broadway side of City Hall Park and DeShays alighted, still puzzling over the discrepancy between what Evans had suggested from the *Herald* and the report in the *Argus*.

He'd passed through the doors of City Hall and was heading towards the stairs when Old Honan stumbled towards him, holding up a warning hand. Reaching into his pocket he shoved a folded-up newspaper at DeShays as though it was a summons. "You might not want to go downstairs without a priest, sonny. Seems like it's blood they're after."

Unfolding Honan's *Morning Herald*, DeShays read the story from start to finish, then read it again:

The Floating Theater at Moore—Attempted Police Exposure of The Temple of the Muses—Its Miraculous Last Minute Escape—Highly Interesting Particulars.

As night's icy mantle fell over the city yesterday we received word that a party of policemen led by officers Harrington and Speight of City Hall was fast descending upon the Moore Street Pier, home to the floating theater which has recently concluded its season: the Temple of the Muses. Though the novelty of this man-of-war turned theater has rendered it a modest success during one of the dullest theatrical seasons in memory, there have lately been whispers concerning the vessel's true character, which were perhaps inevitable given the moral taint attached, fairly or unfairly, to the acting profession.

So it was that we forsook the fireside and hastened to Pier 3, in order that we might learn of the inner-workings of a supposed floating laboratory of vice, a ship which, we were told, has been devoted to lewd and infernal moral experiments in which some of our leading citizens are rumored to have taken part. Alas, the theater's departure for Baltimore occurred sooner than was scheduled, as word circulated that the authorities were eager to penetrate its manifold mysteries.

It was nearly seven when the Municipals arrayed themselves at Pier 3 for this purpose, too late, as it hap-

138

pened. The man-of-war turned theater could be seen churning upriver, having departed just several minutes hence. Undaunted, the agents of the law seized the Adelphi, a broken-down steamer moored at Pier 4, and attempted to bear down on the deceptively seaworthy playhouse. Meeting no resistance from the authorities, we entered the chase alongside them.

The night was bright and bitterly cold and, as our craft embarked, from the shore could be heard the uproarious jeers and shouts of a motley crowd whose sympathies lay with the fugitive theater. Into a howling wind we sailed, the waves crashing against the hull of our proud if overmatched relic as it struggled to overtake the man-of-war steamship, whose crewmen stood aft with their fingers raised towards us, in derision at our ineffectual attempts to overtake them.

By the time we reached the bay the contest's outcome had long been decided. With frost clinging to their whiskers and the bitter taste of defeat in their mouths, the fallen "stars" abandoned chase and turned back to shore. Bitter imprecations were muttered against the Temple's captain, Bradbury Farnham of Sag Harbor, but also an unnamed adversary who, judging from the context of their tight-lipped exchanges appears to be no less than a traitor among them. Though the redoubtable officers decline to offer particulars, we gather that one of their own had earlier been spied in conference with the Temple's crew, presumably paving the way for their timely escape. Prepare apartments in the Penitentiary.

At some point Honan had laid a gentle hand on DeShays's shoulder and retreated downstairs, as if taking leave of a friend facing the gallows. Now he saw why.

"Why if it ain't Misseur Jacques!" exclaimed Mags, as DeShays entered the room. "That's the one, that's him alright." Swathed in her purple shawl and seated in Hewison's chair by the stove, she obviously reveled in her new role as turncoat. Gathered around were the chief, Harrington and Speight, whose cold stares fell on DeShays as those of judge, jury and executioner.

"Fed me a line about writing a book for foreigners," Mags contributed eagerly, looking to the chief as a pupil might regard a teacher when answering a question. Matson nodded slightly but said nothing, keeping his elliptical gaze fixed on DeShays.

"Playing policeman is not a game for little boys, Jacquey," sneered Harrington. "All along we knew a Benedict Arnold was in our midst."

"Got you copped dead to rights this time," added Speight, in the toneless voice of a man making his ten thousandth arrest. DeShays felt like a schoolboy being softened up by toughs for the head bully. From his desk across the room Willoughby whistled a bar of Frère Jacques.

"Should've known never to trust a Frenchman," concluded Mags, huddling beneath her shawl as if chilled by DeShays's deception.

"Come now," said the chief, offering DeShays a smile which seemed a perfect facsimile of the death rictus. "It's time we had a little heart to heart." His slowly curling index finger seemed to coax forth the acid in DeShays's stomach.

Behind him DeShays felt a thud as the chief's door closed, suggesting journey's end. Approaching the wide mahogany desk, he had the feeling of attending his own funeral. At Matson's prompting he sat.

The Chief settled his massive bulk into his chair with an agonizing creak. For an interminable moment he said nothing. DeShays's eyes flicked between a patch of wall to the left of the chief's head, the heel of his own boot, the crystal inkstand and the absurd lead hand resting on the desk. Slowly the great head began to shake from side to side like a pendulum. The place took on the feeling of a sickroom with DeShays the patient. At his bedside sat the doctor, all hope extinguished, hugely grieving at the loss of one so young.

"Your uncle is a fine man," at last the words came, "and this department owes him a great debt. I've no desire to trouble him over what has passed here. In fact I saw him last week, at the mayor's reception. He asked after your progress." Matson paused as if to let DeShays digest his meaning.

"He's told me much about you, though I confess that until today your motivation has always been a puzzle. No doubt you possess certain talents, DeShays, but these are wasted here. In fact, your presence seems to mock us time and time again. Yours is the mentality of an actor, and always will be."

"Please, sir, I can explain," DeShays interrupted. Even to his own ears it sounded feeble. The schoolboy who hadn't done his homework.

The Chief leaned back, fingertips touching as if in prayerful contemplation of his girth. "Until the moment he takes the stage, the actor is like a somnambulist. You live your days in a twilight world, divorced from everyday concerns. And to think," striking a note of infinite self-pity, "I gave you every chance. I put my reputation on the line. I entrusted you with an important task, and you—"

"—discovered who was murdered in Cuyler's Alley!" DeShays grasped the edge of the desk like a defendant in the dock.

For a stunned few seconds the chief stared at him. "Don't pretend to be clever, DeShays. Explain yourself."

"I've done my best to take advantage of the chance you gave me," he heard an odd ring of truth in the stale appeal. "The man's name was Rutherford Bewly. A native of Albany."

"Bewly? Albany?" the chief sounded skeptical, "No relatives have contacted this office."

"His line of work explains why. He was traveling, representing his family's glove business. He took a room at the Astor House on the last day of October, and paid through the day before yesterday. But he only stayed two nights and abandoned his effects."

"Why have you waited until now to mention this?"

"I've only just found out. Give me a few hours, sir, and I'll have the proof right here on your desk. And,"—he would curse himself roundly for his impetuosity—"by the weekend I'll have the case solved!"

The Chief reclined as though to weigh matters from a

distance, his jaw outthrust perhaps to balance his thoughts. "Very well," he remarked distastefully. "Today is Thursday. Should your investigation produce no further results by end of business on Saturday you will be moving upstairs. There is a vacancy for an officer in the great courtroom there. I proposed as much to your uncle at the reception last week. It should keep you out of trouble."

A living statue six days a week? No thanks! Suppressing a reflexive instinct to shake the chief's hand, DeShays rose to leave. Without a word, Matson picked up a knife and tore the seal on a piece of mail.

Smug satisfaction turned to something more like bare-faced dismay in the outer office as DeShays, like Daniel of old, emerged uneaten from the lions' den. Mags was gone. To Honan, lingering in the hall like a relative awaiting the result of an operation, DeShays gave a surreptitious thumbs-up. Yet it was far from sure that what he had in mind would work. Carson, for one, would not be happy.

CHAPTER 22

Taking the steps to the lobby of City Hall two at a time DeShays became aware of grunting and wheezing in his wake. "Whoa there, sonny," puffed Honan. "A woman was here to see you. Didn't choose to wait. Left me this."

Fumbling to unfold the piece of paper Honan thrust at him (Pauline perhaps?) DeShays found a scrawled summons from Kate, bidding him come to the studio without delay.

"Quite a one, she was. Some of the boys were mighty curious."

"Strictly business, I'm afraid." Aware of the old man's eager scrutiny DeShays feigned nonchalance.

Honan assumed an air of amused disbelief. "You'll be telling me the whole story sometime no doubt, sonny. And we'll be having a word about that horse of yours, too." DeShays drew a momentary blank.

"Black Joke." Honan leaned close, his morning coffee announcing itself. "A worthy specimen of *equus caballus* indeed. Took your advice and won a load of chink. And I thought he was just a pacer."

DeShays forced a smile and hurried off towards Chatham Square. The wooden sign hanging on the studio door said that Kate Felton was closed for business. DeShays listened warily, but heard no sounds from within. His knock triggered footsteps.

"Yes, who's there?" Kate asked haltingly. A heavy blue shawl was draped across her shoulders, and she had on the same blue dress as on the first day he'd seen her. Despite a subtle application of make-up, dark circles were visible beneath her eyes. "I found the lock picked when I got here this morning. I listened for some time before venturing in,

143

frightened half out of my head. My camera is the most expensive thing here, and as you can see it wasn't taken. What on earth could anyone want here? I asked myself. I could think only of Mr. Bewly's portrait, and that man who's been lurking around."

"I'd say you're right. It's my fault—my room was ransacked by the same man yesterday afternoon. I should have guessed he'd try here next."

"And have you discovered who he is?"

"A policeman." Kate winced. "He identified himself to my landlady. His name is Dick Poole. Though why he gave his real name is a mystery; he knew I wouldn't be home."

"Perhaps it was his way of warning you off. If you ask me, he must have been jealous of Mr. Bewly. Perhaps over Pauline; she's lovely, you must admit."

"That's a point I hadn't considered!" DeShays laughed dismissively. "And why didn't he ask for a warrant to search here? Did anyone in the building see anything?"

"No. I've asked the lithographer downstairs, the clerks in the paint store, and the hatter on the ground floor. I come here at first light every morning, so it was probably after everyone had closed for the night."

"May I have a look around?"

Kate led the way, DeShays noting a certain tightness in her walk, as if she sensed something of the trespasser still in the air. The light from the darkroom window was blocked by a layer of yellow tissue paper. "This is where I prepare my plates first thing every morning." With a small globe lamp, she highlighted a couple of boxes sitting next to each other on a work table. "Mr. Poole is evidently unfamiliar with the Daguerrean process, as well as lacking a sense of smell." The boxes, she explained, held the iodine and mix of bromine and quicklime used to sensitize her photographic plates. Their tops had been taken off and not properly refastened. A tall cabinet had been rummaged through too, she said.

Walking DeShays into another darkroom, she explained how the plates were developed after exposure, descriptions that seemed to have a therapeutic effect. He didn't interrupt.

144

A long table held more tools of the trade, an iron vessel shaped like an inverted triangle and a little spirit lamp. The light fell on a basin, then over a range of shelves holding numerous bottles. DeShays knelt down and picked up a small green bottle with a charcoal stopper. "I hadn't noticed that," said Kate, placing it on a shelf. "Glad it didn't break. It holds pure mercury."

"I'll make good on any earnings lost today." DeShays stepped back into the hall, thinking how inadequate the words sounded.

"It's too cloudy to take pictures anyway. Unless it clears I doubt anyone will come."

DeShays followed her into the room where she did her color painting and kept her accounts and watched as she lit the bright Argand lamp. The drawers of a tall cabinet were in various stages of open and shut, with a few cases piled on the floor. "Empties," she said.

"And you're positive nothing is missing?"

"Nothing, so far as I can tell. I keep the portraits waiting to be picked up in alphabetical order, which they're out of. And my account book was probably opened as well," she added, indicating a shelf on which a ledger sat next to a row of cases from which identifying slips protruded. "But nothing was taken. Tell me, what has become of Pauline? Where does she live?"

"No idea. She's not in the directory. She may have left town."

Kate paused as if to let him go on. "That's right," she said, sounding a little remote as she turned to put her plates back in order. "You did say you met aboard a ship."

Though it was Carson he needed to see, as DeShays climbed the stairs to the First Ward station he braced himself for an encounter with Dick Poole. The important thing, he told himself, was to avoid a confrontation, because this was precisely what Poole's behavior seemed aimed to provoke.

Stepping into the office he was relieved to see that the man seated on the dais overlooking the benches was not Poole, but

Carson. He was talking with a young officer whose back was to DeShays. Seeing him enter, Carson called out hello, a ring of surprise in his husky voice.

The man was introduced as Officer Sam Greene. Sam had keen eyes and a firm grip. Irontop slapped him on the back, asking him to take his place for a minute, then led DeShays into his office and closed the door, taking his chair with the air of a man having something else on his mind. Sitting himself, DeShays glanced sideways at a daguerreotype of Carson with his wife and baby on the desk, and Irontop turned it towards him for a fuller view.

"You have a beautiful family," he commented, asking the daughter's name.

"Penelope, after my wife's aunt." He pulled a cigar from a drawer, offering it to DeShays, who declined. Carson looked at him as if to say "your choice" and lit up himself, his face suddenly a mask of concentrated attention. "Well?"

"It all began last night," said DeShays. "I was following a thread related to our case. It took me to the floating playhouse at the bottom of Moore. Unknown to me, Harrington and Speight had their eyes on it too. Some sort of raid was planned."

"Good of everyone to tell me," said Carson, clutching the cigar as he licked the inside of his cheek. "I did chance to read about it in the *Herald*. This is my ward, you may recall."

"You and I've been working towards the same end," DeShays said, extracting a nod of agreement. "As you'll have read, the ship took off somewhat precipitously just before those two launched their raid. As I was seen on board earlier, they have the idea it was me warned the captain."

"Hold it Miles. I didn't realize you were the one supposed to be the trouble." Carson put down the cigar, squinting as he considered. "It's been sitting there for weeks, and they just missed it? Sounds like you're an ideal scapegoat."

"The upshot is Matson wants me out. He'd have done it then and there if I hadn't told him about Bewly. That's why I've come—he wants the proof on his desk yesterday." He added, "Oh, and I told him I'd have the case solved by Saturday. It just slipped out."

146

"Yea, he does have that effect on one. But don't worry. Shouldn't be long now, the rate we're tuning him up."

"McGlone?" DeShays could scarcely believe that Carson was still clinging stubbornly to his original suspect. The look on his face said as much.

"He's talking alright," said Carson, his voice hardening. "Confessed to three more assaults so far, and there's plenty more where that came from."

"And what about Miller? Any luck there?"

"Miller's was a perfect murder: no witnesses have come forth, nothing to link the two of them either. We're still looking for a third man, the one who hushed him. That's my job. Meanwhile we may save yours just yet. After Miller washed up I sent Greene to his place to gather a few more things. The togs you found happen to be part of 'em."

They agreed to meet at City Hall in an hour. "And when we're with the chief," Carson cautioned, "I'll do the talking. For instance: we ran into each other at the big fire on Front Street two nights ago." A warehouse had gone up in flames, DeShays had read of it; two firemen died when a floor collapsed. "Later we got to talking about the case over at the Mug."

At the foot of the stairs DeShays asked Carson where Poole was to see where the subject might lead. "Ah, you haven't heard? Poole's been transferred to that new harbor patrol hatched by the chief. An experiment, started this Monday over by Whitehall Slip."

As they stepped out Carson nodded and walked east into a chill wind; DeShays veered west along the side of the market. The idea that Poole might be doing the chief's bidding set off alarm bells in his mind. If Poole had been the man who'd preceded him at the Temple yesterday and Poole was working for the chief— What a damned fool he'd been not to get the man's name. It occurred to him too that Carson hadn't asked what it was he was doing on the ship. Wasn't it an obvious question?

He pulled out his watch. If he moved quickly there'd be just time to take care of something he should have done days ago.

CHAPTER 23

Muted beams filtered through the barred skylights, giving the prison an undersea aura, an impression encouraged by a pervasive dampness that seemed to settle on DeShays's coat and creep deep into his lungs. The Tombs certainly lived up to its name. He sensed a nervousness in the quiet, a suspension. Somewhere someone hawked, triggering spasms of coughing throughout the narrow hall, reminding him for a second of the theater. Conscious of scrutiny coming from nearby cells, he took the iron stairway to the second tier, home of those charged with the worst crimes.

A new field of eyes fastened on him as he turned onto a short bridge connecting the galleries. Two such bridges spanned each of the three upper tiers, and none were directly above or below the other, so that keepers were able to maintain close watch. The guard whose permission DeShays sought sat facing him on a stool midway along the bridge, an older man, dressed in a cap and coat much like his own. Though they'd never met, something, perhaps the like garb, seemed to kindle a certain familiarity in the man's eyes.

"I'm to see McGlone." DeShays held out his copper star.

The man gave it a cursory glance. "Foul disposition, that one." His heavily creased face made DeShays think of a pocket map that had seldom been folded the same way twice. Getting to his feet, pressing on his haunches as though he hadn't risen in hours, the guard adjusted his belt. He nodded to a counterpart posted on a bridge one tier up and across, who responded with a little salute.

Indian file they moved back along the narrow walkway. McGlone was all the way in the southeast corner, the keeper explained, his bowlegged gait accompanied by the jangle of keys, his truncheon bobbing gently in rhythm. With a propri-etary air, he pointed out a newly arrived wife poisoner, who shrank into a dark corner of his cell like a bashful animal. Others stood by the bars, ordinary-looking men with glazed-over expressions. DeShays had the sense of being in a dormitory for clerks gone wrong.

Before the last cell the keeper stopped and turned. "Now you'll be wanting the fetters on this one. I apologize, sir, your name again?"

"DeShays. Assistant Captain," he added shamelessly. "There'll be no need for any fetters just yet."

The man shrugged, suggesting otherwise. Behind the bars a huge heap lay covered in a gray blanket. The guard called out and received in response a loud snore. Drawing his truncheon, he rapped smartly on the bars. "Wake up, sleeping beauty!"

The gray mass stirred then went still again. Blearily, John McGlone rubbed his eyes, then propped his head on his elbow. "Ain't a man allowed a moment's rest in this hole?" he whined drowsily. "I ain't heard sleep's against the law."

"Time for your singin' lesson, Johnny Boy. Captain DeShays is here."

The keeper unlocked the barred iron door, venturing in. DeShays stepped in after him. Greasy brown bangs were plas-tered across the prisoner's forehead. He had a thick growth of beard and his right eye was ringed with a large yellow bruise. He looked to be about twenty-five. McGlone didn't move, meeting his interrogator's gaze with a certain curiosity, as though he wasn't quite sure of what he was seeing just yet.

"Lovely weather we're having, ain't it, sir?" McGlone opined, glancing in the direction of a narrow slit in the wall meant to admit a little light but not wide enough to see out of.

"Sit up, idiot," said the guard, whacking the edge of the mattress with his stick. McGlone yanked his legs away, seem-ingly part of a routine. Disgust etched his face as he assumed an upright posture, the blanket draped across his shoulders.

"I'll be alright," DeShays told the guard.

"Holler if you need me. Mark my words, this one's

touched." DeShays heard the door slam behind him, the key turn in the lock. He pulled up a little stool and sat opposite the bunk, regarding McGlone almost as he might consider someone he meant to impersonate. He knew the type, cocky with a street-corner wit; had run across them as extras playing guardsmen, even policemen.

"New man, are ya?" asked McGlone, evidently a little uncomfortable at his unspoken examination. "Hope you don't mind me saying it, sir, but you look a bit too genteel for a policeman. One of Carson's?"

"Have any others been here?"

"I suppose not, sir. A stupid question, that."

It wasn't hard to get McGlone talking. "Tell me John, how long were you working at 65 Front?"

"Two and half years."

"And before then?"

"Odd jobs, back in Ireland. Bit of roofin' from time to time."

"And when you came to this country? You've got quite a history, I hear."

"I used to knock around some, sure." McGlone seemed to wrestle with himself for a second. "I been in here before. I'm not proud of it, but the past's the past. Not a spot on my ledger the last year or two. I keep remindin' everybody, but they ain't interested. I've nothin' to do with this business, and nothin' can make me say so."

"Your treatment of some of Johnson's customers has attracted a certain notoriety, John."

"None of 'em complained, did they?"

"What do you do with their clothes?"

"Give 'em to charity, those that are worth it."

"Know a man by the name of Miller? Eli Miller?"

"Miller? What's his line of work?"

"Night watchman."

He shook his head. "They had it coming to them. Thieves, caught in the act. I hung 'em out to dry as a warnin' to those who would do likewise. Why one of 'em tried to lay his hands on my girl!"

"Your girl works at 65 Front?"

"Not any more. Betsy done the wash—she's at home now. I don't get out of here soon, she'll be back to work, and her and my little Mary'll be in with her mother—a fine thing, that."

"Married long?"

"I was getting around to it, when all this happened. Trying to get in the carting business. Sometimes I work as a porter as well."

"You've recently admitted to a couple of assaults, John."

"I'll admit to being assaulted a couple of times recently." He touched his bruised eye, adding bitterly, "Prison makes you say funny things. It's all ancient history too. I's on the square for years. Ain't no one going to bring charges, none of your 'corroboratin' witnesses' neither. Now let me ask you a question, sir: if I was to hush this feller, not that I ever settled anyone mind you, why in the name of heaven would I leave him layin' on my own doorstep? Tell me that!" McGlone's brogue rose to high pitch.

"What would you have done?"

McGlone considered the question. "Fed him to the fishes. That's what. You'd have pinned it on the tobby coves then. Another thing: if I snabled that swell, why were me pockets empty when they collared me? I was dead broke, that's a fact."

"Swell, you say. What swell?"

"The one that was settled."

"And how do you know he was a swell?"

McGlone appeared puzzled. "How did I know?"

"Don't ask me. I wasn't there."

"You're a wily one. You're playing games with me."

"Nobody knows who the cove is, except you know he was a swell."

McGlone was silent. DeShays could almost hear his brain creaking. "They must've told me. Someone must've."

Nobody knew. Well, almost nobody. And, DeShays realized, he wouldn't put it past Carson himself to have fed McGlone the line. No wonder Irontop still counted on a con-

151

viction. "Any idea who might have done it, then?"

"Whoever it is that's tryin' to pin the blame on me, that's who. They knew you'd tumble to me right away. I'll tell you one thing: no thief would have been so stupid as to snable the cove, not that way. They'd want to get away, and quickly. It wouldn't fadge, wouldn't fadge at all. An' another thing: if I done someone in, why would I stay around as if all was right with the world? I'd have made meself scarce. An' being so close to the water, I'd have dumped the cove in the drink— not that I ever done anyone in, mind you."

"Are you suggesting the work of an amateur then?" asked DeShays, sounding a skeptical note. He hated his part but was used to that.

"I hadn't considered until now, sir. You may have a point there. I couldn't say one way or another." McGlone simmered down. "I just couldn't say." He scratched his beard, squinting at DeShays curiously. "You're a funny sort of policeman. You'd think I was in your shoes, the way you ask things."

DeShays offered a wan smile. "Anyone you can think of that might have it in for you, John? Think carefully. Someone with a score to settle—one of Johnson's customers, perhaps? Perhaps an old crony of some sort? Anyone your woman knew before?"

McGlone laughed. "I got a list as long as both arms. Who doesn't?"

"But no one who'd go out of their way to pin a murder on you?" McGlone shook his head. "I been on the square for years. Never was involved with anything like that, mind you." DeShays would have liked to talk more, but time was pressing. He got up and nodded down at the prisoner, as though a lesson had been concluded. "I think that'll do for now, John."

McGlone extended a huge hand as if to shake, pulling it back midway as he realized DeShays wasn't going to reciprocate. Sorry as he felt for him, he was a policeman. A policeman, he suddenly realized, who was having his first experience of being locked in a cell. Standing at the bars, he called out for the keeper.

"Lock the door," said the chief, and DeShays rose to obey. Carson helped clear the desktop, piling stuff on chairs. So far the chief had accepted Carson's account of his fortuitous meeting with DeShays (interspersed with a stirring description of the Water Street blaze) without asking questions. And though he'd tested DeShays with a stabbing glance as Carson spun his tale, DeShays hadn't flinched.

Strange to see Bewly's clothes emerge from his own battered valise; a small part of him wanted the bag back. As Carson laid the items out on the desk to silhouette a figure, DeShays felt as though attending a post-mortem where he, the reigning authority on the disease, had to remain silent. Pre-empting the chief's question, Carson mentioned that the tailor's labels had been slashed out.

"Let's have a look at his face." The Chief had deferred the moment of truth, as if to savor the opening of a vintage bottle of wine, something he was said to stock an entire cellar's worth of. DeShays handed him the daguerreotype, watching Matson's stubby fingers open the delicate case as if it were an ancient prayer book. Gazing at the glassy image, his mouth slightly open, looking back to the clothes then again at the colored portrait, Matson ventured no opinion.

Carson spun his theory of Miller's complicity in the murder and of a possible third man still at large, McGlone being in prison at the time. Though the chief nodded in accord, a distance in his eyes suggested to DeShays that his mind was casting the matter in a wider frame of reference, though to be sure he complimented Carson for his dogged application. He himself heard no such praise. When Carson insisted that DeShays was due his share, Matson smiled emptily.

The Chief bound both men to secrecy on the matter, again complimenting Carson, this time with a pat on the back. The clothes he tucked away in the valise, bound for the safe, which he turned to open, his hulking form obscuring its mass as the tumblers clicked.

DeShays was following Carson out when Matson, as if struck with an afterthought, called him back. "Tell me, DeShays," he asked, with the door shut and Carson unceremoniously on the far side, "what exactly led you to believe that the subject of the daguerreotype was the dead man? From the beginning," he quickly added, as if suggesting a refreshing change.

Somewhat startled by this sudden shift, DeShays fumbled for words. "To start with, sir, this man Bewly was due to pick up his portrait that Monday, the day after the body was found. He'd left it for coloring with Miss Kate Felton, the daguerreotypist who made the portrait. He never appeared. I should add that Miss Felton's note was among those you handed me."

"Excellent," said the chief, sounding pleased at his inclusion in the story. "Go on."

"I paid the studio a visit, and placed a notice in the newspapers under Miss Felton's name: I wanted to see if anyone else was looking for him."

"Creditable. And?"

"One result was a visit from the Astor House detective. Apparently Bewly paid in advance for a two-week stay, but remained only two nights, leaving his belongings. As I mentioned earlier, he was down from Albany, where his family runs a glove and leather goods business."

"Incidentally," the chief interrupted, "who, besides us, knows he's dead?"

"No one, as far as I know. And I certainly didn't tell their detective." Best not to mention Kate Felton here, or indeed Pauline.

"Good. Say nothing of the matter to anyone till further notice."

DeShays then told of Augustina Mullins, and the distraught appearance of Pauline Dowling at Kate's studio and subsequently at his lodgings, not omitting a nutshell account of their prior acquaintanceship. The Chief's face hardened to a grimace at the fecklessness of Bewly, then displayed forgiveness and concern over Pauline's misfortunes. At the business end for the first time of his boss's father-confessor persona, DeShays couldn't help but feel a burden lifting as he told the tale. Though an inner voice warned him not to get carried away and, in particular, to leave Poole out.

154

"Did Bewly's belongings tell you anything? I assume you examined them?"

"I found a receipt for a diamond ring, and a recent letter from a woman signed 'Pauline.' The writing was identical with that on the note she left at my lodgings. I assume the daguerreotype was for her."

"Perhaps," said the chief. "Do you have the letter?"

"Not on me," he lied.

"Now, this so-called Temple of the Muses," the chief bore down. "What brought you there?"

"Miss Dowling's last engagement was there." Pointless to mention La Rue's cryptic note. "When the season ended, select gatherings continued on board, in an elaborate ballroom below decks."

"These 'gatherings' have generated considerable interest," the chief remarked dryly, "Not to put too fine a point upon it." For a while—it seemed to DeShays—the great man stared inwardly, a blank, almost lost expression clouding his face. Then, as if roused by a startling thought, he seemed suddenly aware again of his visitor.

"You've done exceptionally well so far, DeShays. From now on you will report to me, and me alone. Understand? Share nothing with anyone else, not even Captain Carson. He can proceed along his lines, and we along ours. And by the way," he called softly as the other reached the door, "I had a word with your uncle the other day. In case you're thinking of writing any more letters."

In the grounds in front of City Hall a gardener struggled to rake dead leaves into a huge unruly pile. DeShays, relieved at his tacit reprieve if alarmed at the reference to his uncle, found himself buoyed by a stiff west wind at his back. He acknowledged a touch of pride on being complimented for his work, even considering the source. The need for praise is deep-seated indeed, he was thinking, when—"Mr. DeShays?"—a voice behind him called.

DeShays turned as a stout ruddy-cheeked stranger in top hat and brown coat caught up to him. "Miss Dowling had it dead on, sir, if you'll forgive the expression. Tall, hand-

155

some, everything you could wish for in a Rob Roy."

"Did you say, Miss Dowling?" DeShays stopped in his tracks. "And you are, sir?"

"Bennett's the name." The man raised his hat. "As for the lady, sir, she'd be glad of a word with you if you can spare the time. If you'd care to accompany me?" He gestured to where, just visible above the park's iron railing, a half-dozen drivers sat frozen atop their cabs—the regulation that drivers be seated and not stand around on the street was officiously enforced by Inspector Harrington during office hours.

At the end of the line was a seventh carriage, its driver's seat empty. "Where is Miss Dowling?"

"I'm requested not to reveal that, sir. But if you'll step aboard we'll be there in a matter of minutes."

DeShays, hesitating, saw A.C. Speight, young Willoughby in tow, crossing Broadway towards him, returning no doubt—in Speight's case at least—from the usual liquid lunch. Willoughby, noticing DeShays, drew him to the other's attention eliciting a shared corner-of-the-mouth sneer. A pox on all police, thought DeShays. Out loud he said, "Very well. Let's go."

CHAPTER 24

The coachman's promise of a matter of minutes proved altogether accurate. DeShays had hardly time to get his bearings when the carriage turned into a narrow lane off Gold Street and slowed to walking pace. Other than a silver crest of some unfamiliar origin emblazoned on the door, the vehicle betrayed scant clue as to the identity of its owner. Upholstered in plush green leather, well-sprung, his guess was some rich older admirer of Pauline. One of those self-inflated blowers that in her heyday, jostled for her attentions. Relief that she might be safe and ready to talk filled his thoughts to the exclusion of any concern for himself.

DeShays was therefore a little surprised to find himself ushered into what looked like the rear entrance of a shabby factory building by a bear of a doorman swathed in a thick cloak, and delivered into the hands of a preoccupied clerk with stuck-out ears who did not bother to introduce himself. Up the broad wooden stairs they climbed, floor by floor, as men rushed by shouting, cursing, shoving, banging doors, till the very building seemed to tremble and DeShays realized he was in a newspaper office, most likely J. Phineas Brunton's , since that was the only publication in sight. Fingering his star, he wondered if he'd walked into a trap.

On the sixth and topmost floor DeShays was handed over to a smooth-faced Negro boy who relieved him of his outer garments and sat him, wordlessly, in an ante-chamber. Here all was polished oak paneling, dark oil paintings in gilt frames and deep armchairs. Distinctly more Pauline-friendly, the hush contrasting with the hubbub below as if, through layers of hell, he'd attained Parnassian heights. He wondered through which of several doors she would make her entrance, knowing all the while she wouldn't; that wherever Pauline was, it wasn't here in this busy building. And that one way or another, whatever was afoot, he would have a lot of explaining to do.

"Mr. Brunton is ready, Master," squeaked the smooth-faced boy holding the door for DeShays.

The person advancing towards him down the length of an oriental carpet, arms outstretched in welcome, was hardly DeShays's image of the man he'd heard Chief Matson on occasion call "the embodiment of all that is blackest in the black craft." Something about him conjured for DeShays the science master at his old school, a man of experimental enthusiasms ending as likely as not in small explosions. Perhaps it was the gleam that burned in his eyes coupled with the curtain beard that straggled from his chin. DeShays found his hand enfolded in the double clasp of one perhaps twenty years his senior and half a foot his inferior. "My dear Inspector, how kind of you to come in answer to the call of a distressed damsel. Brunton's the name. Your most humble and obedient servant."

"Your servant, sir, I'm sure." DeShays struggled to adjust to the tenor of the occasion. "But where is the person I came to see?"

"Of course, of course." Brunton ushered him towards a couple of armchairs. "You are whisked from your usual rounds into—you anticipate—the presence of a fragrant flower of our stage, and are confronted instead with an old boor of a newsman who, no doubt, you feel every reason to distrust."

In a nutshell, thought DeShays, taking the proffered chair. "I've been concerned about Pauline's—Miss Dowling's—whereabouts. Admittedly, I hardly expected to find her here."

"And you were right. As you see, she's not here." Brunton spread his arms. "She has, however, put herself under my care, and as her protector I feel I must obtain answers to certain questions before admitting you to her presence."

As Brunton pulled up his chair the boy servant re-appeared and set a tray on a low table before his master—a glass of some milky green substance and a dish of raw carrots. Brunton glanced at his pocket watch, then, ruefully, at his guest. As the boy departed he said, "Damn the little fellow. He's like clockwork." Then, sliding the dish towards DeShays, "I trust you'll partake. A vegetarian regime is said to alleviate the stress of city life by simulating the feeding habits of our ancestors. Our stomachs, they tell me, were designed to respond to a steady intake of vegetable matter rather than the massive doses of cooked food we shovel down two or three times a day. The catch being that vegetables don't grow on city streets, particularly in November."

DeShays, though his own stomach could be heard protesting vociferously its long neglect, politely slid the dish back. "Miss Dowling has the highest regard, she tells me, for your erstwhile acting ability, instanced in the several roles in which you played opposite one another. She was therefore somewhat surprised, indeed confused," Brunton grimaced as he sipped the green liquid, "at your reincarnation as a member of our so-called new police when she responded to a notice concerning a Mr. Bewly. Once over the initial shock, however, she had every intention of confiding in you and enlisting your help."

"We were to meet yesterday. She never appeared."

"She came to me. Circumstance conspired to force her to seek cover. She felt herself to be in danger." To DeShays's quick glance, he responded, "The exact nature of our relationship I shall leave to Miss Dowling to explain, should she so choose. But tell me, if you will, the nature of your involvement with this Bewly. My source at police headquarters has come up dry. Is this an official police matter, or is this a private inquiry?"

"I'm afraid I can only discuss Bewly with Miss Dowling, sir. As you can imagine, it's a matter of some delicacy. Surely," he added, "with the resources at your command, you'll have learned something of him?"

"On Miss Dowling's behalf, I've sent inquiries to Albany, where he's from. As far as anyone there knows, he's traveling for his company in the South. Incidentally, I'm told you visited Miss Dowling at the floating theater?"

"I was under the impression that she'd asked to see me."

"She sent for you?"

"I was under that impression." DeShays felt a growing sense of exasperation.

"It wasn't a police matter?"

"She'd no idea, till I told her, that I was a policeman. As far as she knew I was living in Cincinnati."

"Ah yes, she told me," he commiserated. "You weren't by chance involved with last night's aborted raid on the boat? You've seen the papers?"

"That was Inspector Harrington's little escapade." He couldn't resist adding: "Though I see the *Argus* didn't carry it."

"Which reminds me," Brunton ignored the bait, "I need a good man at police headquarters. Someone I can trust. Interested?"

DeShays smiled. "It's hard enough to have one master."

"It could be worth your while."

"My expenses aren't high."

"Think about it. Your loyalty may be misplaced, DeShays. I wouldn't give your present employer a snowball's chance in hell to survive beyond the end of the year. And when he goes, his dirty water goes with him."

"I'll take my chances."

Back in Brunton's carriage, heading north to a rendezvous with Pauline (location undisclosed) DeShays reflected on his encounter with the publisher of the *Argus*. Anyone less like Brunton's nemesis, the chief, he could hardly imagine. Though a glint of steel did show itself in his blatant offer. For sure an easier man to talk to, though how his employees felt in that regard he couldn't of course say. As for his relations with Pauline, the obvious conclusion was she was his mistress. But was Brunton her type—indeed the type to keep a mistress at all? One thing did seem certain: Brunton's man at police headquarters was Harrington. With the emphasis on was. Apparently Harrington had failed him—over Bewly and somehow also over the raid on the Temple of the Muses.

DeShays glanced over at the seat opposite where, from a

dark corner, a pair of eyes remained steadily fixed on him. Brunton's servant, Sam, was accompanying him. Minder? Escort? Hitching a ride? Just shy, under orders to keep his mouth shut; or perhaps scared at being knee to knee with the Law? Whatever it was, DeShays couldn't get a word out of the lad and gave up trying. His folks, Brunton had explained, were slaves down South somewhere. He'd adopted the boy, who'd been smuggled north, and was educating him.

Through the sluggish currents of downtown traffic, the carriage worked its way westward then up Second Avenue, as serried city dwellings gave way to streets sparsely settled, bright new row houses in open fields, worn-out farm buildings and shacks, and a few aging country estates. Some half hour after leaving the *Argus*, it labored up a low hill in the fading light past a small shantytown where smoke trailed from chimneys into the frigid air, and pulled into a compound inside a five foot wall. In a trice the boy was pulling out the steps, saying "Welcome, Master!" as if he owned the place, which, with its profusion of towers and bay windows, had the aspect in the pervasive gloom of a medieval castle.

While the driver attended to the steaming horses, Sam led DeShays round the side of the building, away from the porticoed entrance. A door at once opened to his knock. Stepping over the threshold DeShays was greeted by a thick-set woman with a red face and grey hair who embarrassed him by bobbing a curtsey. "An awful chill out today, Officer, I venture to think," she said, betraying her Scottish origins, as Sam, again, took his outer clothes. "I daresay you'd not find a cup of tea out of place."

"I'd be grateful indeed Mrs.—?"

"Lamond."

DeShays rubbed his hands. His breakfast kipper seemed an increasingly distant memory. Following the woman into a small, comfortably appointed sitting room with chintz coverings and a fire in the grate, he wondered if there was a Mrs. Brunton, assuming that this was Brunton's residence. An umbrella stand in the hall, fashioned from the leg of an elephant, seemed at odds with vegetarianism.

"Be off to your lessons, child, this instant!" shrilled the Scotswoman, shepherding Sam from the room.

Alone, DeShays wandered to the window. From what he could see, the land behind the house sloped down to a thicket of bushes and trees. Straining his eyes, no other buildings were visible. By his calculations, the East River couldn't be far away. Fingering the wallet in his pocket, he wondered what Pauline had in mind. What were her real feelings for Bewly? Who had been using who? Was Pauline to follow Miss Mullins to the discard pile? Was she in fact pregnant, as her letter to Bewly implied?

Soon tea and—delight—a pile of buttered griddle cakes arrived. "Miss Dowling will be down presently, I'm sure," said Mrs. Lamond. While that 'I'm sure' sounded a troubling note, at least he was in the right place.

"Has she been here long?" he asked innocently.

"Och, no. The poor lassie came up with him yesterday in the carriage. Such a poor wee shivering thing you never saw in your life. It's a mystery to me where he finds them, the master that is. There's no turning anyone down, such a big heart he has. At least when Mrs. Brunton was alive, bless her soul, she'd put her foot down once in a while." She leaned forward to hand DeShays his tea. "Is it true she was on the London stage? A duel was fought and her suitors did for each other?"

Pauline through and through, thought DeShays. Disloyally, he said, "I believe she is an actress."

Just then the sound of a door closing and steps descending sent the woman scurrying from the room. DeShays cast a longing look at the yet untouched griddle cakes and waited for the grand entrance, ready to take his cue from whatever part Pauline had decided to play. For he couldn't imagine Pauline as just Pauline. Too many layers, like paint on an old banister, obscured that complicated persona.

Dressed all in white, there she was in the doorway. DeShays got to his feet and for some seconds they took each other in. "Don't judge me over-harshly," she began. "Believe me, Miles, I'd not have thrown myself on the mercies of Mr. Brunton had I been anything short of desperate. I don't know what he's told you, but thank you for coming. After what has passed between us, I scarcely expected it."

They sat across from each other. For a minute she said nothing, eyes downcast. He was about to prompt when suddenly she laughed. "I'm sorry, Miles, it feels like the old days and we're shooting lines at each other from a script."

"Let's say we are then, if it helps."

"You probably want to know why I answered that notice."

"Why did you?"

"Mr. Bewly and I are betrothed." Her eyes held a kind of challenge. "He surprised me with a ring. That was more than two weeks ago. I haven't seen him since. From what I understood you to say, I'll not be seeing him again."

"I'm afraid so."

He braced himself for a scene, but she said simply, "What happened?"

"He was found in Cuyler's Alley...."

"The River Mauler!"

He nodded. "We didn't know who he was till the daguerreotypist came forward. He'd ordered a likeness to be colored, and never picked it up."

"A sweet, kind man," she murmured, "who wouldn't hurt a fly. Such beautiful plans we had."

"His things were at the Astor. Among them, this." From his wallet he handed Pauline her letter.

After a quick perusal she clasped it to her bosom in what struck DeShays as an embarrassing excess of theatricality. Are you really carrying his child? is what he felt like asking. Instead, he said, "I'm obliged to put a few questions to you, Pauline. Please don't take it amiss."

Dabbing her eyes, she said, "What sort of questions?"

"You say it's been over two weeks since you last saw Mr. Bewly?"

"A Sunday, it was. November the Second. He came to me at the Temple, took me out for a spin. We spent the day together." She sniffed and blew her nose. Her hand, he noticed, was ring-less.

"And he asked you to marry him?"

163

"The night before, at the hotel."

"So he knew where to find you?"

"Oh yes, he knew the Temple. We met there in July when we were anchored up-river near Albany."

"So Sunday he returned you to the boat, and you've not seen him since?"

She hesitated. "I told him not to come. I begged him. I said it was dangerous after dark. I said I wasn't well, that we'd meet next day. He didn't listen. Close to midnight—it must have been—he came. He was so happy, he said, that he could-n't sleep. He was afraid I'd disappear like a dream. And in the end, it was him—" She broke off. "I wouldn't admit him. I wasn't well. I sent him away to his death."

"You weren't well, or you weren't that eager to see him?"

"I told you—" she flared, then subsided. "Oh what's the point of all this?"

"Did anybody see him board the boat that night?"

"There was no one else around."

"The watchman?"

"I suppose so."

"With the season over, what was the Temple used for?"

"You should ask Mr. Brunton that."

"Why Brunton?"

"The floating theater was his idea. After the company disbanded he hired me to help with an experiment he was carrying out. I continued to live onboard."

Did he detect a certain smugness in her smile? "What sort of experiment?"

"It's about what happens when people give themselves over to their true passions. Animal magnetism, he sometimes calls it. I played the glass armonica for the gatherings."

"That contraption with all the glasses?"

She bristled at his tone. "Its ethereal harmonies sent them to seventh heaven."

He recalled the mysterious vat with its protruding metal rods and the rope. "And what happens when they get there?"

"It does work, Miles. I've seen people find their ideal match when the proper magnetic flow was restored—as often as not in someone else's spouse."

"Otherwise known as 'free love.'"

"Mr. Brunton's words exactly." She ignored his sarcasm. "And since society isn't ready for the idea of free love, secrecy is essential. Only people who were prepared for the consequences were welcome. By the way, if you're not going to finish those cakes—?"

"Please," he waved a weary hand.

"I declare that woman is trying to starve me," she spluttered through a mouthful. "She doesn't care for me. Probably thinks I have designs on her precious Mr. Brunton."

He watched her eat, intrigued at the change that seemed to have overtaken her during their talk. From nervous and suspicious to relaxed and confiding. "Why did you seek Brunton's protection?"

"I was threatened. I was afraid."

"To do with the Temple?"

"In a way."

"Passions got a bit out of hand?"

She scowled. "It's none of your business."

"You knew that the Temple sailed last night?"

Clearly, it was news. "Sailed? What do you mean?"

"To Baltimore. It was in all the papers. Well, not quite all." And now he saw why. "There was a midnight raid planned by the police."

She was clearly shaken. "But the police knew all about us. Mr. Brunton saw to that."

"Meaning Brunton paid them?"

"He squared with them somehow. In case people came snooping around. You know how gossip spreads."

DeShays heard again Carson's complaint to him that very morning, "Good of everyone to tell me. This is my ward you may recall." Apparently Brunton hadn't bought them all.

Pauline was saying, "I can't bear to think of Rutherford in that filthy alley. That just isn't him. He was—what's the word—just very meticulous. He knew how to look after himself. Is it true you've got the River Mauler locked up? Will he hang, do you think?"

"Nothing's final. They're still questioning him. It could well be it wasn't who they think."

"Oh, do you think so?" Pauline turned ashen. She pushed the griddle cakes away. She'd left a few, DeShays noted.

"It's possible."

She seemed to consider. "Are you really a policeman?"

In response, he held out his star. She leaned forward, gazing at it. Once again, he noted an almost tangible change come over her. What was going on in that devious mind? Was Billy Holmes's remark really so far-fetched, that she'd have had Bewly followed and clubbed after accepting his ring?

"I think I'm going to faint," Pauline announced, abruptly standing up. "Don't touch me!" she cried as DeShays made towards her. Then she ran from the room.

CHAPTER 25

"This'll do!" DeShays lifted the trap and yelled up to the driver as the carriage inched along the Bowery with traffic slowed to a crawl at the close of the business day. He jumped out by the corner of Hester Street, where a hefty brown woman with a yellow bandana wound around her head had set up shop. "Hot corn! Hot corn! Some for a penny, some for two cents, corn cost money and fire expense!" DeShays got the large variety, devouring the succulent ear in the minutes it took to reach Chatham Square.

No sooner had he started up the stairs to Kate's studio when he heard what he took to be her own steps descending, and soon she appeared, wearing her brown hooded cloak, her hands buried in a fur muffler.

"I hoped I'd catch you in time. No more visits from big, hairy policemen I trust?"

"No one at all. I spent the day putting things back to rights."

"Supposing I walk you home?"

She tilted her head, assessing him with a curious smile. "Eventually, if you want to. Actually, I had my heart set on some ice cream. You're welcome to join me."

"Why not?" Though ice cream was hardly what he had in mind. A juicy steak and kidney pie chased down by a few mugs of ale was more the ticket. Soon he found himself following Kate up a broad flight of steps to a second-story establishment situated over a bedding warehouse.

They walked past a long counter, where cakes, cookies, fruit and pies were on display. A young serving girl gave Kate a discreet smile of approval which caught DeShays by surprise and oddly cheered him. Clearly, she was a regular here. A sturdy-looking older woman churned out her order from a bucket, working the crank on its side, while DeShays settled for a slab of butter cake. The tables were small, mostly occupied by women, probably wives and daughters of local tradesmen waiting for the breadwinner to get off work. DeShays made his way to the back, as far from the others as possible.

"I'm certain you didn't stop by just to walk me home." Kate dipped her spoon into a plate of vanilla ice cream.

"As a matter of fact, you're right. I'm in need of a little womanly insight. A commodity hard to come by in the department."

"Have you found your actress?"

"Exactly." He briefly described his visit to Brunton's. "And this is where you can help me. You've met both Bewly and Pauline. Do you see them as a likely match?"

"Ah, a most interesting question." Kate held up her spoon as if reading in its smooth oval some hidden message. "I'd say that Mr. Bewly was likely the solution to her problems at the time they met. She is unmarried, beautiful but getting on in years now. I doubt she possesses a great deal of self-knowledge. It's painful for her to look inward. But I see her going in for a stronger-looking type of man, if she had her way."

"That's my impression too," said DeShays, seeing as if yesterday Pauline swooning over George Hamilton Powers's well-oiled muscles on that ill-fated night. Talk about animal magnetism: an electrical circuit joining two energies at full charge.

"You seem lost in a few insights of your own," said Kate, tapping her spoon against the plate. "May I ask the reason for your question?"

"It strikes me as strange that, right after their engagement, she sent him away. Why? Knowing Pauline, a sudden fit of moral scruples—or, as she maintains, not feeling well—seems an unlikely explanation."

Kate smiled. "Knowing her a lot less well than you, I'd say it was a man. She had a man coming to see her she didn't want Bewly to know about." She added a touch crisply, "With someone like that, it's always about men."

168

DeShays pushed his chair back in a sudden gesture, causing a flutter at a nearby table, where a newly-arrived trio of shop girls had been eyeing them with interest. "That's it!" he cried, as Kate stared at him quizzically. "Kate—Miss Felton—I can't thank you enough."

"Kate is fine. You might at least start by telling me what you're thanking me for."

"That man you mentioned—surely, he killed Bewly."

"Yes, but who is he?"

"I'm going to find out."

The sound of iron beating against wood seemed to resound not just through the front door but through the very timbers of 488 Greenwich. A series of three knocks, repeated three times at even intervals, coming just after midnight. DeShays awoke in dread, convinced that the knocking was for him. In darkness he threw off the covers and lifted the sash of his dormer, his heartbeat quickening as he stuck his head out into the frigid night. Nearby other sashes scraped open, and from across the street a man shouted a German obscenity.

Two men stood at the front door, unrecognizable, swathed as they were in traveling cloaks, the hoods pulled up. In the street a sizable carriage was parked, the horses steaming in the gaslight almost as though they were on fire. Struggling into his pants and boots and grabbing a coat, he raced downstairs. Evans appeared in his doorway in his nightshirt, and Mrs. F too was at her door, dressed in a nightcap and gown, her expression demanding of an explanation. With his hand upheld DeShays said all was well, to get back to bed.

The front door opened to an unfamiliar face. "Is Mr. DeShays in?" The man's tone seemed to suggest that some notoriety was attached to the name.

"I am he. What the devil do you mean by calling at this hour?"

Before the man could respond came a voice from behind him. "Come now, DeShays," coaxed Chief Matson, leaning forward in the open door of the carriage so his face caught the light. "It's best if you just get in."

Death always comes in the one way you don't anticipate, thought DeShays, the cold settling over him in the doorway. "Let me get dressed, Chief," he called out, as another Germanic oath pierced the night.

"Get in. Now. That's an order."

Barely had DeShays sat down beside the chief than the door was slammed shut and the carriage jerked forward. As he draped himself in the horse blanket thrust after him by one of the coachmen, he could hear the driver on the box roundly cursing his steeds. They took the corner into Broadway at speed and DeShays, flung haphazardly against the solid bulk of his companion, mumbled apologies.

Every so often the pale light from a glassed-in candle flickered across that stolid countenance, till finally, in mid-sentence, as though continuing a conversation already underway, Matson broke silence. "... who all along I knew was whispering in Brunton's ear, though I had no proof of it. Your transgressions I took to be the errors of a wayward young man, though in truth you are no longer so young."

"I am not in with Brunton, Chief, that I swear."

"Don't deny it, DeShays. You were seen getting into his carriage. You were seen entering the premises of the *Argus*. It insults my intelligence, and that is one—"

Hitting a rut in the pavement, the coach lurched hard and the light wavered. Speight and Willoughby. They must have followed the carriage. "I can explain, Chief," DeShays blurted wildly. "You recall my telling you about Miss Dowling, the actress from the floating theater who disappeared, who was engaged to the late Mr. Bewly? This morning she sent for me. Brunton has her at his house. He sent his carriage. It was a chance I had to take."

"You are a fool, and that is precisely what Brunton has played you for. You see, DeShays, I bear unfortunate news. Tomorrow morning, the *Argus* is going to steal your hard-earned thunder. The name of E. Rutherford Bewly of Albany will at length be proclaimed, that scurrilous rag having conducted its own 'independent investigation,' the police having failed entirely and so on and so forth."

"It was Miss Dowling I told, not Brunton."

The Chief cut him off with a curt wave. "Would it be news to you that the man behind the sordid shenanigans at that so-called Temple is none other than your friend Brunton? Or that Miss Dowling was the principal seductress in that den of iniquity? Oh yes, Inspector Harrington has given me a detailed report."

"Then he's got it all wrong. It was a harmless experiment. Miss Dowling told me all about it."

"Animal magnetism. Free love. Exchanging spouses." Disgust warped the chief's face.

"It wasn't what you think."

"Tell that to the schoolmarm at her desk, the shopkeeper at his till, the milkman on his rounds, the churchman in his pulpit— which, by the way, is exactly what we intend to do if Brunton doesn't pull his so-called revelations from the pages of tomorrow's paper. His isn't the only rag in town. Winston, full speed ahead!" he called through the trap.

Whip smacked against horsehide and the carriage bounded forward, the horses breaking into a gallop. DeShays sank into his corner, his mind a whirl. Matson was right. Brunton had played him for a fool. The man was like a trial lawyer, caring not whom he hurt as long as he won, exploiting a fragile woman who'd run to him for protection simply to embarrass the police.

Streets rumbled by until the road turned to mud. The candle guttered and went out and moonlight spilled over barren fields, disappeared behind lonely houses or peered through dense thickets. The road grew rougher but the carriage kept speed with a rattling din like giant chattering teeth, as though it might burst apart at the seams at every bone-jarring rut. It was impossible to hold a steady train of thought.

For some time now DeShays had guessed at their destination and one part of him was agog to witness the clash of two such titans. What was to be his role in the coming drama? To hold the chief's coat while he took Brunton apart? It would be a painful yet compelling scene, a scrap between two seasoned predators. But it was not to be. "Stay here," ordered the chief as the carriage slowed and pulled up by Brunton's front entrance. One of the coachmen jumped down from the box and helped him out then slammed the door in DeShays's face as if to reinforce the point.

The chief's leaden steps crunched along the gravel path as though to grind it into powder. All lay dark and still. Again three loud knocks reverberated through the night. After an anxious wait the door inched open. A further pause, and the chief was admitted. The door closed behind him. Silence descended.

The two coachmen busied themselves with covering the horses, then conversed in low voices, smoking. DeShays listened, for what he didn't know. From inside the compound came a dog's barking, quickly transformed into a low whine. A moment later light shone palely in a bay window.

Nearly fifteen minutes later, at half past midnight, the front door opened and quickly closed behind the chief. With a certain amount of pushing and heaving he was assisted into the carriage, which sank to his side. On his face DeShays saw the satisfied look of a man who'd wined and dined well. Whatever silent celebration stirred within that vast frame stayed there and DeShays knew far better than to ask.

One by one streetlamps and brick buildings returned and the city assumed shape again. "See me first thing, in the office," grunted the chief before the two parted company.

CHAPTER 26

Descending the stairs that Friday morning, DeShays saw his landlady busying herself with an arrangement of dried grasses that had stood for weeks on a side table in the hall. "Good morning, Mrs. F," he said. "About last night, I'm—" But he got no further.

"Mr. DeShays," she turned on him, pointing the stem of a bulrush toward the parlor, "shall we continue our conversation in there?"

"Very well." Meekly he held the door for her. "But—"

"Mr. DeShays, the time for 'buts' is over. Wasn't it only yesterday you gave me your word? I'm giving you till the end of the month to find alternative accommodation. I run a respectable house. Already I've had a complaint about last night. There are sure to be others." In the face of DeShays silence, she lowered the bulrush. "I'm sorry, but there it is."

As a chastened DeShays entered the breakfast room, Evans glanced up from his *Argus* and slid a soft hand across his throat. Little doubt who was the complainant. Jenkins, whose table manners were impeccable, concentrated on maneuvering a kidney onto his fork, while Eliza examined her nails. Clearly the word was out.

Taking his seat, DeShays leaned slightly sideways the better to scrutinize the *Argus*'s front page. Whatever the chief had hashed out with Brunton would surely be reflected there. His eye caught the letters "LING!" before Evans—in a further display of pettiness—folded the page in. "DOWLING!" at once came to mind: "Mauler Victim Betrothed to Miss Pauline Dowling!"

It was not till he reached Broadway, en route to his appointment with Chief Matson, that DeShays was able to get his hands on a copy of the *Argus*. "CLIPPER IN RECORD CROSS-ATLANTIC SAILING!" he read. For the time being the chief's stalling tactics seemed to be holding.

The chill of the past day or two had surrendered to a soft mistiness, surely to the relief of the few trees he passed, buffeted almost bare by those icy winds. Only the brown oak leaves seemed reluctant to fly away. As the door closed firmly behind him, courtesy of Honan's unseen hand, DeShays anticipated at least some acknowledgement by the chief of their midnight sortie and its apparently successful denouement. But no; tilting back in his chair, Matson stared as if wondering who on earth his visitor might be.

"Ah, DeShays," he said at last in a casual tone that at once put his listener on his guard, "no doubt you've heard the news."

"I've seen the *Argus*, sir, if that's what you mean."

With the wave of a meaty hand, the chief swept the *Argus* aside. "McGlone's talking. Captain Carson was just here. You must have missed him."

For a moment DeShays was speechless, as if the air had been punched out of him. "It wasn't him," he heard himself protest, "It couldn't have been." He might as well have addressed the Sphinx. "Then what about Miller? What about the third man?"

"There was no third man. Miller was an accomplice. His death was unrelated."

"But—"

Like some leviathan slowly breaking the ocean's surface, the chief rose from behind his desk, shrinking it to insignificance as he leaned across. Under the weight of those silent staring eyes, DeShays felt himself submerging towards nothingness. At last, in measured tones, soft and frightening, the great man gave utterance. "Young man,"—DeShays felt a hand clamp down on his shoulder—"if you would leave this office a policeman, as you entered it, you will keep your opinions to yourself."

A half hour later, jolting north in the Harlem omnibus, DeShays still felt the imprint of that steely grip. He felt too

174

the hard outlines of his star of office nestling in the right hand pocket of his coat. Surprising himself he'd not this time given way to impulse, though he knew—as surely as he knew any-thing—that John McGlone, whatever else he'd done, hadn't killed Bewly. Their brief conversation had assured him of that. And very soon, if he played such cards as he held astutely, he might find out who had.

At ten o'clock on a misty morning with a pale late Novem-ber sun rendering the ghostly battlements of the night before faintly ridiculous, Castle Brunton—as DeShays had dubbed it—appeared deserted. At the side entrance a maid answered his knock, her eyes wide at the sight of the copper star. No, Mrs. Lamond was out, the same for Mr. Brunton, and yes, Miss Dowling was upstairs.

Standing once again at the window of the cozy sitting-room, DeShays waited for the familiar footfall. An hour later, he was still waiting. It was early, he knew, for a self-respecting thespian to be up and about. He'd told the maid to announce merely that a policeman wished to speak with Miss Dowling. And when at last Pauline stepped into the room she seemed relieved at the sight of him. "Oh Miles, I can never think of you as a policeman."

Which led immediately to his first question, the time for niceties being over. "How many policemen do you know, Pauline?"

The question seemed to catch her off guard. "What business is it of yours?"

"Personally, none. But since I'm investigating the murder of your fiancé, perhaps you'll answer me. Which of my col-leagues did you think might be calling on you at this hour?"

"Why Miles, do you know every single one of them? Come to think of it, I'm not even sure he is a policeman."

"Does he have a name?"

"I assume so. Most people do."

"Pauline, I'm here to help you. Sometimes I feel you don't want to be helped."

"He had a nasty mustache. There, does that help?"

"It narrows the field. Tell me more."

175

"He came to the boat the day before yesterday. He said he'd come back. Poor little Pauline was so scared she ran to nice, kind Mr. Brunton to protect her."

"What did he want?"

"He just wandered around picking things up and putting them back down. How should I know what he wanted? Perhaps he didn't even know himself."

Into DeShays's mind came Kate's account of that first visitor to her studio, her "awful man" and "the very soul of contempt." A thought struck him. Should he voice it? How would she react? "Forgive me, Pauline, but we're talking about a man who killed, possibly twice, so I have to ask. The man with the nasty mustache—was he at any time your lover?"

Watching her face so washed of expression, he feared she was gearing up again for her fainting routine. But it was rage, pure and simple, that lurked behind the mask. And not, he thought, the stage variety. "You filthy bastard," she screeched, coming at him, fists flailing, so that, to defend himself, he reached out and grabbed her wrists. Behind her, in the doorway, the maid appeared then quickly vanished.

With comparative ease, his chin dribbling her spittle, he forced her onto a chair and stood over her. It was now or never. "Pauline," he said, "tell me one thing and I'll go and not bother you again. You wouldn't let Bewly stay with you that night because you had a tryst with someone else. It's obvious. Who was that someone else? Was it Dick Poole?"

Pauline was breathing hard. "You know something, Miles?" she gasped, "You're pitiful. You were pitiful as an actor, you're pitiful as a policeman." In such close proximity, looking down, he saw how thickly caked her makeup was. His glance to the doorway where the maid had reappeared with Sam must have drawn Pauline's attention for she looked around. "You," she commanded, "show this man out and never let him in here again."

DeShays walked west by a long picket fence, occasionally deflecting a protruding spiky branch with an upraised arm. The landscape of desolate lots and lonely ramshackle houses which lay off the rutted track did nothing to raise his spirits.

He'd gone but a few blocks when the sound of pounding hooves made him turn to find a small carriage gaining on him. The driver he didn't recognize, but as the coach caught up to him he saw that its sole occupant was little Sam. He gave the boy a friendly salute, but Sam just looked at him from behind the glass, and the carriage sped on.

Some minutes later an approaching rumble signaled a stage pulled by two horses barreling his way. It shuddered to a halt several yards ahead of him. Stepping lively he entered through the back, to find just a young couple with an infant and some luggage, and a uniformed ticket boy, whom he paid. Returning the husband's pleasant nod, DeShays gratefully stretched out his legs. Before long the young wife was feeding her infant, while the ticket boy fed himself from a bag of nuts, looking young enough to be at school.

How much of what Pauline said was motivated by pride and how much by fear? DeShays asked himself. If Poole hadn't been her lover, what was his involvement? Some sort of blackmail, perhaps involving Pauline's favors? Hadn't Kate suggested as much the previous day? He'd pooh-poohed the idea, but now he wasn't sure. Who was Poole working for that he could afford to be so brazen? Carson? The Chief? Brunton? Had Brunton paid him to protect the floating theater? Though surely that would be Carson's prerogative as ward captain. Should he beard Carson, layout his suspicions of Poole, demand to know why he'd gone ahead and sacrificed McGlone?

Rolling noisily into the city, the stage picked up and deposited passengers at every corner. As it crept along the Bowery, DeShays grew restless, looking out at pedestrians moving faster than himself. Since his thoughts seemed to be taking the form of statements or questions addressed to Kate, at Chatham Square he stepped off and made for her studio.

"Well?" Kate asked, looking like a druggist in her white smock with her hair up, as she'd been buffing copper plates in the darkroom. "You don't look too pleased with yourself."

"You're right about that. I can't seem to keep out of my own way." He described his midnight ride with the chief and the news of McGlone's confession that prompted his return visit to Pauline.

"I'm pretty sure that Dick Poole called on Pauline the day before yesterday, though what he wanted she either couldn't or wouldn't say. It seems the promise of a return visit sent her into hiding. Questions as to the nature of his interest resulted in my expulsion."

"If that's the one who came here, he's enough to send anyone into hiding. Even the name—it makes you think of a pool of blood, doesn't it?"

"Can you honestly see those two in a love affair?"

"I said I could see her with a strong man, not a primate. Though certainly he would make for an obsessive suitor. One often finds that the case with men to whom words don't come easily. Your Pauline's not a well woman—in a moment of weakness she might be vulnerable to anything. God, it makes me shiver to think of those killer's eyes of his."

DeShays glanced towards the little portraits on the wall. "A pity we don't have his daguerreotype. There's someone I'd like to show it to."

Kate hesitated. "It's possible that I can sketch a reasonable likeness. I used to attend drawing classes but I never have time for it anymore. My sketchbook sits gathering dust in my office."

"Time to dust it off then. Do you have a moment?" He followed Kate into the room where she colored portraits and kept her account books. Among these was the sketchbook, which she opened and propped up at an angle on her desk.

For a time before starting Kate sat gazing at the blank page, a stick of charcoal in her hand. Looking discreetly over her shoulder, DeShays watched her weave black strokes into Poole's likeness, including a small mole over his right eye that he'd forgotten about. "That's him all right. This is incredible, Kate," he said as, after about twenty minutes, she lay down the charcoal. "It deserves to be framed."

"Just be careful not to hang it opposite a clock," she said, tearing out the page.

Horns, tubas and trombones grew louder with each step DeShays took down Park Row. He found it hard not to walk in lockstep with the music which was coming from the American Museum. At the corner of Ann a knot of people stood gaping up at a brass band blaring out a march from the third story balcony draped with colored portraits of exotic beasts and freaks. As DeShays approached the ticket booth for the second time in three days, the clerk barely glanced up. "If it's the Quaker you're after, he's not here. Come back tomorrow," he said, before DeShays even opened his mouth. "Show begins at seven."

"Any idea where he lives?"

"Up in the beanstalk."

"Is the proprietor in?"

The man gave the counter a tired slap. "No." Mindful of his mistake with Pauline, DeShays checked his urge to have it out with him. "Try asking him."

Turning in the direction indicated, DeShays saw what he took to be a child approaching. "Pardon me," he took a step back, "do you work here?"

"On occasion." The voice was that of a child, but the face, on closer scrutiny, was a man's.

"Do you know the Quaker Giant?"

"I do have that pleasure."

"Could you tell me where he lives."

"I couldn't say where he lives exactly, sir, but most afternoons you'll find him working at the Home for the Forgotten."

What God-forsaken creatures washed up there DeShays could only imagine. "Can you direct me?"

"It's on Pitt between Broome and Delancey, closer to Broome on the west side. Look for a big white house set back a ways from the street. And when you get there, ask for Obed; that's his right name."

179

CHAPTER 27

At first glance the Home for the Forgotten had itself the look of a survivor. At one time a country house, it faced sideways on Pitt Street behind a picket fence, flanked by a tiny shack and a row of cottages that had also seen better days. A small yard with a few adolescent trees was all that remained of the surrounding landscape.

DeShays opened the gate and walked along a slate path and up a few steps to the porch. From within, instead of the preachy voices and croaked-out hymns he'd half-expected, he was surprised to hear the high-pitched squeals and stamping feet of children at play. Stepping left, he looked in through a tall window and was transported back to schooldays.

Amid miniature stools and a pair of little benches, small girls were absorbed in arranging wooden animals spilling from a large toy chest. At the far end of the room, surrounded by a half dozen or so screeching boys, lay the Quaker Giant. Rolling gently to and fro he deflected their tiny blows with tucked in elbows as though a boxer practicing defense.

DeShays's rap was answered by a pleasant-faced woman of middle age dressed all in black. "Yes sir, how may I help you."

"I'm here to see Obed. Would he be in?"

"He's presently very busy," the woman warned, to a chorus of squeals. "Who shall I say is here?"

"Miles DeShays."

"May I ask your connection to Obed?"

"I'm from the police." DeShays showed his badge, then tucked it away as if something best unseen.

"The police! What on earth do you want with him?"

"I assure you he's in no trouble, Miss—?"

"Rebecca Martland. I run this establishment."

"An orphanage?"

"A transitional home for orphaned and homeless children. We provide for them until they are placed with a proper family." She eyed him doubtfully. "Well then, I suppose I'd best tell Obed you're here."

She closed the door on him and a moment later the commotion subsided. After a couple of minutes Obed appeared, his head recoiling slightly as it seemed to dawn on him that he'd seen DeShays before.

"Yes, we met at the floating theater," DeShays affirmed, mindful of the curious faces crowding at the crack in the side door Miss Martland was attempting to shut. "If you can spare me a few moments, I'd be very grateful."

At Obed's prompting DeShays followed him upstairs, the Giant's stride spanning three steps at a time. At the top he stood aside to let DeShays precede him into a spacious loft lit by a row of dormer windows and equipped as a carpentry shop with pine planks propped against the walls, and jigs, planes and saws. Wide unvarnished floorboards lay coated with a thick layer of sawdust in which huge footprints were traced.

Sitting on rough benches a few feet apart, the men eyed each other curiously. Obed's smooth, slightly fleshy face betrayed little. With his hairless head and red suspenders pulled over a grey flannel shirt he looked like an overgrown baby.

"They said at the museum I'd find you here. Miss Martland told you I was with the police?"

The Giant gave a slight nod.

"I happen to know a couple of people who perform at the museum: T.J. Winchell and a man named La Rue. Would you know these men?"

Frowning curiously, the Giant again nodded yes.

"Know them well?" His hand wavered indicating so-so.

"Ever tell them that you worked as a watchman at the floating theater?"

Obed shrugged as if to say he couldn't remember, appearing to shy away from the question.

"There was nothing illegal about the job, Obed. You're in no trouble as far as the police are concerned."

The Giant pressed his hands to his temples as if in a futile effort to recall.

"How did you come to work at the museum?"

He slapped the coins in his pocket.

"I need a dollar as well as anyone else, friend. Tell me, how long were you at the ship?"

Obed signaled four or five weeks.

"And for how many nights a week?"

The Giant held up four fingers.

"Sundays?" Yes.

"Did your shift last until morning?" It had.

"And how did you come to work there?" The Giant shrugged noncommittally. "Please tell me, Obed. Who hired you?"

Obed hesitated, showing signs of agitation. Finally, he reached down and traced in the sawdust the letters: B-R-U-N-T-O-N.

"And how did you come to meet Mr. Brunton?"

Obed pointed downstairs, and with his hands made bountiful gestures.

"A benefactor, then?" Exactly. "And would a Negro boy named Sam have stayed here for a time?" The Giant bowed his head: precisely.

"Having worked at the ship for a while, I imagine you must have gotten to know some of the visitors." Reaching into his pocket for Kate's sketch of Poole DeShays passed it over. As he unfolded the paper something in Obed's eyes turned inward.

"Seen him before?" The response was a confusing series of hand signals. "He's a policeman, right?"

Obed nodded yes, and pointed at DeShays as if to say, "So are you." Describing a sketching motion he pointed at him again.

"Ah, I see. No, an artist friend of mine drew it from memory. So tell me, did this man ever come to visit Miss Dowling? Anything you say to me will go no further than these walls, Obed. That's a promise."

The Giant held up his hands, indicating uncertainty.

"Were you friendly with Miss Dowling?" Smiling, he shaped a halo above his head and gave a deep nod.

"I've know her for many years. We've acted together on stage. I'm out to protect her. So tell me, Obed, how often did you see the man in the picture?" The Giant shrugged, and with his fingers gestured two, perhaps three times.

"He used to come around midnight?"

The Giant hesitated then jerked his thumb sideways.

"Before?" A nod yes.

"Always at the same time?"

Obed's left hand wavered, indicating different times.

"Two Sundays ago, around midnight, did you observe anything out of the ordinary while you were on watch?"

Frowning as if struggling to recall, Obed shook his head, no. He had begun rocking back and forth on his hands as if to keep warm, a sign, thought DeShays, of jittery nerves.

"And do you recall seeing this man at the boat late that night?"

The Giant shook his head, as if remembering the comings and goings on a night two and a half weeks back was beyond him.

"Think, Obed; did no one board the boat that night? I know someone did. Miss Dowling told me so."

The Giant threw up his hands in exasperation.

"Try to think back. A man she was not expecting: perhaps he asked for her by name?"

After a pause Obed held up his right index finger. There was one.

"And how long was this man with her?"

He made a sweeping motion as if to say the man came and went in a hurry.

"What did he look like?"

Obed pointed to DeShays.

"Me?"

He shrugged.

"And you saw no one else?"

With his arms folded across his chest for emphasis, the Giant firmly shook his head.

DeShays rose to his feet. "The man you saw that night was murdered, Obed—I believe he was killed shortly after you saw him. Someone is liable to pay for that crime who had nothing to do with it—a man with a wife and child, who lies rotting in the Tombs. You have no choice but to remember!"

With a look of contrition, Obed held his palms up help-lessly: he had nothing more to offer.

DeShays gave him a thorough look, tinged with disappointment. "Obed, two men have been killed already, and Miss Dowling is in hiding in fear for her life. Should anything jog your memory, remember that nothing will be shared with the man whose picture I showed you. I work out of the chief's office at City Hall, but at night you can find me at 488 Greenwich Street. Remember that address, and expect to see me again."

The Giant bowed his head and let out a tense breath. Holding open the door to the stairs he let DeShays descend first. At the front door his handshake was limp, and he seemed to shrink as DeShays looked him squarely in the eye.

Outside a stiff wind animated the washing hung from backyard clotheslines, and late afternoon shadows lengthened and merged, the light fading from the sleepy old houses with their worn coats of paint. DeShays would be glad never to visit this corner of town again.

Obed was frightened. He was holding something back. Only when pressed with Pauline's admission of Bewly's visit had his memory of that supposedly unmemorable Sunday magically returned. And despite their brief encounter, the Giant had remembered him perfectly well. Memory was not his problem. He would have to let time do its work and press the man again tomorrow.

A few drops of rain on his face and shoulders caused DeShays to turn up Grand Street where for stretches he might walk beneath the awnings if the heavens opened. The sheer volume of merchandise stored in the shops and warehouses, few of which seemed to attract takers despite salesmen who barked vacantly at every passer-by, conspired to depress him. A metaphor for the futility of human endeavor. His next stop was shaping up to be a glass of Scotch.

For several blocks he passed stores displaying cheap glass and china, hats and caps, used clothes and furniture. A string of shoe stores had huge boot-shaped signs hanging outside, boots painted in large silhouettes on their pitched roofs and, on the sidewalk, boots and shoes shelved in glass cases. Something drew him towards the window of a store occupying an old frame house, and he stopped to look.

How long the face in the glass had been staring back at him he couldn't have said. He turned sharply.

"Time for new boots, DeShays? The way you've been getting around, yours must be worn clean through."

It was the first time DeShays had seen Poole wearing a top hat and he felt an urge to take a backhanded swipe at it. "You must be in need of a new pair of beaters yourself, Poole, the way you've been walking in my steps. Long days spent visiting other people's homes, rummaging through their belongings, watching their every move. Tough on the feet, isn't it?"

"I just wouldn't want to see any harm come to the nephew of Morgan K. Allaire. A person such as yourself needs special looking after."

"I'll be just fine on my own, if you give me half a chance."

"The way your nose gets into corners where it don't belong, I wouldn't give spit for your chances. Take my warning and stop behaving like a fool. Else they'll be putting you to bed with a shovel soon enough."

"Just like Eli Miller?"

Poole cackled, and not for effect. "You should only come up floating soon as he did—otherwise what a time they'd have identifying you."

"I imagine you'd be able to lend a hand there."

Poole lingered an instant with a feral glare, his condensed breath fuming in the cold. Then he turned and stalked off up the street. His tight black clothes and his wrestler's walk emphasizing his powerful build, he seemed at once absurd and explosive, the sort of man people comment on from a safe distance.

A gentle tug at his elbow surprised him. He turned to find a thickset, jowly man backing away with his hands upheld as if in surrender. Much shorter than DeShays, the isolated strands of dark hair spanning his scalp were reminiscent of kelp on a rock. The man's eyes sparkled as he began speaking in a warm German accent.

"Pardon me, sir, I meant no offense. My name is Kling, and mine is the clothing shop next door. I am not one for pulling strangers off the street, my good fellow, but you see I have for you an excellent pair of pantaloons, with matching vest too. Clothing of the latest fashion, tailored as if just for you. How odd! I say to myself, watching you speak with that nice chentleman. Not often do I find such things for a man your size. All the more reason we may come to terms, if you'll step this way."

Kling bowed obsequiously and gestured towards his shop as though to usher in royalty. About to shake the fellow off, it dawned on DeShays that here lay an answer to the dilemma that had crept up on him. The shop must have just opened; a freshly painted sign, gilt letters on black, hung above the second floor windows and read, "Henry Kling Fine Second Hand Clothing." With the dealer a step behind him, DeShays crossed the threshold to find dim aisles packed tight with cast-offs, and that familiar musty smell.

Not many minutes later a graybeard, bent with age, could be seen emerging from the self-same shop. Leaning on his cane, his head swathed in what might have been a bandage, his body draped in the padded silk dressing gown of a bygone era, he tapped his way up the street intent on some urgent business known only to himself.

CHAPTER 28

It occurred to DeShays as he lay limp as a spaniel's ear in what was almost certainly his own bed, judging by the shape of the damp patch in the ceiling which had helped reduce his rent, that Pauline had a point: as an actor he must indeed be pitiful. With an effort he tried to piece together what had happened.

After leaving the shop on Grand Street—Henry Kling Fine Second Hand Clothing, he recalled the name—he'd retraced his steps as fast as his disguise allowed towards the Home for the Forgotten. He couldn't ignore the possibility of Poole— had he tracked him there—wanting to do a little investigating of his own. And, once inside, making mincemeat of Obed.

He remembered deciding on the short-cut through the open-air market at Essex Street, deserted at that hour, the stalls closed and bare, the lingering smell of poultry and offal, a pig snuffling at a pile of rotten vegetables. And after that, nothing. A big blank. From the smarting pain when he moved his head, that's where the blow must have fallen. How naive he'd been. Far from leaving him, Poole would have continued to watch him. "A person such as yourself needs special looking after." Well, he'd as good as asked for it.

But what possessed the man to bring him back here to Greenwich Street? For surely it was Poole, not some passing Samaritan, since he'd nothing on him to say where he lived. Was he wrong about Poole? Had he jumped to conclusions? Had Poole tried to help him? His mind strained after a glimmer of clarity. If only he could reach it, but it stayed stubbornly just a glimmer.

When DeShays came to again the room felt washed in a grey light and a not unpleasant smell invaded his nostrils. He struggled to sit up.

"Oh, Mr. DeShays!" At once the flushed face of Eliza Fitzgerald floated above him, her ringlets almost brushing his cheeks. "Oh, don't move Mr. DeShays. Let me run and fetch Mama!"

In the time it took for his landlady to mount the stairs DeShays managed to heave himself into a sitting position from which he woozily surveyed his surroundings. Draped over the foot of the bed in mute accusation he recognized the padded silk dressing gown of his aborted escapade. Gingerly probing his crown, his fingers investigated what felt like a considerable bandage.

"Well, Mr. DeShays," began Mrs. Fitzgerald, "A fine state of affairs." She inspected the bandage. "We're going to be a very dull household when you pack your bags."

"Oh, Mama," protested Eliza from the stairs.

"Now run and tell cook to send up one of her hot toddies, there's a good girl. Off you go. For a policeman, Mr. DeShays, I must say you have some exceedingly colorful associates." There was a speculative edge to her tone. "That foreign piano player—I forget his name—then that poor actress, Miss Dowling. And now this Mr. Obed, a storybook giant if ever I saw one."

"Obed? Here?"

"Half way through dinner—weren't we?—when he burst in. By God's mercy, Mr. Jenkins and Mr. Evans were dining out or they'd have given notice on the spot."

"And you didn't let me know?"

"Mr. DeShays, you were there. Over his shoulder like a sack of coal. It took me a minute before I realized the creature was dumb and not in the vice of demon drink. He wrote his name down on this piece of paper."

DeShays held the scrap of paper with a single word, OBED, printed on it. "What day is it?"

"Today? Why, Saturday. You'll have till the end of the month to make other arrangements." Her glance fell meaningfully on the silk dressing gown.

"Mrs. F, I know what you're thinking, but it's not so. The fact is I was attacked doing my duty as a policeman; investigating a murder in which this man, Obed, happens to be an

188

innocent witness. This is just between ourselves, please,"—she bent her head—"he's a God-fearing man who may well have saved my life."

"That's as may be," Mrs. Fitzgerald sounded unconvinced. "Oh, and you had a caller last night, it almost slipped my mind. A Miss Felton. I told her you were indisposed."

"Miss Felton?" He felt himself coloring under her gaze. "Did she—? Was she—?"

"She left no message, Mr. DeShays. But it's nice to know that some of your friends seem, well, regular."

It was lunchtime before DeShays—under the expert care of Eliza and little Millie—began to feel anything like his old self. With the door of his room propped open he heard the doorbells chiming downstairs as they had off and on through the morning. Only this time there followed sounds of a scuffle and the screech of girlish disputation, and in short order his two nurses burst unceremoniously upon him, Millie clutching to her stomach something which Eliza seemed intent on wrestling away.

With a semblance of order restored, DeShays received from Millie's hands a by now somewhat creased fold of paper addressed he saw, smoothing it out, to THE POLICEMAN AT 488 GREENWICH STREET. CONFIDENTIAL. Under the severe gaze of two sets of eyes he broke the seal revealing, in neat capitals, the words, SIR, SHOULD YOU BE WELL ENOUGH AND WILLING MEET ME THIS NIGHT AT THE AMERICAN MUSEUM. YOUR SERVANT OBED.

"Is it a secret?" demanded Millie.

To which her sister replied, "Of course, silly. That's what confidential means."

"I need some confidential help," DeShays said. What had happened to change Obed's mind? There being no shortage of volunteers, he gave instructions, distributing a handful of coins. "Be sure to tell your mother."

"But it's a secret," objected Millie.

"The annoying thing about mothers is they know everything anyway. There are no secrets from mothers." He pretended not to see Eliza blush.

A little while later, thanks to his willing accomplices,

DeShays was catching up on the news. "RIVER MAULER WAS NIGHT WATCHMAN, VICTIM FROM ALBANY," announced the *Tribune*; "MAULER UNMASKED," blared the *Herald*; while Brunton's *Argus* trumpeted (incredibly), "POLICE SOLVE CUYLER'S ALLEY SLAYING, VICTIM IDENTIFIED." Bewly was described as "an itinerant salesman from the Albany area" whose name was being withheld by the police pending notification of his nearest and dearest.

Captain Carson took the lion's share of the credit and was quoted as attributing the death of the killer to drowning due to his well-known over-familiarity with the bottle. It was the victim's bloodied garments, he said, discovered in Miller's possession that sealed the case. McGlone would be held on an unrelated charge of creating a disturbance. The populace were assured that earlier speculation that an accomplice was still at large could be put to rest. Chief Matson issued a statement to the effect that law-abiding citizens could sleep peacefully in their beds secure in the knowledge that their protectors were ever-vigilant on their behalf. And so on, and so forth.

DeShays was livid. He could hardly believe his eyes.

Ducking beneath a banner proclaiming "GRAND AND GLORIOUS ATTRACTIONS!" DeShays flashed his copper shield at the ticket booth clerk, a man he hadn't seen there before.

"Performance over yet?"

"You'll catch the finale. Grand Parade of Giants and Dwarfs." He nodded towards the stairs. "Watch out on Two," he warned, as DeShays turned to go. "Wild Indians. Harmless—s'long as they're fed regular."

He ascended a broad staircase, at first finding no one among the darkened galleries. A glass case containing the famous Fee-Jee Mermaid, a creature part mummified monkey part fish, shared wall space with The Three Men of Egypt, their blackened grinning skulls sticking like scorched babies out of funeral wrappings. Beyond an archway, at the far end of the floor, a gently heaving mass must be the Indians, dossed down for the night. On the third floor a few scattered lamps shone dimly

190

through rows of towering glass cases filled with macabre relics. The lecture room and stage were on the floor above, and from the sound of it the show was building to a climax.

All afternoon, since getting the note from Obed and seeing the papers, DeShays had felt as if suspended in time and space. One minute he'd be sad and resigned, knowing his days in the police were over and how useless, in the face of the powers that ran things, his efforts were; the absurdity of ever having thought otherwise! (Though it was Saturday, a workday, he felt no compunction about not contacting the department. To hell with them all.) The next minute anger surged and his head throbbed as he thought of Carson, and how he'd proved no better than the rest of them, running roughshod over their compact. Meanwhile Dick Poole, the likely killer, was free to prowl the streets, bashing people on the head, just as he'd sent Eli Miller conveniently to the next world. Judging from the report in the *Argus*, the chief had bought Brunton's—if not support, at least neutrality—by agreeing to withhold Bewly's name, suppressing potentially embarrassing associations with Pauline and the proceedings at the Temple of the Muses.

Feeling he'd go crazy if left to these morbid deliberations DeShays slipped out of the house in the gathering gloom of late afternoon, evading the ministrations of his nurses. Destination: Pelham's. A way of filling the hours till meeting Obed. He'd considered visiting Kate, knowing she'd be wondering what was happening. He owed it to her, he knew, but what did he have to report? A feeling of shame came over him, of not coming up to expectations, that somehow he'd let her down.

Pulling the front door quietly to, DeShays hurried down the street. A cold wind was blowing the leaves around and the few people about, chins thrust into protective scarves, kept lowered eyes. So that they were almost abreast before recognition set in and both started talking at once.

"I thought I'd look in on the way home, see how you were," said Kate.

"I was just thinking of you," echoed DeShays. "I owe you an explanation."

And so it was that Kate and DeShays ended up at Pelham's

and he was able to fill her in on all that had befallen him since their parting the day before; and that Billy Holmes, when Kate had stepped out briefly, was able to remark, "My God, old man, you're smarter than you look. Where did you find her?"

"Don't get ideas, Billy. She has that daguerreotype studio. I told you. She's been helping me on that case."

"Helping you? She's mad over you. And you, if I'm not much mistaken, are quite partial to her. Miles, do I hear wedding bells?"

"You forget. I'm a married man."

"You told her?"

"We talk about daguerreotypes."

"Well, if I were you—" But at that point Kate returned.

Later, as DeShays walked Kate home through the dark, cold streets, it seemed only natural for him to take her arm.

DeShays passed a case of boa constrictors. He was just yards from the doors of the lecture room when they burst open and disgorged as bizarre a parade as ever he'd seen: four giants got up as horses with dwarfs dressed as jockeys strapped to their backs. The jockeys egged on their chargers with whoops and shrieks, making much play with their whips so that DeShays had to spring back to avoid a cut. As the troupe disappeared around a corner the audience, in high spirits, piled out after them. DeShays pushed his way through the throng which was headed for the stairs, and went in search of the performers.

He found them in a noisome area behind the lecture room. One of the giants, a swarthy Chinaman, had a dwarf by the throat and was dangling the screeching sufferer whose arms and legs rotated like pinwheels. A colossal fat boy, blubbing his eyes out, was comforted by a thin man with no arms. In a makeshift pen an orangutan rocked on his haunches while working his way through a stack of carrots, calling Brunton to mind.

A tattooed man leaving pointed out Obed. He was dressed soberly as a Pilgrim Father and was helping extricate a fellow giant from his horse's head. DeShays bided his time, observing the man's big-boned ruddy looks and his considerable girth.

Spotting DeShays, Obed strode over and greeted him warmly, examined his bandage and shook his head sorrowfully as DeShays thanked him for possibly saving his life. Guiding him back into the still illuminated lecture hall, without any preamble the Giant took a folded paper from a pocket. In the same meticulous hand he had seen earlier, DeShays read as follows:

"On the night of Sunday the Second of November last I, Obed, known as The Quaker Giant, was on guard duty at the Floating Theater at Moore Street. After the audience quit the theater, Miss Dowling sometimes entertained visitors. On this night she had one such caller, a man I had never before set eyes on. He stayed for only a few minutes, maybe ten. I watched him off the boat and lost sight of him amid the crates awaiting loading at the dock. About an hour later I heard noises coming from the place where the crates were stacked. Thinking perhaps thieves were at work I went down to look and discovered a man in the act of hoisting a load wrapped in tarpaulin onto his shoulders. Accordingly I approached nearer and made my presence known. The man, a stranger, at first cursed me, then held out what looked to be a policeman's star.

"Notwithstanding this, his furtive behavior made me suspicious. I trailed him at a distance along the waterfront until he turned into Cuyler's Alley. Not wanting to reveal myself, I tarried several minutes before venturing after him. Lying on the cobbles was a man's body. He was nearly naked, his head badly bloodied, but from the cravat still tied around his neck I recognized the caller who had earlier visited Miss Dowling on the boat."

After ascertaining that Pauline received no further visitors, police or otherwise, that night, and that a deeply troubled Obed had spoken of the incident to La Rue, it seemed to DeShays that it only remained for the Giant to present his evidence to Carson for Miller to be exonerated and the unknown policeman—who Obed swore he'd never seen before—to be identified and arrested. "If you're willing," he told the Giant, "there's a man I'd like you to meet, and no time to lose about it."

CHAPTER 29

Despite the lateness of the hour, the Iron Mug was doing good business as a diehard crowd of revelers sought a head start on their Sunday boozing. Still in his Pilgrim Father getup, the Giant by his very presence cleared a path to the counter. Like Moses parting the Red Sea, thought DeShays. Hammer Lang, not one to be fazed by the eccentricities of his fellow men, nevertheless looked up from the pint he was drawing with a questioning glance aimed in DeShays's direction.

"Boss around?" yelled DeShays above the din, coming straight to the point.

With an upward jerk of his head, Hammer indicated Carson's whereabouts while mouthing something about beauty sleep that DeShays didn't fully catch. Turning to Obed, he motioned him towards the back of the saloon and thither the two fought their way.

Late as it was, he had no qualms about interrupting Carson's sleep, beauty or otherwise. Confronted with Obed's eyewitness account, Carson would have little choice but to concede.

Once through the door into the hallway a semblance of quiet prevailed. To the left a flight of stairs ascended to the family quarters while to the right steps led down to the kitchen and cellar. DeShays half listened for the crying of a baby, then recalled that Carson's wife and child had gone to the country and were likely still there.

Anxious to avoid another run-in with Izzy, he motioned to the Giant to stay put and started gingerly up the stairs. At the first creak however came the sound of a thump and a shuffling overhead followed by the little half-barks of an inquisitive dog. Old Caesar took his stand on the top step and peered myopically down at the intruder below, growling. A voice—Carson's—came indistinctly, calling the dog, asking what was the matter.

"It's me, Irontop. DeShays. Apologies for the late hour but you know I wouldn't do this if I didn't have to." Hearing nothing, he climbed a few more steps. "Something's come to light on the Bewly case. Thought you'd want to be the first to know."

"Wait there, Miles," came Carson's muffled reply. "I'm coming down."

DeShays turned back to where Obed was standing and signaled to him that Carson would be down soon. All at once, before his eyes, the Giant seemed to reel backwards, legs flailing, arms useless at his sides. Behind him, framed in the entrance to the cellar steps, appeared the grimacing countenance of Izzy. He must have crept up behind the presumed intruder and surprised him. But clearly Izzy hadn't reckoned on who he was up against. Before DeShays could do anything more than gape, Obed, with a sharp bucking motion, shook his attacker off, the two ending up facing one another locked in a weird arm's length hold, with Izzy's chin neatly cupped in one of the Giant's great mitts. Moments later, giving vent to an unearthly gurgle, the Giant swung Izzy round and sent him crashing down the cellar steps. There came a thud, then silence. Then Caesar set to howling and Carson's voice sounded from above, commanding both servant and dog to cease and desist. Obed, meanwhile, had vanished into the gloom at the end of the hall and appeared to be trying to break down Carson's front door.

Torn between pursuing the Giant, seeing to the unfortunate Izzy, and enlightening Carson who now, partially dressed, was starting down the stairs, DeShays settled for the latter.

"What in tarnation's going on?" thundered Irontop, holding aloft an oil lamp and peering down the hallway. "Where's Izzy? Who in hell is that?"

"His name's Obed, night watchman at that floating theater that was moored at Pier 3. I brought him along because he saw something that sheds a new light on the Bewly murder."

196

"Saw something? What are you talking about, Miles? Where've you been? That's all sewed up. I told you. History."

"Seems like he saw who did it," DeShays persisted. "Bewly wasn't killed in the alley. He was killed on the docks at Moore, three blocks away."

"You don't know what you're talking about. Anyway, what's it matter where he was killed, we've got our man, haven't we? Thanks in good part to you. Izzy! Izzy!" Carson called down but got no answer. Starting down the cellar steps, he turned and looked back. "If you know what's good for you, Miles, you'll keep your theories to yourself. You're up for my assistant captaincy, you know." Holding his lamp, trailed by faithful old Caesar, he disappeared.

DeShays was stunned. Sensing a presence, he glanced around. Squatting near the top of the stairs was a young woman wrapped in a blue shawl. "What happened?" she asked in a scared voice. DeShays didn't attempt an answer, but ran to where Obed had finally managed to unbolt the door.

Together they passed the entrance of the Iron Mug where merry-making continued oblivious of the drama taking place next door. It felt good to get out, to walk in the empty street, to breathe the cold, damp, slightly smoky air. He was aware of his companion's agitation, that he was eager to tell him something, and assumed that the Giant was rattled by his run-in with Izzy. Indeed, that proved to be the case. Under the first gaslight they came to Obed laid a detaining hand on DeShays's sleeve. Pulling the statement he'd written from a pocket and holding it up to the light, he pointed out the words, "The man was a stranger to me." Then, nodding in the direction they'd come, he mimed the choke hold he'd had on Izzy's neck.

"Are you telling me that that was the man you saw carrying the body into Cuyler's Alley?" DeShays asked, perplexed.

The Giant nodded.

"And he showed you a policeman's star?"

Emphatically, he inclined his head.

"But—" DeShays touched his bruise which had begun to

throb. "That means—" he began again, but the implications of what Obed had just said overwhelmed him and words failed. "It means," he tried a third time, "it means we've another call to make tonight."

Where do you find the Chief of Police of the City of New York at one o'clock on a Sunday morning when you need him? At home, presumably in bed. But where did Chief Matson call home? DeShays had no idea. There were not a lot of people on the street he could ask, but one man he might reasonably expect help from came to mind. And DeShays had a notion where that gentleman might presently be found.

Sebastian readily admitted the two to the Christian American Bible and Tract Society though Billy Holmes had not yet arrived. Obed resisted all offers of the house brandy and DeShays reluctantly followed suit, much as he felt the need, deeming sobriety the better part of valor. They took a table in deep shadow far back from the stage to avoid drawing attention to their somewhat eyebrow-raising appearance, though Seb remarked that, should the law arrive, the Giant had the perfect costume. And arrive it soon did, in the shape of Daniel Hewison, the chief's brother-in-law.

DeShays allowed him a few minutes to get in the mood. After sitting through a tableau of Aphrodite rising fully-formed from the foamy sea, he crept up beside him and re-introduced himself, noting with satisfaction the spasm of nervous coughing his presence produced. In the spirit of "one favor deserves another" (how proud of him Billy would have been; how ridiculous he felt) it was agreed that Hewison accompany the two of them to Matson's home in his carriage, parked discreetly in the neighborhood.

The Matson residence in the wee hours of a late November Sunday morning presented a somewhat gauche face to the world. One of only a handful of houses bordering newly developed Gramercy Park, it stood bleakly in its lot like a rejected suitor, all dressed up and nowhere to go. It was the chief himself who eventually thrust his night capped head out of an upper window to ascertain who was calling at that ungodly hour. Seeing who it was, however, and perhaps assuming some family crisis (DeShays and Obed were hidden in the carriage) he came down to open up; though his displeasure at the sight of them standing on his stoop was vociferous. And when Hewison at once drove off and Matson realized he'd been played for a fool, he was fit to explode.

"Forgive me, Chief, but I hope you understand that I wouldn't have disturbed you—and brought along my friend here—had not the interests of our new police been uppermost in my mind."

"Pretty words, DeShays. I understand no such thing. Who is this man?" Without his spectacles, in his nightshirt and slippers, the chief seemed a lot less fearsome. Or maybe it was simply that, next to the Giant, he shrank.

"A carpenter and a Quaker, sir, an entertainer and, more pertinently, a night watchman of impeccable credentials."

The Giant bowed his head respectfully as the screech of a woman's voice sounded from above. "It's nothing, Mother," came the chief's shouted response, "Go back to bed." Glaring at his visitors, he said, "Say what you have to say, and leave," adding viciously, "It's a nice walk back to town at this hour." Picking up his lamp, he led the way towards the rear of the house.

Back in what appeared to be his study, Matson poked viciously at the grey remains of a fire before settling himself at his desk and turning the wick up on the lamp. In its glow DeShays glimpsed all manner of decorative objects—paintings, plaster busts, a stuffed owl. "Well?" He looked from one to the other of his guests who remained on their feet.

Stepping forward, the Giant laid his statement on the desk. After locating a pair of glasses, Matson held the scrap of paper to the light and scrutinized it as DeShays watched for any hint of a reaction. Letting the paper fall dismissively from his fingers he sat back as if inviting an explanation. DeShays then recounted their visit to Carson's leading to the encounter with Izzy Mendoza and the Giant's reaction.

"Is this so?" Matson addressed the Giant, who inclined his head. "Speak when you're spoken to, sir!"

199

"He can't, Chief" DeShays intervened. "He's mute."

For a while the chief sat slumped in his chair to the point where DeShays felt a slight prick of pity to see the great man so utterly diminished. Was this one chestnut he'd not be able to pull from the fire? For surely he saw the implications of what they'd told him. Suddenly, from the embers in the grate, a little flame hissed forth. The Chief rose. "I shall send for Captain Carson." he said, "In the meantime,"—indicating the note—"I'll keep this." As the front door closed on his visitors, he added, "It may interest you to know, DeShays, that I am not altogether surprised by what you've told me."

In pitch darkness and silent communion, like a pair of burglars on a mission, they crossed Union Square to Broadway. Here the gas lamps shed an intermittent glow, and of the few miscreants and revelers they encountered, none bothered the tall, slim man and his much bigger companion. At Canal they shook hands and parted, the Giant turning east, DeShays west.

CHAPTER 30

Just how long had the bells been ringing, he wondered. For a while DeShays lay prone in bed, hands clutching his pillow as though it was a floating log. At length, pulled by the reverberations from the doldrums of semi-consciousness, he recalled what day of the week it was. Yet this was more than the habitual come-to-service Sunday peal. Under it there boomed out darkly, insistently, over and over, the count of five. It could only be the bell in the cupola of City Hall, its massive weight ensuring its sound carried to the furthest corners of the city.

Rolling out of bed, DeShays threw up the sash and poked his head out. Searching the spires and housetops he looked in vain for visible signs of fire, because the tolling of the big bell meant that all Manhattan's fire companies were summoned to the Third Fire District. From the direction of Canal Street came bawling and shouts, the clatter of wheels, the blowing of a horn and the sound of a jingling bell. Pulling on his clothes as fast as he could he rushed downstairs through the eerily empty house. Everyone would be at Sunday worship.

Already congregations were emptying into frigid streets. DeShays ran for several blocks in the direction of general movement till, from behind him, came a deep rumbling of scraping wheels and the whooping and hollering of young voices. Skipping into a doorway, he let the onrushing engine pass. It was an old gooseneck pumper, dragged along by a squad of leather-helmeted young men, an enthusiastic gang of boys following in its wake. When one of the youngest stopped to retrieve his fallen cap, DeShays called out to him to ask where they were headed. Coffee House Slip, came the answer, confirming his worst suspicions.

Minutes later a winded DeShays spotted a carter driving an empty one-horse two-wheeler. Flourishing his badge and shouting "police!" he jumped aboard and sat on the floor taking a bumpy ride all the way to Wall and Front, where he hopped off, the way being blocked by the gathering crowds. Merchants and clerks in their Sunday best were emerging from offices clutching great ledgers to their chests like girls carrying their schoolbooks, while the street echoed with chaos, smoke and flame coloring the eastern skies. The wind was driving hard to the southeast, and word on everyone's lips was that the fire might spread to the docks and warehouses.

Coffee House Slip was partially closed off by a cordon of stalwarts with copper stars pinned to their chests. DeShays showed his and passed through the line. The spectacle of the Iron Mug transfixed him—its windows replaced by sheets of yellow flame, thick ropes of black smoke streaming from its dormers carried by the wind towards the river. Carson's place and the two buildings east of it were going up like tinderboxes.

Adjusting his muffler over his nose and mouth, DeShays joined onlookers on the south side of the street which, despite acrid smoke stinging eyes and nostrils, boasted the best seats in the house. No one could survive such a fire, yet scanning the crowd he saw no sign of Carson, nor for that matter Izzy. Incandescent flames playing wickedly in the blackened hole which once was the Iron Mug's doorway seemed to comment on their fate. From inside the well-stocked barroom came small explosions, heard against a backdrop of crackling flames, streaming water, sparks and hollering firemen.

The engines were arrayed in three lines going down to the river, those on the street drawing water from counterparts two hundred feet east, who were in turn sucking water in from the river. On either side of the engines teams of eight men clad in red flannel manned long brakes, one group rising as its opposite fell, suggesting to DeShays a strange ritual of prayer. As the men grunted, the brakes made violent rocking sounds with each stroke, and a man staggered back clutching a broken hand, to be quickly replaced in the line by another.

The men were pumping out streams of water faster than it could be taken in, while firemen manhandling hose pipes aimed them onto the blazing buildings. A foreman in a drab-colored coat was calling out garbled instructions through a silver trumpet. Men clambered up the fronts and sides of buildings via tall ladders, while great lengths of leather hose were uncoiled across the cobbles, in places leaking at the seams. The fire had jumped to a building to the rear of the Iron Mug, and from the back windows of a tall warehouse next to that firemen were training their hoses on the buildings below in the hopes of containing the blaze.

Pulling himself away DeShays moved through the crowd looking for signs of anyone familiar. A pair of well-dressed mercantile types were comparing the blaze to another of recent vintage, arguing over which was grander, while flames could be seen reflected in the windows behind them. At the front of the crowd youths were urging on their favorite fire companies, yelling "Go it 22!" and the like, as elsewhere young women cried inconsolably. A knot of hard cases who might have been the Mug's regulars looked on grimly, one of them daubing his eyes with a handkerchief.

Standing against a building was a hollow-cheeked codger in a woolen nightcap, an overcoat thrown over his pajamas. This old man, thought DeShays, might have been among the first on the scene. "Pardon me, sir, but can you tell me what has happened to Captain Carson?"

"May God rest his soul," said the man, most of whose teeth seemed to be lacking. "He ran back into the fire to get that hound of his and never come out." Next to him an old woman with a coarse shawl draped over her made the sign of the cross. "Ashes to ashes," she said, shaking her head. "He was a decent man," croaked a second crone with heavily creased features. "Always ready with a helping hand for those less fortunate."

"Did any of you actually see him run back in?" asked DeShays. There was a hesitation as the threesome looked at one another. "Matter of fact, I did," said the toothless man, a trifle unconvincingly to DeShays's ears. "Must've been out for a while," he added, "otherwise I bet he'd have had that dog with him. Ain't come out since, and the dog neither."

A shower of glass turned their attentions back towards the fire. A movement within the crowd caught DeShays's eye—a small boy was being led away by the arm by a policeman. Likely a little pickpocket, he thought, following their course through the crowd but eventually losing sight of them.

It was then that DeShays laid eyes on the chief. He was standing with Chief Fire Engineer Braddock, ringed by a bunch of men, some of them reporters DeShays had seen around City Hall. Working his way around the back of the crowd, he stood at a discreet distance, near enough to catch some of what was being said without giving himself away. At this point he'd have sorely liked to grill the big man himself. A brief nine hours ago they'd parted upon his expressed intention of sending for the very Carson whose house was now in flames with Carson himself possibly dead inside it. He heard again the ominous words, "It may interest you to know, DeShays, that this is not exactly a surprise to me." The big man was up to something, but what?

"... an earnest and fearless man," he was saying, "embodying the finest aspirations of our new police." Could he really be talking about Carson? "... always the chance of a fire being deliberately set ... something we have to investigate ... matter of routine ... went back for the dog" the chief elaborated as the newsmen scrawled his every word.

"Fishing for pearls, DeShays?" The soft voice in his ear caused the eavesdropper an involuntary wince. "Oh, don't worry, I come with an olive branch this time, not a cudgel. I'm happy to see no permanent damage done. No," perhaps catching the spreading look of disdain on DeShays's face, "it was a bad mistake. I entirely misjudged you. We were on the same side all along, you and me. But you got there first, and I tip my hat to you, sir. I didn't have the proof, see. It was you that nailed him. That dumb-fool giant, who'd have ever thought? You put us all to shame. As I say, I misjudged you, thought the two of you were hand in glove. Jesus!"

"The two of who?" DeShays was confused. Suspicion turned to curiosity.

Poole nodded towards the conflagration just as a supporting timber collapsed into the street in a shower of sparks. "A good man, but vain. A politician, not a policeman. But in the end, brave. I'll give him that. Took the honorable way out."

"What are you saying?"

"We won't see him again," Poole declared matter-of-factly. "Chief let him choose: do it yourself or we'll do it for you. 'Course, being who he was, he went a bit too far. Jesus, and all for a woman."

"Pauline Dowling." So Poole and the chief had spoken.

"Almost fell for her myself." Poole's harsh laugh cut DeShays. He didn't like this man any more now than before. "That's when I realized what he was up to. Poor fool. Look what he had going for him. All gone, and for what?" He spat. "Ah well, to every man his Achilles heel."

"In all honesty it was the furthest thing from my mind. Till yesterday, that is. How did you come to suspect him?"

"Watched him like a cat. I knew his routine. Knew something happened that night. Came in next morning with his right hand all bandaged up and some cock-and-bull tale. I reckon that toff didn't let him off scot-free. And the way the face was todged in, there was a reason for that. Your everyday robber don't do that. I'll wager that was his doing. And the way he stuck it to McGlone like that, and tied the whole thing up so neat. Hell, I know McGlone. A bad egg, yes, but not a killer. And when that wasn't going anywhere, he turns on the old watchman." Poole shook his head, more in sorrow than anger it seemed to DeShays.

"But how did Bewly's clothes end up at Miller's?"

"He'd have planted them himself back when he first went looking for him. I reckon it was his man, Izzy, who stripped the corpse and mashed his mazzard. On Irontop's say-so."

DeShays watched as the Chief Engineer left Matson's side and went down the street, where flames licked through the edges of closed shutters on the top story of a tall counting house, the building farthest east. A massive engine, Southwark No. 42, painted green with gold trim, was stationed there out front. Soon a fireman with a tin trumpet slung across his back grabbed an axe from the back of the machine and banged in a door panel, reaching in to open the lock. Several men followed him inside, lugging a length of hose.

"Seen the chief yet?" asked Poole. "He'll be wanting a word with you."

They made their way to where Chief Matson still stood alongside another man DeShays didn't know, reflected firelight flickering in his lenses. "Ah, Miles, the very man," he boomed, sending DeShays into high alert. He'd never been addressed thus by him before. "Meet Assistant Chief Engineer Norville. Inspector DeShays is one of our finest recruits, nephew of our esteemed Alderman Allaire. And of course you know Captain Poole. He'll be taking over the First Ward from poor Carson. Big boots to fill indeed. Cut down, like Lycidas, in his prime. 'Who would not weep for Lycidas?'"

Captain? DeShays thought, as the chief recited a few more lines of Milton. Surely, a little premature.

"Naturally the wife and child will be compensated. A mercy they were with her people across the river. I've dispatched Inspector Harrington to break the sad news."

There was shouting in the street as firemen emerged from inside the counting house. Minutes later Chief Braddock returned to the chief's side and DeShays was introduced to him in the same glowing terms as before. In assured tones Braddock told them how the men had been playing a stream up the hatchway but had been scalded by the water splashing back on them. He'd ordered some of them to the back of the building to prevent the fire from getting to Pine Street, and soon Engine 42 was pouring a powerful torrent into the building, checking the fire's progress.

"I think we can all congratulate ourselves on a job well done," the chief's gaze swept the little group and descended firmly on DeShays. "Eh, DeShays? At a cost, yes, at a heavy cost, but I think we can all agree that justice has been done."

"Amen to that," echoed Poole with a piety that did not become him. And with the strict injunction to take the following week off, DeShays found himself dismissed from the Presence.

In numbed amazement he merged back into the crowd gathered opposite the fire. Then a fireman was running towards him, shouting and gesturing westward for everyone to clear off. The tall counting house across the street might collapse, someone said. The south side of the street was swept clear, and DeShays found himself caught up in the general flight west. He remained among mesmerized onlookers on the southwest corner of Wall, unable to pull away, though to him alone the glowing flames and dashing firemen seemed the extension of something infinitely more terrible.

Gradually there dawned on DeShays a sort of impotent rage which spared no one, least of all himself. Not only had his best efforts gone for naught, they had been ruthlessly preempted by the chief to turn murderer into martyr. His own introduction as the chief's protégé had been a crowning insult. Out in the cold, left feeling like a puppet after the puppeteer has released the strings, he turned towards home. And came face to face with Old Honan.

CHAPTER 31

Every so often the southbound train would slow to a standstill as it approached a curve, and each time DeShays picked up the newspaper lying at his side and read the same column, though had he wanted to he could have memorized it in short order. It was, he knew, a symptom of his mind feeding on itself, a condition which he feared might persist indefinitely. After five days, his astonishment at the way Chief Matson manipulated reality with the ease of an artist positioning his model had only grown. How fascinating it was to witness this in newsprint, which lent the chief's falsehoods an indelible quality. Perhaps between the lines, DeShays feebly hoped, there might appear some trace of what had happened between the time he and Obed had left the house on Gramercy Square and the moment that the Iron Mug went up in flames.

The idea to get away for a breath of fresh air, while not his own, had proved a sound one. No use sitting around town stewing in his own juices. So that Monday he had paid an unannounced visit to his mother up in White Plains, taking his first trip via the railroad that had only extended service that far in the past year. And it was true that her joy at seeing him at her doorstep had reminded him that there were other things in life—at least until he began reading the accounts that were appearing in her local paper, which were reprinted from none other than Brunton's *Argus*.

As the train idled by an abandoned sawmill, he once again read of the "noble and undying bond of loyalty that exists between man and his best friend" in reference to Carson's supposed attempt to save Caesar, though no trace of the dog had been found. Perhaps dog and master "might together enjoy their Eternal Reward." He read of "man's ingratitude to man"

208

in reference to Izzy Mendoza, who was now wanted for murder and arson, the prime suspect in both the murder of "E. R. Bewly, late of Albany" and the burning of the Iron Mug. "The New Police had acquitted themselves triumphantly" in the course of the investigation, "a fantastical affair" in which a "strange mute Quaker, a giant employed by the American Museum" had, through a chance encounter, identified Izzy Mendoza as the man he'd seen hauling Bewly's unconscious form into Cuyler's Alley. There Izzy had performed his "ritual of shocking and brutal degradation, fully consistent with his former profession of pugilism," which was condemned as "evidence of all that is base and inhuman." No sooner had Carson discovered "the viper in his midst" than was his "noted generosity towards certain rougher elements repaid with treachery." As for Irontop, his hulking frame had been so badly charred that he was identified only by the diamond stickpin which lay near the body, one DeShays himself had noticed a few weeks back, and his copper star and gold wedding ring.

Up ahead the signalman waved his white flag and the train churned forward. DeShays laid the paper down, and as he looked out over the somber landscape, viewing through a veil of drizzle and mist a lonely little settlement or a factory of wet stone, he imagined Carson's funeral. It had been set to take place the previous day, moving down Broadway to the Battery. He pictured Carson's wife Sarah marching bravely at its head, followed by the mayor, Chief Matson, Poole and the others, members of the fire department marching with their engines in full polish, with his own uncle doubtless prominent among the mourners. Would the mysterious woman in blue that he'd briefly glimpsed at the top of Carson's stairs be among the onlookers? (Twice later on DeShays would experience a strange mixture of excitement and misgiving when he thought he'd sighted her, only to find he was mistaken as he drew closer. He never did see her again.)

As the journey progressed DeShays grew increasingly restless. New passengers boarded his carriage at each junction; a farmer and his wife, a pair of priests, a mother with five children. One of these, a small boy, persisted in sticking his head up over the back of the seat and fixing DeShays with an inscrutable stare, an act he performed repeatedly despite his mother's admonitions.

Eventually the locomotive pulled into the Yorkville tunnel, and for a moment DeShays and his fellow travelers were alone together in the dark in that feeling of communal isolation unique to passengers. Withdrawing his watch as the train emerged into waning daylight, he saw that it was just after four, time enough to drop off his portmanteau before his dinner appointment. Meanwhile there was still more soggy farmland before the train chugged into yet another tunnel and pulled into the Madison Square depot. Grabbing his bag, DeShays rose on stiff legs and transferred to a horse-drawn railway that tugged him through the familiar cityscape, dropping him off by City Hall. His appointment was for six at Sherwood's over on Broadway and Walker, a fine saloon noted for its Chesapeake Bay oysters.

DeShays pushed open a door set with panes of multi-colored glass and stepped in, feeling the pile of a red plush carpet beneath his boots. A number of fine chandeliers of ground glass cast a shadowy gleam over a spacious room. To his right several fashionably-dressed men stood by a long counter of veined white marble, on which sat an array of decanters and silver pitchers. Some slapped down cards while others just smoked, drank and laughed, clearly the regulars. Behind the counter a bartender in a red silk vest and shirtsleeves was shaking up halves of a mixed drink, and as DeShays glanced over the man's shoulder at a painting in which a classical heroine was having trouble keeping her drapery attached, he was acknowledged with a nod.

A row of boxes stretched to DeShays left, ornately carved in gold-painted wood. Blue silk curtains revealed mirrored walls. While none were now drawn, judging from the sound of a woman's already tipsy voice and the look of some of the drinking and dining couples, it was just a matter of time.

Old Honan was sitting in the very last of the boxes, facing the door. With a napkin already fastened to his collar and a decanter and partially consumed plate of oysters before him, he appeared at one with his surroundings. On sighting DeShays he signaled a waiter. "I trust you've enjoyed your stay in the country, sonny," he declared, pouring his guest a glass of iced brandy punch and calling for more oysters, "Plenty of rest and fresh air; don't say I don't give good advice. Did you find your mother well?"

"As well as a widow woman fussing over her wayward only child can be, thank you."

Indeed, it was Honan who had urged DeShays to get out of town. Wandering away from the fire that Sunday he'd encountered the old man who had similarly been drawn to the conflagration. Alarmed by what he called DeShays's "death mask" face he'd insisted on escorting him to his own nearby lodgings where in his room he uncorked a bottle of medicinal Armagnac. Matching his host tumbler for tumbler DeShays had observed through dulled senses that Honan appeared remarkably sober. Succumbing to the wreaths of cigar smoke he even joined him in a smoke himself.

Naturally the talk was of the fire, agreement prevailing that there was more to Carson's demise than met the eye. But Zeb, as he insisted on being called, was not at all sure what could be done about that. "What's done is done, especially so if done by the Father," he said, though he did promise "to keep an ear to the ground." And on that note, and with the incentive of a possible further tip on the horses from DeShays's unimpeachable source, they'd agreed to meet in a week here at Sherwood's where Honan apparently had some longstanding business with the owner.

"And may I assume, Zeb, that you've kept your ear to the ground?"

Honan leaned back in the booth, anticipating his moment. "Not an easy thing, mind you. The Father has it all under tight control—no one except the fire department and a few policemen selected by the big man and Poole were granted access to the scene once the ruins cooled off. Fears of looting along the slip and all that, they say. Vandals running off with scorched timbers and the like. Through discreet inquiry, though, I did discover a few points of interest that you won't read about in any papers."

"The *Argus*, at least, seems to have been written by the chief himself. I take it he and Brunton came to terms."

Honan nodded agreement. "No matter about that. The point being that where there's fire, there are firemen. It so happens that I know the foreman of Phenix Engine Company 22. They were first at the scene, of course. Care to venture a guess as to why?"

DeShays's mind harked back to Eli Miller's sad little room, probably already rented, and the old helmet he'd worn in his days with Phenix No. 22. "Would I be wrong to say that Carson had a policy with the Phenix Insurance Company?"

"A modest one it was. No hint of the fire being set to realize the policy, and as the benefits go to Carson's wife the company wouldn't dare dispute it anyway. In any event, it's not the fire department's job to investigate cases of arson, that falls to the police. Nonetheless, it's this fellow's job to poke around in the aftermath, and relate any suspicions to our department. And he likes his job—a little too well, if you ask me. What this fellow doesn't know about fires; it's amazing, the things he sees. Right away, he tells me, he knew something wasn't right. Just from the sounds of the wood burning, he knew that something had been doused on it."

"Nobody's claiming this was an accident, Zeb."

"Drink up and listen, will you? This fresh air has done you no good."

"Pray continue."

"Now fire leaves behind patterns, which our man reads like music. And the pattern of the charring points to the origin of the fire itself. Fire, of course, burns up, and in a V-shaped pattern, which points back to its source."

"News to me."

"That's what makes our case so very interesting: the origin of the fire was precisely where Carson's body was found, you see."

"I did wonder about that; there was no word in the papers as to where that was."

"He was at the foot of the steps, before the cellar door. Now keep in mind, even the char pattern around a door jamb will reveal the direction that the fire came from. The door itself was completely burned, of course, but the side of the jamb facing the stairs was charred to a far greater extent than that facing the basement. All Carson needed to do to escape was to walk through the door to the basement and right out the backyard, for Christ's sake. What's the matter, sonny—you're white as a sheet!" Honan called over to the waiter for some water.

DeShays was back in the Iron Mug, frozen in time, watching Izzy and Obed scrap like desperate bears. With all his strength Obed had thrown Izzy, who'd crashed to the very spot where Carson's supposed remains had been found, and when Carson had called down to Izzy there was no response.

"It's nothing, Zeb. Something went down the wrong way, that's all."

Honan watched DeShays sip his water, then continued. "Now if you ask me, here's how it all happened. Once Carson realized that your Quaker friend had spotted the link back to him, Izzy was living on borrowed time."

"In other words, we may suppose that Carson lent Izzy his badge one final time."

"Well said, young man. In my opinion, Carson is halfway to Texas, with Izzy resting in his coffin."

"Well then, Zeb, what are we to make of the chief's ultimatum to Carson?"

"Don't think for a moment that the chief communicated with Carson directly—he never dirties his hands through direct contact. No doubt he left the matter to Poole's discretion, promising the considerable weight of his support for the vacant captaincy."

"There's nothing to be done about it, as far as I can see. Despicable as Poole is, I still can't believe that he'd allow Carson to start such a fire."

"What passed between them is beyond our reach, though I don't believe this nonsense of 'you do it yourself or we'll do it for you' for a second. Carson would have known why Poole was at his door and made short work of him had such an ultimatum been given. My guess is that when Poole came calling Carson offered to disappear and promised to make it look good, though perhaps he tricked Poole as to how good. By then Izzy would have been dead, and the course simply presented itself."

"In a way I can understand about his striking Bewly. They likely had words over Pauline and we all know Irontop's temper. But to turn on old Miller like that?"

"Instinct tells me that Izzy was the one that settled him, on Irontop's orders. He'd have todged his mother on Irontop's say-so."

It was a joy to see Old Honan using his powers once again, like watching layers of grime and varnish being stripped off a portrait by an old Dutch master. Here was what policemen once were and ought to be, not miserable lackeys of politicians or Jonathan Wild-like creatures of the underworld. He would have liked to enlighten his companion on the point concerning the Giant and Izzy, and absolve Carson of at least one murder, but it wasn't until much later that he brought himself to do that. For a while they sat eating, with DeShays now and then discreetly checking his pocket watch. At last, having consumed a dozen oysters, he undid his napkin and got up to excuse himself for the evening.

"Good God, sonny, you've hardly taken a sip of punch! Sit you down this instant!"

"I'm sorry to leave you, Zeb, but what say we do this again next week, eh?"

"I hope you'll stay awhile next time," the old man grumbled, pouring himself a quantity of liquid and raising the glass, quickly emptied, to his younger friend. "Perhaps long enough to recall an item of sporting business on the agenda. That fresh air seems to have had an altogether too drastic effect." On the way out, DeShays settled the tab with the waiter.

Outside it was drizzling again. The touch of rain on DeShays's face had a cleansing power. Walking east, he reached the Bowery. The same sort of avid young faces were in evidence as those he'd seen the night he ventured into

Spider Murphy's, which he passed, wondering where old Winchell might turn up next. The doors were closed, but out on the street you could still hear the sound of a fiddler scraping away. Passing Kate Felton's studio a short while later, he didn't so much as look up, instead crossing the square.

As he ascended the long staircase, a trio of loudly dressed girls spilled down in high spirits, and he stood aside to let them pass. Looking back up from below, one called out to thank him, curtseying for the amusement of her friends. DeShays responded by doffing his cap and bowing, which sent the girls out into the night laughing.

At the top of the stairs he was met with the warm smell of baked goods, which always seemed to fuse into something more delicious than any one treat could possibly be. Behind the counter a ruddy-faced older woman, with brawny forearms and her hair up, was busy churning out ice cream from a bucket. She noticed DeShays, and with a knowing look tilted her head towards the tables in the back.

THE END

www.ingramcontent.com/pod-product-compliance
Lightning Source LLC
Chambersburg PA
CBHW031952170626
46807CB00006B/2457